Life As A Journey

Two short novels

Yaron Broon

ISBN: 9798453251810

Cover design by: Yaron Broon

To my Dad,
You are the inspiration.

And

To Maia,
You make it all worthwhile.

Contents

Life As A Journey

"That's life, that's what all the people say
You're ridin' high in April, shot down in May
But I know I'm gonna change that tune
When I'm back on top, back on top in June

I said that's life, and as funny as it may seem
Some people get their kicks stompin' on a dream
But I don't let it, let it get me down
'cause this fine old world, it keeps spinnin' around

I've been a puppet, a pauper, a pirate, a poet, a pawn and a king
I've been up and down and over and out and I know one thing
Each time I find myself flat on my face
I pick myself up and get back in the race

That's life, I tell you I can't deny it
I thought of quitting, baby, but my heart just ain't gonna buy it
And if I didn't think it was worth one single try
I'd jump right on a big bird and then I'd fly

That's life, that's life and I can't deny it
Many times I thought of cuttin' out but my heart won't buy it
But if there's nothin' shakin' come this here July
I'm gonna roll myself up in a big ball a-and die
My, my!"

Gordon Kelly L / Thompson Dean K

Prologue

Stride after stride she walks; the shape of her legs and her panoramic vision allow her to determine her steps, so she'll never step on an object that doesn't belong. She will always follow me. From time to time, I give her a piece of pita bread, so she'll feel good; the pita tastes to her like chocolate to a child.

We are both walking in the endless desert; the wind caresses both my hair that grew recently and her elegant body. I smile at her and feel that she smiles back. The formidable cliffs in shades of red and black and in a variety of shapes and forms call me, "Come and climb us!" However, I know the danger of deterioration and that the stones only appear to be a solid part of the rock. The wadis and ravines meander like ancient giant snakes and among them sparse vegetation of thorny acacia and weeds to which survive the dryness with great difficulty. Every so often a fox crosses the road searching for prey, and when it sees us, it runs away in a panic. Heads of giant Spiny-tailed lizards, that a lash from their tail can be very dangerous, peep from crevices in the rock, and in the distance, we see a small herd of mountain goats grazing for pleasure. We approach closely; a few feet away, almost within easy reach of them, until they jump to the nearest cliff, climb effortlessly and gracefully as if it was a flat surface, and walk away from us.

In the silence, only my footsteps being heard, her footsteps barely audible, despite the eight hundred pounds of her weight. The feeling is that only we are in the world; us and the nature that surrounds us. Above us in the sky a beautiful giant Bearded vulture glides, looking at everything from above, probably laughing at the limited creatures that stuck to the ground. Occasionally, it plunges at an incredible speed and then rises again on a hot air stream. Herbal plants such as Micromeria, Undulate Fleabane and Fragrant Oxeye, which are used to make tea, appear in ravines that are also full of other tiny flowers that I don't know their names. They sparkled after the last rain, which is rare in this region, where the annual average is 25 millimetres of rain per year.

The marvellous harmony that is occasionally interrupted only by huge man-made steel birds or by an SUV of a status-seeker Yuppie that didn't follow the instructions and lost his way, fills my heart with perpetual excitement and calm. The past and the future don't exist; time disappears down the mountain shoulders that look like a woman's breasts, and up the gully that creeps between them. The innocence and naïve lines are in everything; from a grain of sand to the massive boulder that rolled downhill thousands of years ago. The only belief that remains is in the sun that rises in the morning and sets in the evening, and our experience of time. When the sun stops, we will cease to exist.

Most mornings, I wake up at sunrise, light a campfire, and brew a pot of tea from the herbs I have picked on the previous day. Then I do my morning workout that maintains and improves muscles and flexibility—followed by a meditation that includes a peaceful sitting and watching the waking wilderness, the disappearing nightlife, the appearing daytime animals, and the colours of the sunrise that is different every day. Then I reflect on myself in relation to all the above. Later I load on her saddle the small number of belongings and gear that I own and get on our way, and she is behind me, ready for the day's experiences that await me. When I get tired of walking, I kindly ask her to sit down, and I climb and sit on the wooden saddle; one crossed leg embraces the saddle's horn, and the other is loosely swinging toward the ground. After she stands up again, at seven feet tall, we are becoming one creature with two heads, six legs and four eyes that see everything.

At lunchtime, when the air is so hot even breathing is a task, and you can cook an egg on the bare rocks, we find a shady creek, a broad tree, or every few days a water spring or a deep pond of water that was formed after the last rainfall. I ask her to stop, take off the saddle and gear, and allow her to enjoy and cud the vegetation in the area. Then I prepare lunch that contains pita bread which I make from flour, water and salt, a salad from tomatoes, cucumbers, onions, Za'atar, olive oil and a Labneh which is a sour soft white goat's milk cheese. I knead the dough well, divide it into four pieces, flatten them, then with a movement similar to pizza making I open them carefully, so there are no holes. When the dough is a large thin circle, I place it on the hot Saj, which is a convex metal plate placed on top of the fire, wait a few seconds, flip it, and after about five minutes I have four beautiful pitta bread. I cut the vegetables into large pieces, add a bit of salt, and a lot of olive oil, and mix the best salad in the world. To the Labneh, I add olive oil and a large amount of Za'atar which is A Middle Eastern mixture of herbs and spices, then dip a piece of pitta in it, and eat. It's a tasty and satisfying meal. I usually devour the salad and two pittas, the other two I wrap with fabric, so they don't get dry out and keep for dinner. In the afternoons, my thoughts wander to the past and the future; pondering with longing at the moments of happiness and recalling the difficult and sad parts of my life.

After all, the only property that really belongs to us is our bodies, our past, and our memories. As they are our most precious possession, we must guard and nurture them. The misconception in our society is that those material things, such as houses, cars, money, and clothing, are our property. Still, it is only an apparent illusion that we have developed owing to the fear of dealing with the real property that is us. All material things are not ours; they are borrowed from nature and will come back to it in the end. If we misuse those borrowings, nature will strike us twice as strong. The collective addiction and the worship of objects, which are usually prepared by others, make us feel empowerment and comfort, especially compared to those who have less but weaken the real power that comes from ourselves and the awareness and respect to our surroundings.

Reminiscing about memories gives me a feeling of fulfilment. It reminds me of how I got here, what I went through and done to be who I am now, with all the accomplishments, bitterness, pride, frustration, love and suffering, which are in my perfection.

In the evening, I'm climbing to the highest peak in the area to watch the sunset. This is the ultimate experience in the desert; the changing colours of the sky and the mountains in all the shades of red, yellow, pink and orange excite me every day. The sunset is never the same as the previous day. Sometimes I dance madly, screaming, singing, laughing or crying uninhibitedly and out of control from my sense of freedom and life and the staggering view of the world around me.

In the evening I descend from the mountain, light a fire again and play the guitar or just listen to the sounds of the night; the wind whispers through the acacia tree branches, the singing of crickets and the crackling of the burning wood. Each voice speaks to me, tells me a different story, and sings me a lullaby until my eyes shut, and I fall asleep to the sound of silence.

A girl in a gully

One day, I came across a small hidden water spring with a few trees and some desert vegetation that Nadya, my camel, could munch. I decided to settle down for a few days, take a walk in the area, soak up some water and mostly rest. In the morning, I woke up at sunrise and had a dip in the pool. After drying myself in front of the campfire and a cup of coffee, I decided to change my routine and take a short walk to release my muscles from the night's sleep; I felt that something different would happen today.

I was walking out of the quiet hidden spot… boom!!! Rowdy music disturbs the morning tranquillity of the waking desert, so I walked toward the bass noises, the banging and the screaming. About a mile away, on a high hill, I saw a group of about a hundred people dressed in tight clothes of all the colours of the rainbow, dancing like nothing but the music exists. The music almost blew out my eardrums, and I felt a powerful urge to turn around and return to my quiet and secluded spring, but I forced myself to move forward and explore this extraordinary phenomenon. The dance floor was delimited by four huge piles of speakers, each of which had several people clung to, they were in a total trance and probably deaf, as no mortal person whose ears function properly could withstand the noise and decibels from such a distance. Most of the people in the party danced with themselves, oblivious to the surroundings, praying to the God of Ecstasy, Speeds, and the LSD. Dozens of empty water bottles were laid scattered on the floor. The nightmarish experience was fuelled by the D.J. who shouted to the crowd that answered back with screams and hand-lifting, like a sect of believers in an uncontrolled fanatical cult. One of those creations of darkness; a shaky hybrid of a human, a neon sign in Las Vegas, and a mannequin from a shop window, approached me with a silly smile and a glazed look in his eyes and offered me to join them. "Hey bro, come and join, I've got Acid, Molly, Shrooms, whatever you want."

He took out of his pocket some coloured pills and pieces of cardboard and showed me.

I shook my head and refused politely.

"Ok, smashing buddy, whenever you want some, come to me. I love you, bro!" shrieked the walking Parkinson's disease and disappeared into the crowd.

The combination of state-of-the-art technology and super-primitive tribal rituals fascinated and disgusted me at the same time. It strengthened my understanding that as for the social conditioning from our "enlightened and advanced" culture, our fundamental need for a release of joy and pressure can only happen through technology and drugs or alcohol that artificially unleash our compulsions and bliss. I asked myself, "What the hell is wrong with us? Why can't we go into an ecstasy without Ecstasy?"

I looked, dumbstruck, at the phenomenon for a while before leaving the place back to my big friend who was sitting and chewing cud in silence. I sat down opposite her, looking into the peaceful big black eyes, and calmed down. The inner peace of the camels and the wisdom in their eyes is one of the most magical things in the world.

She looked at me with a maternal look that said, "Sit down, chill, the world is beautiful, you don't have to get stressed from anything. Breathe deeply, just breathe; nothing in the world is more important than now."

King Solomon was probably sitting and looking at the camel when he wrote in the book of Ecclesiastes:

"Vanity of vanities, says the Preacher, vanity of vanities! All is vanity.

What does man gain by all the toil at which he toils under the sun?

A generation goes, and a generation comes, but the earth remains forever.

The sun rises, and the sun goes down and hastens to the place where it rises.

The wind blows to the south and goes around to the north; round and round goes the wind, and on its circuits, the wind returns.

All streams run to the sea, but the sea is not full; to the place where the streams flow, there they flow again.

All things are full of weariness; a man cannot utter it; the eye is not satisfied with seeing, nor the ear filled with hearing.

What has been is what will be, and what has been done is what will be done, and there is nothing new under the sun.

Is there a thing of which it is said, "See, this is new"?

It has been already in the ages before us.

There is no remembrance of former things, nor will there be any remembrance of later things yet to be among those who come after."

My eyes closed, and I sank into a nap that was interrupted by strokes on my leg. I looked down and saw a small fox pulling my pants. I kicked it to chase it away. It moved about ten feet away and came back to bother me. After a few minutes, I realised it's trying to signal me to follow it. Curiously, I went along with it. The fox ran, but every few hundred feet stopped to make sure I was behind it and then continued. We played that game for about half an hour. Suddenly, I saw a man lying on the ground in one of the gullies. I got closer and found out it was a young woman; she was unconscious. I looked for the fox to thank him, but he had already gone. The girl was in her early twenties and was wearing tight vinyl clothing. I touched her neck; she was still alive, but her pulse was weak, and her breathing was slow. I realised she was at the party and was probably dehydrated. After I stripped her from the tight top, so her body could breathe, I loaded her on my shoulder and returned to the camp where I stripped her from the rest of her clothes, then wrapped her body in a thin blanket and wet her face with a bit of cold water. She woke up disoriented and confused, looking at me with dread.

"It's ok," I said. "You were dehydrated and passed out. I'm here to help you. Here, you need to drink this; it will make you feel better."

I gave her a bottle with a cocktail of water, salt, and sugar to give her body back the minerals, sugars, and fluids she had lost at the party. She turned her head and spat the drink onto the ground, then shook her head, refusing to drink.

"Drink slowly, I know the taste is horrible, but if you don't drink, you'll die."

She looked at me with blurred eyes, sipped the drink slowly, finished it, then closed her eyes without a word and fell asleep again.

I woke her up every half an hour and made her drink a little. By the evening, she gathered more strength and sat in front of the fire, wrapped in a blanket and shaking slightly from the cool breeze. She looked at me; "Where am I and who are you?"

I told her how I found her. She lowers her eyes, "I remember going to a rave in the desert, and my friends convinced me to take acid; it was the first time for me. At first, it was mesmerising; all the colours became brighter, and things were changing in front of my eyes. I danced for hours, frantically. The music was beautiful, and so were all the people that surrounded me. After a while I started to feel unwell; I felt everyone was closing in on me, that someone was watching me and trying to touch me all the time, and the people around me were getting unbearably smelly. I felt claustrophobic; I had to get out of there. The music also started to bang in my head like a hammer. So I ran away before it would split my head in half, and I'd lose my mind. I can't remember much since then; just that I was walking for hours, feeling that someone was following me and trying to kill me. I was thirsty but didn't dare go back to the party. I couldn't remember the way back anyhow."

"The next thing I remember is your face and a salty drink in my mouth."

"Are you hungry?" I asked, "I made dinner; not a home meal like your mother probably makes, but it's nutritious."

She nodded; "I haven't eaten since yesterday at noon, I can eat an elephant right now."

She demolished two pitta bread, a whole bowl of salad, and half a box of Labneh.

"Thank you." She smiled at me. "It's the most delicious meal I've ever eaten."

I smiled, "I can't argue with that."

All that evening, we sat and talked. Her name was Noa, twenty-two years old. She lived in Tel Aviv and was working as a secretary in a law firm and was pretty bored with her job. She had a family in a village near Tel Aviv; parents and two younger brothers. Recently, she broke up with her boyfriend of five years and was looking for a new purpose and substance in her life.

At one point, she looked into the blanket that was wrapped around her and blushed. "Did you strip me?"

"Yes, I had to take off the condom that covered you. Your body had no way to breathe; it's a miracle you didn't get a heat stroke. If you want to put that rubber fabric on again, your clothes are here." I pointed to the folded bundle by the fire.

"Thanks, but I'm comfortable with the blanket in the meantime, and I'm sorry I doubted you. I'm just pretty shy. Apart from my ex-boyfriend, no man has seen me naked."

"Shyness and embarrassment have been created for one thing."

"What is it?" She looks at me with wide eyes.

"To rise above and overcome it," I replied, and put another piece of wood in the fire. "This is not the first time I have seen a naked girl, and you can take pride in what you have. Maybe you're right, but I still don't want to show my breasts to every man." She answered and checked that she was all wrapped up with the blanket.

"But you don't have to get angry with yourself or be embarrassed if someone sees your boobs by mistake." I poured another cup of tea. "Also, if you are so ashamed of your body, why are you wearing clothes that emphasise every curve of your body?"

She started to fidget uncomfortably. "Well, let's leave it now. I'm sorry, you're still recovering from the trauma of the acid trip, and I'm getting on your case, let's talk about something else."

The night had come down. It was the end of the month, and the sky was moonless and full of stars.

"Look at the sky; you don't get a sky like that in Tel Aviv."

She laid back on her elbows and looked up in astonishment. "Wow! I have never seen so many stars; it's breathtaking."

"I'm pretty certain you've never taken the time to sit still and actually look at the sky. If you look long enough, you might also see a falling star."

A minute later, a line of light appeared in the sky, "Look," she shouted, "You were right; there's a falling star."

"Did you make a wish?" I asked with a smile.

"Sure, but I think it's just nonsense, superstition. Do you want to know what I wished for?"

"No! The wish is just for you; if you say it out loud, it will not come true. It's not nonsense; these are the things that give us hope and dreams, allowing us to yearn for something better. Without our ability to dream and hope, even in the most innocent and naïve way, even if it's silly and childish, we would be meaningless and indifferent. When you judge everything rationally, you lose the mystery, the surprise and the fun of being a child. Look at me; I know I will not walk here in the desert forever, but this period that our society classifies as an escape, is for me the true essence of being.

The total experience of who I am and the world around me, without the defences that one needs to develop in order to function in human society. Here, at the hard times, I only need to struggle with myself or with nature."

"What are you actually doing here on your own in this forsaken wilderness?"

"First, I'm not alone; I have Nadya." I pointed at the camel. "She is a better and more loyal companion than most of the girlfriends I had so far, and more trustworthy than most of my male friends. Besides, the desert is full of life; whoever saved you wasn't me, but a fox that dragged me to where you were laying. Second, what am I doing here? I'm living through and experiencing, I'm cleansing myself of the filth and dirt that human society has soaked me with; hypocrisy and jealousy, power trips, and shame. I am slowly breaking the walls that social games have forced me to build, forcing all of us to build, so we could cope with the cynical and ridiculous world that technology and communication have unfortunately produced. Life here is simple, without cars, TV, telephone, and newspapers. I write, play, sing, and observe the world and myself. I'm doing what the fast-paced modern external stimulations have castrated in most of us. Tomorrow, I'll let you feel the sensation I'm talking about. Tomorrow, all your senses will work".

"And how did you come to the decision to live alone in the desert?"

"As I said before, I'm not alone, and how I got here is a lifelong story. Anyway, it has been a hard day for you, go to sleep and gather strength for tomorrow; we will get up at sunrise."

"I'm not tired, let's talk some more." She answered me and opened her eyes wide to show me she's not sleepy.

It got nippy as the evening turned to night; I asked her if she wanted another blanket, but she refused; "It's nice and cosy like this. It's been a long time since I felt so good and so calm. The silence here is amazing! You can literally hear it; it's like a vacuum in my ears. I feel like the silence is, in fact, noisy, but a pleasant noise." She snuggled even more into the blanket.

"I see that you are cold; do you want another cup of tea?"

She nodded her head shyly; "Can you please hug me? I only know you from today, but I feel very free and safe with you as if nothing bad could happen."

I poured another cup of tea and put my arms around her. She was small and fragile; so innocent. I hoped people's cynicism and Powerfulness would not break this naivety, as it was so easy to exploit it.

"You told me you are unhappy, and a little bored with your life at the moment, but you didn't tell me what you want to do."

"I would like to work with tribes in Africa or the Amazon and help them; teach reading and writing, or to work in a clinic. I would also like to be an activist for environmental conservation in these places because the modern world is destroying the habitats and heritage of these unique cultures." She stroked my hand and huddled even more in my arms.

"So why don't you do something about it? Become a nurse or study environmental conservation, you can always volunteer with one of the international organisations that deal with human rights, conservation or aid in the Third World that provides educational or medical aid."

A fox's cry sounded from afar. She clung to me more; I stroked her hair, and she relaxed. "You know, Noa, it's easy to fantasise and dream about what you want, but the difficult thing is to turn it into reality regardless of the difficulties and obstacles on the way."

"Yes, I know, but I'm not sure if I can leave my friends and family and settle alone in another country. I've never been alone."

"Regarding the 'Not sure if I can'; you can do everything, you just need the confidence to go for it. It's all depending on what you are willing to give up and what you are ready to compromise. Anyway, if you join an organisation, it will generally take care of you and ensure that you land on your feet. About your loved ones and your country; you will not leave them forever; you can always come back. So all of what you said are excuses to uphold the security and comfort you have now, which according to you also sustains the boredom and the lack of meaning in your life that I think causes degeneration and mediocrity. Don't think this problem is only yours; in my opinion, this fear of being away from familiarity and comfort is a fundamental problem of the culture and education at these times. For example, notice how your senses work here, away from technology and mechanisation. Notice your hearing, vision and smell, how you touch, how you feel when you touch."

"Yes, I feel a lot stronger here." She whispered. "I feel more, listen and pay attention to the smallest sounds and noises. You're right; I suddenly realise that in the city, with all the noises of phones, TV's, computers and cars, the senses degenerate."

"Not only do the senses degenerate," I continued, "but also the will and intention; we hear but don't listen, see but don't look, and many people I have met cannot stand to be touched. Also deflating is the desire to do and learn what you want, the curiosity to experience new things that are sometimes uncomfortable but can be highly satisfying and exciting. The fear of pulling away from the ordinary and changing what is wrong. The television that cooks the mind with stupid reality and game shows is encouraging a useless sitting in sophisticated armchairs, which deteriorates the muscles and causes obesity. Look at those who call themselves 'sports enthusiasts' who sit and watch sports every night, screaming at the screen, eating crisps, drinking beer, and getting fat. The last time they even played any sports, though, was in PE lessons in school. The noises of the cars and other machines fuck up our hearing. We no longer know how tasty vegetables and fruits can be, because nowadays, we prefer the looks over the taste, so the farmers blast the fruits and veg with chemicals and supermarkets throw away any item with the tiniest defect.

Look, I'm not against progress and technology, but they are tools to improve ourselves and not the other way around. I think the craving for money and materialism, and the education for them, cause us to go back in many ways; it makes us somewhat numb, so it is easier to control us, to wash our brains and to block the uniqueness of each one of us.

This entire speech was for you to overcome the fear of changing your life, to be who you want to be. Do not be afraid to do what satisfies and excites you, and experience as much as possible. Even if sometimes the experiences are not great or convenient, take them as a learning curve."

"Yes, I guess you are right. No one ever said these things to me before."

We sat for a while in silence, curled up with each other until sleep came down on both of us.

I got up at dawn and put the kettle on the fire to make tea. The air was fresh, and a gentle breeze was blowing.

"How did you sleep?" I asked, after waking her up, so she could see the sunrise.

"Like a log." She smiled, still a bit heavy-eyed.

"We have an interesting day today, so you better get up soon; I want to show you the beauty of the beginning of a new day in the desert."

I took off my clothes and jumped into the cold water of the pond and swam a little to release my joints and loosen my muscles. I glanced at Noa occasionally; she was flushed and embarrassed and tried not to look at me, though I caught her sneaking quick peeks at me every so often. After I got out of the water, fresh and alert, I put on my clothes and sat down next to her to have a cup of morning tea.

"You should also get into the water, it's lovely; there's nothing like a refreshing morning dip to start the day."

"The water looks freezing. I'll just go wash my face." She answered uneasily.

I gave her a Bedouin Galabeya that I had in my possession, as her clothes were too tight and too hot for the desert's heat.

"We are leaving in a few minutes; I'm going to collect some wood for a fire later. Meanwhile, please get dressed and get ready."

We ascended to the nearest summit, just as the sun was coming out. The view was spectacular; from the mountain, we could see the entire region, the wadis, canyons and cliffs, even the sea and the high mountains behind it. The landscape was bright red that became orange, pink and yellow as the sun rose higher in the sky. The air was still crispy and nippy. We sat there for about two hours in silence. Her eyes were wide open, absorbing and exploring the creation of a new day; the life dripping from the crevices and caves into the world, the mountain goats that come out to graze, the insects that start their working day, and the birds that chant praises to the desert.

Eventually, we needed to get on our way; the nearest town was a walking day away, and I wanted to pass at least half the way to it before it gets too hot. She reluctantly came down the mountain with me. I packed my things, filled the jerry cans with water, and loaded everything on the camel. Before leaving, I introduced the two girls; Noa was initially scared of Nadya, but I knew they would get along. I loaded her on Nadya's back, despite the screams of fear that came from her throat as the camel stood up. Then we set off.

Most of the morning, we walked quietly without talking; no conversation was needed. Nadya's tranquillity calmed Noa. She had already fallen in love with the overgrown animal. We had a few quick water breaks during the morning, in which I explained to her about plant species, their features, and their ways of surviving in the desert without water. And about the landscape and formation of the desert. Towards lunchtime, I found a cool cave at the side of a mountain, so we stopped for a siesta and a light lunch. Noa was quiet and absorbed in her thoughts. I examined her face as I lit the fire; her delicate features wrinkled, and she seemed to be trying to make some decision. Suddenly, the wrinkles disappeared and serenity of acceptance of a decision appeared on her face. She turned to me with a light in her eyes, "I want to stay here with you in the desert, I've never felt so calm and peaceful, and I feel I can learn a lot from you and the desert."

"Absolutely not! You cannot stay with me!" I said, "I'm sorry, but this is my journey, and I have to do it alone. Although there are many lonely times and hardships, I have to go through the experiences by myself. You have a life elsewhere. If you want to change them and go on a journey, just do it. It should be your journey, and you must be in no doubt about it. The understanding you will find on the way will be yours only, because there is no all-inclusive truth, but only personal truth. Your journey doesn't have to be in the desert, even though, right now, it makes you feel good to be here; you can do it anywhere that enriches you. Don't you worry, we will meet again up the road sometime, somewhere. The world is a small place. In a few years, you will probably see me as another passing episode in your life."

It's hard to describe the disappointment on her face.

"In the evening we will reach the nearest town, from there you can take a bus home."

I pressed on her shoulder gently. "I'm sorry."

Just before sunset, we reached the outskirts of the town.

"We have to separate here and say goodbye, Noa, I don't want to enter the town." I said, "You need to continue on this street to get to the bus station."

She gave me a long hug, "I'll never forget you, and you won't be a passing episode in my life." Tears ran down her cheeks.

"I'm sure we will meet in the future. Until then, just remember not to let the fear of change overcome you. I hope you'll find your way in this brief life."

I turned the camel and walked back towards the desert. I felt her eyes on me as I was walking away from her, but decided not to look back.

Dad

The next day, at lunchtime, while sitting and looking at the distant sea. My thoughts were wandering, and for some reason, revisited that morning a few years ago when he came to me. I would give anything to talk to him again one more time.

It's five in the morning on a beach in Sinai, Egypt. The sun is coming out in the east, painting the mountains in red and orange. The sea is like a mirror; flat, without waves. The village is quiet, with no living soul outside; everyone is asleep. I'm sitting on the beach, crossed legs with a joint in my hand. On my lap is laying a curly head of the girl from last night; Tina, Nina, Lina, I can't quite remember her name. She is sleeping after a long night full of alcohol, weed, and sex. My thoughts spread in different directions that are out of reach in everyday life. In the end, they focus on my father; it is unclear to me why he, here and now after such a long time that I didn't think about him. The ways of the mind and soul are mysterious.

My father passed away when I was only eleven years old. I'll never forget that night when he fell; half an hour before he told my mother that he is not feeling well and is going for a walk. According to my mum, he came back after a while and said that he was feeling better. Then he fell.

I woke up from the sound of his fall, but I didn't get up. Only after about ten minutes, the doctor and nurse arrived and tried to resuscitate him. Then I got up to see what was happening. Half asleep, I saw my father lying unconscious on the floor and several people standing over him. My mum was crying hysterically. My grandma took me back to bed and ordered me to go back to sleep.

All the rest of that night, I couldn't sleep; there was a hustle and bustle in the house, and I also knew or felt that I wouldn't see him anymore. It was only in the morning that I fell asleep for a couple of hours until my uncle woke me up and informed me; "Dad passed away."

I looked at him and only said; "I know."

My father, who was a craftsman, a sailor, built roads with big machines. My father, who left school at the age of fifteen to support his mother and younger brother after his father also died at an early age of a similar heart attack, and learned the school work alone at the house with books that his friends brought to him. My father, who knew four languages and was so funny until he brought people to tears. My father, who smacked me at times, but I didn't hold a grudge for it. My father, who didn't drink alcohol, didn't smoke and rarely got sick. My father, who was strong, and demanded from me a lot, never gave up. Dad left me to grow without a guiding hand, without explanations of why, how, and where to.

"See what came out of me and what I have done with my life, that's all I want. To talk to you one more time face to face and ask all the questions that are locked inside me."

"You came to me several times in my dreams and said that you just came back from a long journey, and now you are going to stay. And I would wake up, not sure whether it was reality or a dream. Eventually, I would realise that these were the dreams of an adolescent boy with no answers; Just questions, all of which I need to solve on a daily basis without your fatherly advice."

At home, we hardly talked about him, even with my friends, my teachers, or other people. I couldn't talk about him; every time he was mentioned, I felt uncomfortable, and I changed the topic of the conversation.

"I didn't talk about you in my youth, Dad, but you were always in the back of my mind."

At the funeral I didn't cry and haven't been crying since; I cannot, I have tried hundreds of times, but I don't know how to.

Sinai, it's five o'clock in the morning, I'm sitting on the beach admiring the stunning red landscape in front of me. Suddenly I see a spot in the sea in the distance, it is growing slowly as it approaches me. My senses are trying to sharpen and identify the strange object in the water; it's not a boat or a ship, it's not a fish. I'm looking harder at the object that is getting closer, and after about a minute, I'm starting to realise that it is a person who walks on the water towards me.

Slowly, I'm able to identify him; he, it's already clear to me that it's a man, is already about three hundred feet away and continues to walk in my direction. His facial feature begins to be distinct; cold sweat is trickling down the back of my head as his face becomes clear.

"It can't be; it's the weed that I've smoked! It's a hallucination! It's a dream!" All those thoughts are running through my mind. The girl on my lap is still deep in her beauty sleep. The figure is coming closer and closer, already about twenty feet away; it's becoming clear that this image is my father walking towards me with a grin on his face. I slap my face until it hurts. I'm awake, it's not a dream. He is getting closer and closer, without a word, putting his hand on my shoulder. I shut my eyes, then open them; my father is gone.

Still feeling the hand on my shoulder, I turn back and see the Bedouin fisherman from the village. His hand is on my shoulder, "Sabah Al-Khair!", "Good morning!" He says with a smile full of rotten teeth.

SUV

A voice of an engine roaring and a man swearing threw me out of the memory. I opened my eyes, and to my surprise, I saw an expensive SUV; one of the status symbols that blocks the roads and ruins nature when the "suits" want to play with rugged machines and feel manly and cool. The front wheels were sunk all the way to the undercarriage in the sand, and a man was kicking and swearing at it as if it was a living being. I stood on my feet, staring, amazed at the bizarre show presented to me.

"You goddamn car, move your fucking ass. Why did I spend so much money? So you can get stuck in the middle of nowhere?" The man screamed while kicking the wheel.

Sweat was pouring from his forehead, and his face was red from annoyance and anger. Suddenly, his eyes spotted me standing and looking at him, and the frenzy stopped. He froze and glanced at me awkwardly, wondering from where I suddenly popped.

"Sorry, sir, can you please help me push the car? I don't understand how I succeeded to sink in the sand; the company assured me that this was the best off-road vehicle in the market, and suddenly it got stuck in the middle of the trip; it's a fucked-up car. I have to get back to the hotel for dinner; I already paid for it."

"I'll help you." I said with a smile, "But first, let's sit down in the shade; I'll make some tea. You can relax a bit, then we'll release the car. Besides, no matter how good the car is if the driver is not experienced enough."

He seemed as if he was going to protest, but gave up and sat on a stone under the large acacia tree. He pulled out a mobile phone from his trousers and tried to call.

"You are wasting your time; there is no reception here. You might get some reception on the top of one of the summits."

He glanced towards the nearby mountain and the blazing sun, and then put the phone back in his pocket.

"Relax buddy, you'll be on time for dinner, and tonight you will sleep in your hotel room. Just have a little patience. You can stretch out on the blanket while the tea is boiling."

"I've heard that drinking herbal tea in the desert is soothing and relaxing." He said.

"No, mate," I couldn't resist laughing. "Taking the time to make the tea, collect the wood for the fire, sit and wait for the tea to boil and then sip it slowly, is soothing and relaxing. The actual action of drinking tea is not soothing. Taking the time and having a break from speed, pressure, agenda, and commitment will give you a few more years before the heart attack. That's why you came to the desert, isn't it?"

"Yes, maybe you're right." He said, stretching the blanket. "Say, is this beast yours?" He pointed to the camel.

"This beast will pull out your car, so you can talk about her nicely. First of all, it's not just a beast; it's a camel, and her name is Nadya. Second, she understands a lot more than you think."

To show him how intelligent she is, I called her name to come to me; she stood up and approached me, rubbing her nose on my arm to his astonishment.

"I was sure these camels were stupid animals." He mumbles.

"That's what most people think, but once you open your eyes, you find that a lot of the things most people think are wrong. The ignorance of: 'That's how everyone thinks' or 'That's what everyone does' is why prejudice is created. The camel, contrary to the general opinion, is one of the most intelligent animals."

"So, did you hire the camel for a few days to wander around in the wilderness? Try to be a Bedouin? A Man of the desert?" He asked in a slightly sarcastic tone.

"Not exactly," I answered calmly, "I've been living here for a while."

"Why?"

"I'll answer you by asking a question; where do you live?"

"I live in Tel Aviv."

"Why?"

He looked at me bewildered, as if he didn't understand the question. "Because that's where the centre is, where things happen, work, entertainment, and girls. What do you have here? Sand and stones? You don't even have air conditioning here."

"What things happen there? Also, which of those you are in fact experiencing or engaging in?"

"Well, you know; cafés, restaurants, concerts, shows, girls, friends, clubs, hook-ups…"

"Okay, I'll bet that you are working in software or an advertising company and earning a nice salary. You're a bachelor without a long-term relationship with a woman. You have short and casual hook-ups with girls, but you're afraid to commit; you're afraid not to be free to do what you want. But on the other hand, you spend a lot of time with friends so you'll not be alone and deal with yourself. You sit with your mates in cafés and talk about girls in general, girls from the previous night, you are looking at girls walking outside and joking among yourselves about what you want to do with them. You talk about the experiences from the last rave, talk about what is 'in' or 'out', try to make an impression on each other with the money, salary, car, size of flat; You probably have a three-bedroom flat just for yourself. Regarding shows in Tel Aviv; I'm confident that the last time you went to the theatre was on a 'culture day' when you were in the military, and opera or dance shows don't interest you. The only shows you perhaps go regularly are of DJ's at parties."

The conceited expression disappeared from his face, and anger lines came upon his lips.

"You're wrong; I have a two-bedroom flat facing the beach and not three."

"I guess that in other things I'm pretty close to the truth, though. You see, before you mock another person's way of life or choices, you might want to look at yourself first. I don't have cafés and pubs here. However, if I feel the need to be around people, I can easily go to the beach where there is a great selection of pubs and girls of all kinds. Even if the distance to the beach is a walking day, it's OK; I'm not in any hurry, I'll end up there in time. I don't miss the company of friends you're talking about; I came here to get away from them because I'm tired of the pretence. Notice how many times you feel lonely, even when there are friends around you. I'm, on the other hand, alone here but not lonely. Loneliness comes from within us, from emptiness and meaningless prospects, and not from the number of people around us. Don't forget, cynicism and ridicule come from disrespect to others that come from your disrespect to yourself that comes from weakness and insecurity. Now my friend, can I offer you a cup of tea?"

"By the way, I know you didn't mean to disrespect me but throughout my life, I've often been mocked and suffered jokes at my expense for walking my path and not following the society rulebook. Even though I know that this mockery comes from weakness and jealousy, at a certain point I've had enough. I do expect that at least here in the desert, far from other people and under my hospitality, my guests will not be disrespectful."

"I'm sorry if I hurt your feelings, buddy, I didn't mean to. I appreciate your help and hospitality, and you know what? There is some magic in life here, even though I don't think I can live far away from the urban noise. Thank you for putting things into perspective. You were right about my friends and me; if I look at it now, our conversations and pastimes are quite shallow, but that's the way it is with most people. However, not every conversation has to have a deep insight and seriousness. Without sarcasm, life will be dull."

He took a small sip from the glass I served him, "Dude, this tea is excellent, which herbs did you make it from?"

"It's a professional secret. I can't reveal the ingredients, but I'm glad you like it."

The chap finished the tea in two sips and got up.

"Do you think we can pull out the car now?"

"It's tough for you to sit back and relax for a little while on your holiday, isn't it? Okay, let's get this cumbersome steel block out of the sand."

I called Nadya, tied the towing belt that he found in the car's boot to her saddle and the other end to the front of the vehicle. Then he sat behind the wheel and within two minutes the car was out of the sand, and Nadya was munching a pita that I gave her for her kind help.

The guy came out of the car with a big smiley face, holding a stack of notes in his hand. "Thanks, buddy! I'd like to pay you for the help."

"No, thanks." I gritted my teeth. "Not everything should be bought with money, mate; help others in trouble, humanity and hospitality cannot be weighed in gold. I hope you'll get to dinner on time and enjoy the rest of your holiday."

He got in the car, waved goodbye, and quickly disappeared into an annoying cloud of dust.

She

Sometimes when the loneliness bug enters, I go back in time to the memorable episodes in my life that most of them have a significant connection to my way of life and solitude now.

A few days after my encounters with Noa and the annoying SUV driver, which were unusual days in my journey, the bug suddenly hit me without notice. My method to get rid of loneliness and depression is not to fight it but to give myself to it. By doing so, they are fading faster.

I sat down under a tree and went back in time to the strange day two years ago on a train from Amsterdam to Berlin.

I'm sitting in a train cabin, the sun outside shining; it is one of the most beautiful days of that winter. I'm busy pondering about my past and future life. The outside is lovely; Fir trees, colourful vast fields, grey country cottages and old towns. I'm excited about going to Berlin, this magnificent city that is awaiting me, with all the history, art and madness that goes wild according to the stories.

I'm not alone; she travels with me. She, with all the history, art and madness we shared. Shared, but no more.

I feared this trip with her; I didn't know what would happen after the crisis in our relationship. I don't know what exactly I feel for her at the moment; I used to love her more than anything, but now that I have opened my eyes, sometimes I can't stand her, sometimes I love her like before, and sometimes I feel sorry for her. One thing I know; She hurt me, more than anyone else in my life, and I'm still angry and don't know how to relate to her.

After crossing the border to Germany, I notice that I'm quite happy; I love to travel, see the world, and learn new things. To feel that the world is my oyster, that there are no boundaries and the feeling of freedom is total. I have always thought borders are a stupid thing resulting from the "Territorial Imperative" element of the weak human. I know that this happiness will soon end. But I don't care.

She sits in front of me and reads a book, "The Alchemist." She loved these sorts of teenagers' philosophies. I'm wondering if there is still a slim chance that we can be together. Fate made it difficult for me that year; every trip outside Rotterdam, my city of residence at that time, we travelled together. In my mind, I know that there is no way we'll be together again. In my heart, though, I'm still fooling myself. I wonder if I still love her or just hold on to the past?

That year was packed with new experiences; I was living in a new country, and for the first time, I lived out of my tiny home country. The beginning of the year was particularly exciting; I met many new and beautiful people from all over the world. I discovered for the first time what love is, so I thought. She was the first person to speak to me at the academy, and I immediately fell in love with her. Then she tore my heart apart.

She decides to go out for a smoke. I suggest that I'll also come, "You better stay and keep an eye on the bags." she says.

So I stayed.

I'm thinking about the professional opportunities that await me in the near future. Will luck finally play out for me?

Momentary happiness is temporary; five days from now, I will have to come back to reality. Fate deceives you, gives you something to look forward to and hope for, and then punches you in the guts. This was my life experience before the trip.

She sleeps in front of me in a small, intimate train cabin, in the small world that belongs to us for only eight hours. She looks so beautiful and peaceful. There is, though, an invisible wall of mixed emotions between us. I feared this trip with her; I had to repress a lot of emotions, a lot of pain and anger. Four months earlier, it could have been one of the happiest trips of my life. However, since then, a lot of water has passed in the Rhine, and our relationship was very fake. At least from my side.

I'm thinking about my good friend Reuben, that this week gets a chance to win the heart of her best friend. I hope with all my heart that he will succeed. I know she is attracted to him, but a woman's heart is unknown and random. Sometimes it goes topsy-turvy, it's unclear why.

The German conductor comes in and asks for tickets. She gives them and speaks to the conductor in English. After the lady walks out, we laugh, as she grew up in Germany. In our profession, most of the time you don't live in your home country, and you speak mainly English, so after a while, you start thinking in English. Most of my colleagues are citizens of the world, as art is more important than the country for them. They don't have a ridiculous connection with a piece of land that was artificially outlined by their species. They are open enough to mingle, get to know and assimilate with other people and cultures. This attribute was the thing I loved most that year; the students at the academy were from all over the world. They all lived for one purpose; to fulfil their goals; be better dancers, teachers, or artists. The integration and communication have been brilliant, even with all the differences.

The landscape is slowly changing; the forests become denser, and a different architecture emerges; we are in Germany.

Naturally, I begin to think about the Holocaust; about this beautiful country immersed in blood, the packed death trains, the thin people with the dim look in the eyes I have seen in films. How did this enlightened culture that raised some of the greatest artists, scientists and thinkers in history, a culture that has advanced the world theoretically, technologically and artistically, perhaps more than any other country in modern times, except maybe Great Britain, its nemesis in that war, produced such monsters?

How did this extreme darkness come out of the extreme enlightenment?

Maybe it's the way of the world, perhaps it's the Yin and Yang, and we have to find the middle point, the equilibrium. If we had stayed in the middle, there would have been no development, nothing to aim for; life and people would be incredibly dull.

I look at her; she isn't so peaceful anymore, and her forehead wrinkles occasionally in her sleep. I would give anything to know what is going through her mind at this moment; what she feels about me?

She wakes up and takes the Walkman; the batteries are empty, and she doesn't have new ones. I'm laughing because she always forgets things like that.

"Stop laughing at me." She says with a lovely smile and goes back to sleep.

The beginning of the year was wonderful. We spent entire days together; went to pubs, sat in the park, strolled in the streets, and hung around in her flat. We would sit for hours talking or just look at each other. I remember the day we sat in the park on the grass on a rare sunny day; she looked at me, "What are you thinking now?"

"Nothing, I'm just having fun."

So she asked, "Do you want to kiss me?"

"Do you want me to kiss you?" I replied.

"I want you to kiss me, but I'm not sure if I love you. I don't want to play with your feelings."

I smiled at her. "So what are you doing now if not playing with me?"

She started getting into all kinds of apologies, so I shut her up with a kiss.

I remember the day she told me she didn't love me; we sat in my kitchen for about three hours; the atmosphere was uneasy; I was trying to figure out what she was afraid of. Her whole being and behaviour that month, her entire body language, the look in her eyes toward me said love. But then she told me she doesn't love me and wants me only as a close friend, like we were until now. I tried to explain to her that we were much more than close friends, even though we hadn't yet had sex because I wanted to give her time to decide and take off her barriers.

Eventually, she just left and went back to her flat.

I went up to my bedroom, despondent and depressed. I put on the CD player Pink Floyd's "The Wall", covered myself in a blanket and tried to disappear.

After about an hour, the phone rang. It was her; she asked if I wanted to come to her flat. I answered no and put the phone down. After a few minutes, I felt I couldn't be far from her. It was stronger than me. All that time since we met I couldn't stop thinking about her, in the street on my bike, at home, in the classes. I kept seeing her in my mind, and every minute I wasn't near her, I missed her. So I called back and said I was coming over.

I will tell you about that night in her flat on another occasion when the censor will approve. I can only say that it was a night full of passion which she instigated, and was one of the most unforgettable nights of my life until then.

The next afternoon we were invited to dinner at a friends' house. Throughout the evening, she did not look at me. When I finally managed to catch her alone, she informed me that she was feeling bad about last night and nothing had changed in our relationship or her feelings for me.

I asked her why she invited me over to her flat? Also, why did she set off the night events?

She replied she didn't want to lose me and didn't want me to stay away from her. So she called me to come and talk but got carried away, and now she regrets it. Though, she still wanted us to stay as friends as we were before.

What goes through women's minds is by far the greatest mystery of creation.

I was still blinded by love and thought she was also, but some fear stopped her from coming to terms with it, until a few days later when she took off her mask and showed me a totally different woman.

At Hanover, a fat German man with a massive mole on his face came into our cabin and sat down next to me, destroying our confused intimacy.

From time to time she smiles at me, her smile is captivating and charming; those amazing big green eyes that look straight into your soul and laugh. I can't resist them. Those times when I feel like I'm going to explode at any minute are the most challenging moments when I'm with her.

Her thin and muscular figure is in contrast to her delicate face and flexible body language; she reminds me of a cat. Her looks together with her mien of a little girl discovering a new world every moment rapt me every time we were alone. In the company of other people, however, she would turn her skin over, and I would become a minor nuisance that existed only for her little nit-picking to make her feel mature and powerful. During these times, I chose to ignore her and concentrate on the other people in our society, some of whom were fascinating and amusing in their own right.

It disappointed me when our hosts told us we would not live together during the week we were in Berlin, because in my foolishness I hoped it might bring back what we had.

We arrived in Berlin; it's the end of the trip. We said goodbye at the station as each one of us was invited to stay in a different flat. The events of that week are less memorable to me. The important thing was that our relationship improved a little and didn't include a complete disregard for each other as it was in the previous months. Though we were still pretty uncomfortable around each other at times. I still had a little hope for something to happen between us, as we both passed the audition, and we were going to work together in the future. Well, this job, ladies and gentlemen, was going to demand us to work intensely close and tight, physically and emotionally.

I opened my eyes, took a sip of water, and looked around to check that Nadya didn't astray. It was still too hot to walk, so I closed my eyes again and floated back in the memory lane.

To remember, it is like watching a video; you close your eyes and drift. If you wish, you can move forwards or backwards in the timeline; you just need to press the right button.

I pressed the button two months forward from the train to Café Dizzy, which is located in a large industrial city called Rotterdam, which is in a country called by most The Netherlands. Inside the Café, sitting by the window, is I. It's Sunday, a day of rest. It's a chilly but pleasant afternoon of a European spring. The place is cosy and warm; on the walls, there are pictures of the jazz giants of the 1950s; Charlie Parker, Dizzy Gillespie, Louis "Satchmo" Armstrong, and more. I'm drinking a cold beer and eating a lovely Dutch apple tart with cream. The sound system in the background is playing a song by Billie Holiday that adds to the calm atmosphere. In my head, the thoughts are racing non-stop, though.

At noon, I woke up from a phone call from my good friend Reuben telling me about the previous night, when he hit it off with a sexy French girl. He was already in love over his head with her. We laughed about the other beautiful girl who rejected him a month ago and lately seems jealous and keeps flirting with him. I'm happy for him, but I'm also somewhat envious; I need to find the one who will love me, but she is nowhere to be found, while he has two gorgeous girls chasing him.

It is not an easy time in my life, I'm about to start working in Berlin which is excellent, but I'm also afraid not to live up to the expectations of the choreographer who demands to drop all the mannerisms, be who you are and find your true self. It is a challenging and frustrating task. Looking back, it turned out to be much harder than I thought. Though the results were fruitful and the crowd loved the shows.

I'm waiting for next week when I'm going to fly back home for a short holiday. I hope that the holiday will give me some time off from the scary thoughts of the future. I'm afraid that the future would continue as my life until now and would not justify its existence.

My life until now was not uninteresting and was full of purpose, but I always felt that I needed something else, something more. Until recently I didn't know what I needed, but lately, I figured out that I need what I have never experienced before, a love of a woman; I needed a hug, a touch, to know that someone cares for me and takes care of me. To be with someone that I could be real around her, without games, pretence or masks. Someone who doesn't try to change me and doesn't play games with my feelings— someone to celebrate the successes with, and to be supported by after failures.

I often think I'm tired of fighting; myself and the world. Tired of doing it all by myself, tired of the disappointments that have been a large part of my life. Nothing ever came easy on a silver platter for me. Sometimes, I think I should take some sleeping pills and put an end to this. However, I know I would never do it. I'm not afraid to die; it is probably good over there, as no one has come back yet. But too many people will get hurt; Family, friends... I don't like hurting others. So the pills are out of the question. Anyway, I always feel that there is hope for something better in the future. Even in the most difficult and depressing times, I've always felt that if I'll go ahead and do not give up, in the end, I will get what I wanted.

I'm probably just feeling sorry for myself for no reason, and I do have a good life. Maybe I'm expecting too much. However, you can't fight your emotions.

Now, a few years later here in the desert, I understood that one thing, such as love, money or success will not fulfil the missing part of life because as human beings who think and feel, we naturally want and seek more and more; there will always be something missing. When there is money, we want to have love or more money. When we get love, we want children followed by a lover on the side. After we get to Mars, we will want to reach Pluto. Our nature always encourages progress, so we are never fully satisfied. Now I understand that doing, not giving up and insisting on not being discouraged is just as meaningful and essential as the objective. When I reach the target, I am improving it or setting another goal so that there is no end or a happy ending.

Looking back, I see how naïve and somewhat immature I've been back then. At that time, I missed the love of a woman, but now it's clear to me that love would give me some happiness, but will not make my life complete.

The day before she called me, I was surprised as we had not been in contact for a month. She is already working in Berlin, feeling good but missing everyone here. I hope everything will go according to plan, and when I join her to work on the project, we will rent a flat together as both of us don't know anyone there. Maybe far from her friends. Something will happen between the two of us again. This phone call, once more, had given me new and naïve hope, yet utterly unreal and not meant to happen.

My angel

Fast-forward ten months from Café Dizzy.

The Christmas period ended, and so did the project I've taken part in. We performed ten times in a theatre in the city and received brilliant reviews, but every good thing has to have an end. She and I worked together and were friendly, but the intimacy was gone. I realised that my feelings for her faded and became like a scar on the body, that every time you touch it, it reminds you of an event or time in your past. Sometimes it is funny how the heart works. I turned the page and concentrated on the present and future.

All my friends and colleagues left the city to seek other opportunities elsewhere, but I've decided to stay in Berlin to keep experiencing this diverse city. A city that is changing at a rapid speed but still remembers its past glory days, a city that has everything; from a wild and wonderful side to the insanely depressing side. My flat is in a small street named Lychener Strasse, in the cool Prenzlauer-Berg district in the east part of the city. It's a cheap and young area, a former old and grey communist quarter that changed its character and became trendy. A lot of fringe art, galleries, small theatres, cafés, pubs, and cheap ethnic restaurants. A sizeable amount of the population is young; it comprises artists, punks that look like a relic from the early '80s that hangs out at S-Bahn and U-Bahn stations or supermarket's entrances and asks for handouts, students, elderly who are living in this borough since their birth, and a large gay community who feel very free in this area of the city to be who they are.

I want to use my time to observe and research the western social or anti-social Homo sapiens that live in a confined area with five million of its kind. The distance from the crowd while performing on stage doesn't meet my needs anymore; I want to feel more connections. So I decided to end my career on stage, and I'm making my living as a busker at Kurfürstendamm, Berlin's luxurious shopping street. I stand on the street corner in a suit with no movement, like a statue. When someone tosses a coin, I juggle for a few seconds and freeze again, waiting for the next coin. Apparently, I'm the one who is performing to the audience, but the real theatre is the audience itself; its responses to the human statue and its attempts to make me move without paying money, which of course fails. Some people shout at me in an effort to startle me. Some people take the hat with the money from the floor, hoping I would run after them; eventually, they give up and put it back. There was a woman who started undressing in front of me, another woman kissed me on my mouth with the tongue; even that was unsuccessful and didn't make me move. It's interesting to see the different reactions, even of those who only watch and do not bother me, or the kids who just touch me, normally on the tip of the pinkie to check if I'm real.

I'm spending my free time wandering the streets or sitting on the S-Bahn or the U-Bahn trains that roam the entire city. I watch people and try to learn and imagine their stories and characters. In the trains, I have seen people from all over the spectrum of society. Thousands of faces of all kinds; Businessmen in suits and briefcases reading a newspaper or talking on their mobile phone and every few seconds looking at their clock because time is money and in their eyes life is meaningless without plenty of it, drunks singing and dancing followed by the looks of pity from the other travellers, weary elderly women who have been through many of the city's turmoil in their lifetime, carrying baskets full of groceries, noisy youth with hormones bursting out of control, junkies handing leaflets and asking for charity, students browsing at textbooks, and just a lonely people that running the long race of life. Some people are still fighting, but most have realised that they are facing windmills and have given up; Living their meaningless insignificant lives in anticipation of winning the lottery or for the redeeming death.

The street experience is more optimistic; lots of couples in love, beautiful art displays by artists who have no money to present in institutionalised establishments, suited yuppies who look full of themselves, street musicians and smiling people filling the cafés and restaurants. On the other hand, there are also those obnoxious noisy punks that harass the public in the streets, and the few racists, who are mostly over sixty (probably former Nazis) that when recognising that you are a stranger, they make a sour face and give you poor service.

The city is changing; my area of residence has a massive renovation project of the houses' fronts, which were neglected during the communist era. Potsdamer Platz is the largest construction site in the world; when I was there, I felt like I was on another planet. The districts that flourished during the golden era of Berlin in the 1920s and were the Bohemian and cultural centre of Europe are returning slowly to their former glory. The German government is soon to move its offices, and the title of a Capital city, to Berlin. The atmosphere on the streets is of anticipation and suspense for what the change would bring. I hope that Berlin's unique alternative culture will not disappear in the face of the commerciality that is taking over our world.

I don't know anyone in town, and I hadn't talked to anyone for a while. Loneliness is hard; the feeling of a small, unimportant creature in the vast orderly bustle can be unresting. Apart from the time I work, no one has any interest in me, no one cares or bothers me, I have no personality, no identity, and no one gives me a second look on the street or anywhere else. Such an experience provides a good perspective on the importance of each one of us in the world. It also allows one to observe from the side without being involved. I insist on staying despite the loneliness. Looking back, without this unwavering determination, I would not have met my angel.

It is mid-March, I'm waiting at the Eberswalder Strasse U-Bahn station near my flat on Sunday evening. Mighty Berlin is covered in white after heavy snowfall in the night; it was unexpected for this time of the year, and probably the last snow of the winter. A remarkably peaceful stillness descends upon the city after a snowstorm. The eyes open, the cold air penetrates the lungs, and there is a feeling of a valve opening in the heart. You can walk slower, relax, and just feel the beauty and peace all around. I cannot explain it, but when everything is covered with snow, and the sun is shining, life seems more beautiful and the world's matters seem insignificant. I've experienced the same feeling later in life where I encountered snow; in Amsterdam, Prague, and Jerusalem.

Light snow is falling, and it's cold outside, below zero, and the sun is setting. A few people are waiting with me at the station; suddenly I hear shouts in the air, "Ausländers, raus!", "Die Juden erobern die Welt!" "Tod den Schwarzen!" ("foreigners out!", "The Jews are taking over the world!", "Death to blacks!"). I turn my head and see a large gang of neo-Nazi skinheads wearing military clothes, their heads shaved, and aggressive tattoos painted on their bodies. There are also a few girls with them, similarly dressed, only with their hair dyed instead of shaved. They entered the station and are now breaking down tickets' vending machines, throwing bins, and frightening the people who are waiting for the train. I'm looking at the big clock hanging over me; the train should arrive in one minute. I'm praying that they will not recognise me as a foreigner before it arrives, as I don't have time to walk away. One of them approaches me, it is still unclear to me how, but he manages to identify the book in my hand as written in Hebrew and shouts to his friends, "Hier ist ein Jude!", ("There is a Jew here!"). In a flash, the entire group is swirling around me, shouting derogatory insults. I'm looking for refuge, looking pleadingly at the other passengers who look at me with pity but are afraid to interfere and help. Suddenly I feel a firm push from behind, and I fall forward into the hands of one of them, who pushes me back with a punch in the face that stuns me. The mob starts to play with me, throwing me from one to the other, kicking and beating me. I'm trying to resist as best I can, but they are ten, and I'm only one. My strength is weakening, and I feel I'm going to lose consciousness. Through the blows and kicks, as I'm getting into a stupor, I see a pair of sad grey eyes staring at me with compassion. Our looks cross for a second, and then one of the hooligans shouts, "Let's put him on the railroad tracks!" and the entire herd follows, "Death to a Jew!"

Suddenly, I hear police sirens. The skinheads turn to flee and throw me on the station floor, almost fainted and covered with blood and spit. I'm opening my eyes that have already started to swell and see the pair of grey eyes leaning over me. With my last breath, I'm asking her in broken German, "Please help me get up and walk; I'm working illegally here, and the police will deport me if they find me here." Two small hands grab me with great effort and help me stand up. Hardly holding the weight of my body, we start to run to the exit on the other side of the station. Every few feet I'm stumbling, but somehow manage to stop my falls. I'm explaining to her with hand gestures the way to my flat that fortunately is close by. I'm on the verge of fainting, she slaps me hard and whispers in my ear in English, "Stay awake, we're almost there."

Finally, after what seemed like forever, we enter the building. She rummages in my pockets and pulls out the flat keys. Luckily it is a ground-floor flat, as she definitely cannot physically take me up the stairs in my current situation. At last, we are entering the flat. She is gently helping me to my bed and asks: "Do you want me to call an ambulance? You don't look very well."

"Please don't call an ambulance or the police, I'm alright," I whispered.

"Do you have family or friends here that I can call?"

"I don't have anyone here."

"I have to go, are you sure you'll be okay?" Her eyes are already looking towards the door.

"I'll be fine, just please bring me a glass of water before you go."

She brings me a glass of water and says, "You look awful, but I can't stay. I'll try to come tomorrow to see how you are doing."

My eyes are already swelling, and I can barely see anything. Before I lose consciousness, I hear the door slam, and darkness descends on my world.

In the morning, I'm waking up sore and bruised. I'm afraid to move; I remember that at night I woke up in pain every time I moved. After about an hour of laying down and staring at the ceiling, I feel I must go to the toilet. I manage to get up despite the horrible pains in my chest and limp to the bathroom. After I empty my bladder, I look at myself in the mirror. Because of the swelling, I can barely open my eyes; they look like two narrow slits. My mouth is also swollen and painted with dark coagulated blood. I'm washing my face and body from last night's filth. Feeling a little more refreshed, I'm tottering back to the bed thinking about my current situation; At least two of my ribs are broken, my right knee is swollen, my entire body is full of black-blue marks, and with such a face I can't go out. I have food in the fridge for three days, and when it is consumed, I'll have no choice but to go out to buy some. I know that in my present state, I'll struggle to do more than ten steps. The current state of affairs is not good.

Hopefully, the girl who saved me would come as she said, though I'm sceptical about it; does she have any reason to return? I can't understand what she was doing with these hooligans. Perhaps she is like them, and just had a moment of weakness and felt sorry for me. Maybe she'll come back with them to finish the job. I remember, though, that her eyes had a genuine kindness despite heavy makeup and aggressive military clothes. I know that if she came back, she would come alone.

I don't want to call my family in Israel; first, I don't want them to worry. Second, I also don't want to hear the: "We told you!" and "Come back home and learn something. We can't always help you; we're not rich."

I convinced myself I would go through this crisis alone. A few days in bed and the swelling would go down, leaving only the broken ribs that only time will mend, as you can't put a cast on them. I just have to be gentle with myself and not strain my body for a few weeks.

I've been in bed for two days now, trying not to move, trying to concentrate and heal my body, sending a recovery signal to it. Most of the time, I'm in a kind of deep meditation; it's my only way to pass the time and stay still without losing my mind. Twice a day I hobble to the bathroom and the kitchen, using the toilet and eating a bit. It's hard for me to chew, so I'm eating mostly yoghurt and canned soup. The food is running out, so I will need to go out to do some shopping soon, but I'll try to delay it as much as I can; my lips are still quite puffed, and my eye is still black.

Around noon, I heard a gentle, almost unnoticeable knock on the front door. I look through the peephole and see a girl with purple hair; she wears worn blue jeans and an army coat and holds a carrier bag from a supermarket. I recognise the sad grey eyes and open the door.

"Hi! I hope I'm not disturbing you. I just came to check if you are ok. I feel awful about what they did to you. I wasn't sure if you were able to go out, so I brought some food."

I stare at her, confused for a moment, as I didn't think I'd see her again, and then I open the door and move aside to let her in.

"Come in."

"Where can I put the shopping?"

"Oh, sorry, you can put it on the kitchen table, I'll put it in the fridge later." I'm pointing to the kitchen on the right. "I'm sorry, but I can't stand for long. We can sit near the kitchen table. Can I make you a cup of coffee or tea?"

She starts to put the food in the fridge. "You look like you are struggling to stand, sit down, I'll make the coffee."

I'm sitting down heavily on one of the chairs. "Thank you so much for the shopping; I'll pay you back as soon as I'm able to go to the ATM."

"Don't be silly! It's the least I could do after what my friends have done to you."

She puts two mugs of coffee on the table and sits opposite me.

"I'm sorry it took so long to come and check on you, I had to wait until Hans let me out on my own after that night when I helped you. He didn't know where I disappeared and thought I ran away and left him. He thinks I'm going for a job interview today, which I have but a bit later."

Her English is good, and she seems well-educated. I wonder to myself how she got entangled with a gang of neo-Nazis.

"Is Hans your boyfriend?"

"Yes, and he is also the leader of our group." She looks down at her mug, too embarrassed to look me in the eyes. "I'm so sorry about what they have done to you, I feel ashamed."

Her vulnerability makes me a bit uncomfortable; she has a gentle face, of the kind that is unable to hide emotions. Her fair skin, blonde hair and childlike face make her look almost angelic. The oversized ragged clothes are in contrast to her natural features as her tiny body looks like it's been swallowed by the large overcoat.

"Well, I'm not sure what you are doing with those animals and how you've got involved with them; but you helped me and got me out of there, and I have to thank you for that. By the way, I still don't know your name. I'm Ari."

"It's Anna."

"Nice to meet you, Anna."

She seems more relaxed, and a shy smile comes over her face. She carefully looks up at me and asks. "Where are you from?"

"I'm originally from heaven." I'm saying with a serious expression on my face.

She looks up again and laughs. "Come on, really, where are you from? With a face like that, you don't look like an angel."

"Oh, thanks! I didn't think my look was so appalling."

A sheepish expression comes on her face, and she moves uneasily.

"Sorry, I didn't mean it that way. I referred to the current state of your face with the swollenness and the haemorrhages."

"I know. I'm just messing with you. I grew up in Israel, though, in the last couple of years, I've been living in Europe in different countries, going to where the wind and work take me."

"Oh, wow! I've never met anyone from Israel. So you are a Jew? It's OK if you are, I'm not like my friends; I don't believe in all the racist mumbo jumbo."

"Yes, I'm a Jew, but I have very little connection to religion and tradition. I describe myself as a human or a person; I'm not categorising myself under any title or group. I'm just me."

"So, what do you do that makes you move so often?"

"Well, I'm trained as a dancer, I was dancing in a project here; we performed in Theater am Halleschen-Ufer before Christmas. But the project finished, and now I'm busking outside Ku'damm for a living. I was doing it until your gang beat me up. You look like an educated girl; why are you hanging with them?"

She looks at her watch and suddenly seems anxious. She takes a last sip of the coffee, stands up and puts on her coat. "I'm sorry, I have to go, thanks for the coffee."

I'm getting up to see her out. "I didn't mean to make you uncomfortable with my question."

"It's OK; it's not you. I'm out for a while now, and I don't want to piss Hans off. I'll see if I can pop in tomorrow."

She opens the door. "Tschüss! Bye!" and runs toward the tram stop.

I look at her running down the street, intrigued; "Who is this girl?" She seems so reserved and scared, but under the surface, there is an energy that seeks to erupt and an inner strength that I find riveting.

The next day, my face looks much better; the puffiness is reducing, and the colour is starting to return to normal. I feel much fresher, although my broken ribs still make it hard for me to breathe comfortably. She knocks on my door in the early evening, again holding a carrier bag.

"Hi, I brought you Doner kebab and chips. I hope you like it with garlic sauce."

"I love garlic sauce. Thank you so much again, you can't keep buying me food, though."

She seems a bit flustered and looks back to the street often, so I invite her in.

"Are you alright?"

"Yeah, Yeah, I'm good now. It's just Hans and the bloody group; Scheisse! Shit!... Don't worry about it; you have enough on your plate. Are you hungry? I'm starving! I'll get us plates."

Before I get the chance to open my mouth, she is in the kitchen putting two plates and two glasses on the table, then taking the food and a large bottle of coke out of the carrier bag.

Eventually, she looks at me and smiles; "You look so much better today; I can finally see your actual face. Come on, let's eat."

The quick shifts between looking agitated, almost frightened, to a bubbly and smiley girl, confuses me, but it also fascinates, attracts and makes me want to know more about her.

"Thanks, I feel better. My ribs are still giving me a bit of grief. It will take a few weeks before I get back to normal. By the end of the week, I'll be ready to go out and face the world again, though I won't be able to return to work until I'm 100% recovered. By the way, the Doner is delicious! Exactly what I needed. Danke schön for everything, Anna."

"Bitte schön, it's the least I could do. Anyhow, I had to get out for a while, away from Hans and his disciples."

"Oh yeah, it's your turn to tell me about yourself and how you ended with them. I really want to hear it."

"I guess I owe you that."

Over the next hour, she tells me about her life story until now, which is an intriguing fusion of a soap opera and the story of Christiane F.

She grew up in Frankfurt to a wealthy family of industrialists that owned steel, textile and food factories in Germany, Poland, the Czech Republic and Hungary. Her father was barely at home most of her childhood; if he wasn't away on business trips, he would be most of the time at work and came home in the late evenings. After dinner, he used to close himself in the study room, where she or her mum were not allowed to disrupt.

Her mother was a beautiful and stylish lady who loved the high life, the money and the status. She hosted fundraising galas, social evenings and parties and loved the attention from Frankfurt's influential figures that saw her as a glamorous diva. There might have been love between her and her husband once, but it was long gone. They pretended to have a good marriage, but behind closed doors, their relationship was cold and formal. Her mother never liked to be a mum, Anna and the boys were a burden on her; she preferred to let someone else raise the children. She used the children only as a showcase, so the world can see what a perfect family she has. Also, there was a family secret; no one except the family and the house personnel knew that the state of her marriage hurt and frustrated her mum, and she developed a mild Bipolar. She turned to alcohol in an attempt to wash the demons away, and it often swung out of control.

Anna was basically raised by nannies that were often replaced, as her mum's snobbish and arrogant attitude, and her mood swings, pushed them to their limit until they left. She went to private schools and got all the expensive clothes, toys, and gadgets she wanted. When she has grown older, no one has given her any limitation; she used to have the freedom to come home late and go to sleep whenever she liked, as long as she brought a school certificate with good grades at the end of the year. There was no love in the house, though; no affection, no hugs or kisses, no lullabies when she was a toddler, no loving hand brushed her hair when she was a child. It was the cook who helped her when she got her first monthly period. The mother was too busy with her parties and booze to give attention to her children, and the father was hardly at home. Her parents spoiled her with material stuff as a substitute for the attention and affection that they were unable to give. When Anna was little, the nannies tried to give her love and affection, but they couldn't replace the mother figure. Her two brothers were much older than Anna and left the house as soon as they graduated. They were busy with their own lives and issues, and she was never really close to them anyway because of the age gap. Although Anna was wary of her father, she adored him and enjoyed being around him; he was this unapproachable respectable figure which she looked up to and cherished every second he spent time with her, and every bit of attention he gave her. In those rare moments, he showed care and tenderness toward her, in his own way. Just at a later age, when she was a teenager, she discovered his true nature.

One day, two weeks before her 15th birthday she passed near his study room, he forgot to close the door fully, and she heard him talking to someone on the phone. The tone of his voice was different and softer than his usual authoritative manner. She stood behind the door and listened for a few minutes. Her father was sweet-talking to a woman; telling her how he loves her, how beautiful she is. He set the time when he was going to pick her up to go to a fancy restaurant the next evening. He told her about his plans for the weekend when he was going to take her to Paris for three nights. Anna realised that her father has a lover and the evenings when he returns home late, the weekends away and probably some of his business trips are lies, so he can spend time with this woman. Her father, who took the role of the patriarch of the family after his father passed away and was entrusted to manage the business and keep the broad family united, turned out to be a deceiving weasel that tore apart the family.

The discovery of her dad's double life was the last straw for her.

Her parents, unsurprisingly, forgot her birthday; her dad was on a "business trip; he was probably in a fancy hotel screwing his lover. Her mum was in her bedroom, probably trying makeup or dresses for the next event and drinking herself to sleep. Anna decided not to stay at home and feel sorry for herself; she wanted to party. It was Saturday night, and the clubs were already open, so she put on the sexiest dress she found in her wardrobe and nicked stilettos from her mum, put on heavy makeup, so she'll look older, then took a taxi to Bahnhofsviertel, which was a centre of the nightlife scene. It was also the Red-light district, but she didn't know that. She entered the first bar she saw and ordered brandy, not because she liked it as she had never drunk spirits before, but because brandy was what her dad was drinking, and it was the first drink that came to her mind. The bartender looked at her oddly but poured a shot. She finished it with one sip and asked for another one. After the third shot, she heard a man's voice from her right side; "You might want to slow down, are you alright? You drink like there is no tomorrow."

She looked in his direction and saw a group of 3 guys and two girls in their early 20s sitting on one of the tables drinking beers and wine.

"It's my birthday today, so give me a break, Mister."

The guy who spoke got up and sat down next to her. He leaned close to her ear and said in a low voice, "Even with this dress and the makeup, I can see that you are not one of the working girls from around here. So you need to be careful. How old are you anyway?"

"I'm 18 today."

He looked sceptical. "I bet you are. Happy birthday! Do you want to come and sit with us? The wolves around here are just waiting for a young pretty single girl. By the way, I'm Ulrich; I prefer Uli, though."

She hesitated for a few seconds, looking back and forth at him and the group, then said, "Sure, why not. I'm Anna" then got up, a bit wobbly, and joined them.

Uli introduced the rest of the group. "Guys, this is Anna, it's her birthday today, and she is looking to party tonight."

"Happy birthday, Anna!" all of them shouted.

Then he asked her. "Anna, after this drink we are heading to the Omen. Would you like to join us?"

It was the mid-90s, and the Omen was the coolest and most popular club in Frankfurt that was the world centre of the Techno scene, so she agreed to go with them without hesitation.

"You might want to slow down with the drinks, though, if you want to get there…"

"Don't worry about me, I can handle myself." She said, then thought to herself; "This is going to be the best birthday ever."

That night, she came to know the club scene and the related drugs that naturally come with it. It was also the beginning of her self-destruction journey that eventually led her to Berlin and me.

After her 16th birthday, because of the lack of parental supervision, she started to go out to bars and clubbing regularly. She got to know many people from the night scene that introduced to her all kinds of drugs, which she happily consumed. In the next year and a half, she lived a double life; in the daytime, she went to school, did her homework and went on shopping sprees, acting like any other rich teenager, although her school work deteriorated, and she was often late. She turned away from her friends as she felt they were immature. The nights she spent out in the streets, in bars or clubbing, coming back home at 2 or 3 o'clock in the morning. She was hanging with night owls that were much older but didn't care if she was underage. After an experience with Ecstasy and hallucinogens, she tried cocaine and other uppers and got hooked. There were weekends that she didn't come back home at all and crashed overnight at friends' flats. Her parents were oblivious and not aware of her decline. They continued to give her a large sum of pocket money, which she spent on Blow and Speed. Until the day that school called and informed her mum that Anna didn't show up to school for over a week.

When Anna returned home that evening, long after midnight, her mum was waiting in her room. She confronted her yelling and screaming, but Anna that was fuelled with cocaine didn't bottle up and answered back. A huge argument erupted that ended with Anna packing a small backpack and slamming the front door behind her. She hasn't gone back to the house since.

All she wanted was to get as far away as she could from her parents, so she took a taxi to the train and with the cash she had left she bought a ticket for the night train to Berlin. The train arrived in Berlin in the early morning, and she got off at Bahnhof Zoo, which is the main train station. She had no idea where to go or what to do next, as she had no money and didn't know anyone in Berlin.

Hans found her standing outside the station, muddled and lost, and asked her if she needed help. She told him that her handbag was stolen, and she didn't have any money. He was kind and offered to buy her breakfast. He was in his late twenties, looked like a nerdy student and came across nice, polite and friendly, and she was starving, so she agreed to join him. After breakfast, he offered to join him for a walk in Tiergarten, which is a vast park near the train station. As she had nothing else to do, and he seemed harmless, she was happy to walk with him. Hans had the gift of charisma and charm; he explained to her about the gardens, about Berlin, the history of the city, how proud they should feel as Germans, how the city became more and more multicultural and multiracial which is killing the spirit of the city. His conviction and passion captivated her young mind. He also mastered the art of gaining others' trust, so by the end of their walk, he knew where she came from and that she had run away from home and didn't know anybody in Berlin. She told him about her parents and the lack of interest they have in her or her life, how the teenage conversations and interests of the kids in her school bore her to death. In the hour they walked in the gardens, she opened up to him about her life and her feelings more than she had shared with anyone in her entire life. She didn't tell him about her drug habit, though. He listened, was understanding, nodded or said the right things at the right time and often related to his own childhood. He was like a spider that slowly weaved his webs around his prey until it was ready to attack.

Eventually, he invited her to stay in the guest room in his flat until she could find work and sort herself out. As she had nowhere to go and had no clue what she was going to do, she followed him without thinking about the consequences. When they got to his flat, she took out the last sachet of cocaine she had left and asked if he wanted to snort a line. His face turned to a mask of rage. He grabbed the sachet from her, poured the content in the toilet and flushed the water. When he came back, he was already calm and told her gently that if she wants to stay in his flat, she must not contaminate her mind and body with substances that were brought to this country by all those foreigners who were trying to weaken the Germans by clouding their minds and sicken their bodies in order to take over the city and country. So if she didn't want to become "Aine Ausländerschlampe", "A foreigners' bitch", she should keep her mind clear, her body pure, eat healthy food, and exercise. According to Hans, this was the first step to fight this foreign invasion that tries to erase the German culture.

For the next two weeks, she didn't leave the flat. Hans helped her cleanse and detox her body from the rubbish she put into it for over a year. He cooked healthy food, and they exercised together. All this time he pumped into her mind his ideas and ideology, and by the end of the fortnight, she became fixated on him instead of drugs.

He had a small group of misfits like her, which he gathered around him and were lured by his magnetism, his passion and the fiery and emotive way he manifested his ideas. It gave them a sense of belonging and portrayed it as they were crusaders on the front line against the forces of evil. They printed leaflets and handouts about his ideas, beliefs and plans for the redemption of the country. He held gatherings and forums in his flat in the north of Friedrichshain, a few streets east from where I lived, where he manipulated the attendees to feel that their thoughts and opinions mattered regardless of the fact that he always navigated and steered the discussion to his agenda and ideology. In retrospect, she realised that he was aiming to build himself an army which eventually was just a gang of thugs, but at the time she followed him blindly like the rest.

She stayed in Hans's flat and became his woman; cooking, cleaning and helping with the chores for the group. His parents passed away and left him a small sum of money and the flat, so he didn't need to work and spent most of his time reading, writing his manifesto, printing handouts and scouting the streets, parks and trains station for lost souls that he could recruit.

In the beginning, their activities were handing out leaflets and putting posters on street bulletin boards and walls. Slowly, as the years went by, Hans became more and more militant and forceful; he encouraged all the guys except himself to shave their heads. Also, the entire group, the guys and the girls, expected to wear military or leather clothes that, as he explained, projected power. Then they wrote graffiti on walls and vandalised shops and community centres of immigrants, even of those who are second-generation in Germany, like the Turkish. She was not comfortable with those activities but was still under Hans's charismatic spell. So she used to join the gang, but stood in the back and didn't take part. Just when they started to have brawls with Turkish or African gangs or just beat up innocent people in the street as they have done to me, she finally acknowledged that there was something fundamentally wrong with their way and beliefs. She understood she had to get out. However, she was 19 years old, didn't finish school and never worked before, so where can she go and what will she do? She was also terrified of Hans; she knew he wouldn't let her go, and if she tried to run away, he would send his goons to find her. So she stayed but kept a low profile as much as possible. When she saw me lying on the freezing station floor begging for her help, she felt she had to help me. Now, she is not sure what to do; she knows she has to get away from Hans and the gang but doesn't know how to do it.

"Wow!" I'm saying, speechless.

"Well, you asked me to tell you what I'm doing with them, so this is my story... it's not what you expected, ha?"

"You can't go back to him, Anna! If you need somewhere to stay until you'll figure out what to do next, you can stay here and sleep on the sofa. They wouldn't find you here"

She looks at me with distrust and fear. "I don't know, I don't know you. Also, Hans might have sent people to follow me, and he knows where I am now."

I'm reaching over the table, grabbing her hand gently and looking deep into her beautiful grey eyes.

"Hey, I'm not Hans, and I won't hurt you. How can I, in my current condition? I just want to return a favour. Anyway, don't you think that if they would know where you are now, they would already be knocking on the door or breaking it?"

"I guess you are right, but you don't know Hans. He is smart and always has a plan. I don't want you to get hurt again. They are getting more and more violent, next time they might kill you."

"Anna, look at me! You cannot go back, you must break the ties with them! Stay here for a while, and we'll figure out together what you can do next. We are in Germany, not in Yemen. I'm sure there are organisations and places that help girls in your situation."

She looked at me sceptically, then looked down at her hands, then at me again.

"Ok, I'll stay, but only if it's not putting you at any inconvenience."

"It's fine, don't worry, it will be nice to have some company, I'm a bit fed up talking to myself."

"But I don't have any clothes and toothbrush, and I don't have any money; I spent all that Hans gave me on the Doner kebab and the chips."

"I have some money. We can go tomorrow morning to buy you some clothes and toiletries."

"Alright, but only if you let me repay you when I get some money. We need to go early, though, when the shops open; Hans and the gang normally get up only around noon, so it will be safer to leave early for the shopping."

"Sure." I got up and pressed the button on the kettle. "Do you want coffee?"

"Yes, please."

For the next 2 weeks, we are spending most of our time in my flat, going out only to buy necessities. We pass the time talking a lot and getting to know each other, listening to music or playing games. There is a nine years age gap between us as she is only 19, and I'm 28, but there is an aura around her that bewitches me. In the first few days, we form a kind of Platonic bond; both of us are a bit lost in this life and ambivalent about where to go from here, and we are hiding from the wolves outside until we'll figure out what to do next.

It changes on Saturday night.

While I'm lying in my bed reading a book, I hear a silent knock on the bedroom door.

"Come in."

She opens the door and asks if she can come in.

"Of course, come and sit here." I move a bit and make space for her on the bed.

"What are you reading?"

"The Metamorphosis by Kafka."

She is looking a bit bewildered. "What is it about?"

"It's about a guy that wakes up in the morning and finds out that he turned into a cockroach."

"Oh!" she smiles. "Die Verwandlungen", I saw it in Hans's study room. He has quite an extensive library. I wasn't allowed to touch his books though, only to clean the room, so I never read this book. If I wanted to read, I had to go to the public library. Can you please read for me a bit?"

She stares at me with a weird look while I'm reading like she tries to make a decision. When I get to the part where Gregor Samsa tries to get off his bed to open the door, she takes the book from me and puts it on the duvet, then leans toward me and kisses my lips gently. The sensuality and intimacy of the kiss astound me. She then lays her head on my chest and closes her eyes. I put my arms around her and slowly drift to sleep.

When I wake up in the morning, she is still sleeping peacefully. I stay in bed lying and watching her sleep, wondering if we are falling in love with each other. When she opens her eyes, she smiles at me then takes my arm, puts it around her and cuddles with me.

"Good morning, did you sleep well?" I ask.

"Yeah, I had the best sleep in years. Can we stay like that for a while?"

"I'm not in a hurry to go anywhere, just be careful." I move a bit, "Don't press too much; my ribs are still painful."

"Oh, sorry, I forgot." She caresses my chest softly.

It feels so nice.

I turn and look into her eyes. She looks back at me, nods and says without a sound, "Yes, I want it too."

We make love, and it's passionate and gentle and wonderful. The physical and emotional intensity is like I never had before; it is like the outside world ceased to exist, and we are the last two people on earth. No one or anyone matters, just us and what we give to each other.

"Are we in love?" she asks after it is finished, and we calm down.

"I guess we are." I'm still a bit breathless.

"Cool! Are you hungry? I'm starving!" She throws off the duvet and gets up. "I'm going to make you a breakfast of champions."

We can't stay in the flat for the rest of our life, we also can't stay in Berlin anymore. Anna needs to get away from Hans's claws, and we agree that it's too risky for her to stay here. A Greek guy whom I befriended lately and owns a small restaurant in Schönhauser Allee, near to my flat, where I became a regular, offered me a while ago to go to the Greek island of Hydra. His family owns and operates a hotel and day-tours on the island, and he promised they will give me a job if I come, cash-in-hand. I've been to Hydra before when I was 18, on the End-of-school trip; it's a beautiful, peaceful island not far from Athens. Exactly what we need now. Also, it's where one of my favourite musicians, Leonard Cohen, lived in the 60s and met Marianne, who became his muse and girlfriend and was the subject to his most beautiful song "So long Marianne". It sounds too perfect, but the risk of disappointment is safer than the risk of encountering Hans's gang in the street.

I've saved a bit of money that should be enough for plane tickets for both of us and a couple of weeks of food and rent until the first payday. So we decided to take a chance and take my mate's offer; Anna can find a job as a waitress, and I'll work on whatever they want me to do.

Anna is so excited; tomorrow at noon we are finally flying to Greece. Last week we prepared for the trip; we went to a travel agency and bought plane tickets to Athens and tickets for the ferry to the island. I went to the bank and drew all the money from my account; most of it in travellers' checks and the rest in cash. I also bought Anna some clothes and a suitcase, and we bought the friend's family thank you gifts. The rest of the week we spent at the flat daydreaming together about the paradise that is waiting for us and celebrating the happiness of our new love with the anticipation for a new life and exciting adventures. She is buzzing all over like a bee all day and can't be still for a minute. I think she packed our suitcases about 5 times. She keeps asking me if I'm hungry or if I want a drink and hovers in the flat like a toddler. Every time she comes next to me, she gives me a kiss or a hug.

At 3 pm someone knocks on the door. Anna freezes and looks at me worriedly.

"Don't worry babe, it's probably a utility meter reader, just wait in the bedroom."

I look through the peephole and see a man in his 50s in a dark grey suit and old-fashioned glasses; he looks like an accountant. I open the door, asking if I can help him.

"Can I speak to Anna please?" He asks with a heavy German accent.

"There is no Anna here, only me. Sorry, you got the wrong address."

He put his hand on my shoulder.

"Look, young man, I know she is here, and I know you are working here illegally, so please call her before I'll call the authorities. I just want to talk to her."

I'm ready to close the door on him when Anna comes out of the bedroom.

"It's ok, Ari, it's my father's assistant, I'll talk to him."

"Are you sure?"

"Yes, it's fine. I've known him since I was a kid; he won't hurt me."

While they are talking in the front garden, the man is pointing at a black Mercedes that is parked in the street. After 5 minutes of conversation, she comes back to the flat, and he walks away and waits next to the car.

"It's my father in the car," she says, "I'm not sure how he found me after all those years, but he is here, and I need to go and talk to him. I'll be alright."

Before I can say anything, she gives me a quick kiss on my mouth and walks to the car. The back door opens, she sits inside and the door closes.

After about 15 minutes I'm starting to worry, I can see the man talking to someone through an open window of the back seat on the other side of the car. The person in the car gives him an envelope, then he walks back to me with it and says: "Anna is going back home with her father now. We are not forcing her, she is choosing to return to her family." He hands me the envelope. "Take this money. I believe it's a large sum for someone like you. Leave Germany! You will never see or contact Anna again! Do you understand what I just said?"

I look at him speechless with my mouth wide open for a moment, and before I get the chance to reply, he turns back, walks to the car, sits in the front passenger seat, and closes the door. My mind is blank and my feet are nailed to the floor. I can't move. All I can think is, "What the fuck is happening here?"

The back window opens, and I see Anna looking at me with her big sad eyes. I can see her lips saying without a sound, "I'm sorry!"

I finally get a grip of myself and run toward the car, but before I can reach her, the car is speeding up and driving off down the street, then disappears around the corner.

It was the last time I ever saw my angel.

Despair

I was suddenly disturbed by something rubbing my shoulder and threw me out of my memory. Nadya wanted some attention and a treat, so she shoved and pushed her nose gently against my shoulder and chest.

"Come on, girl, give me a break, it's siesta time. I'll come to play with you in a bit."

I gave her half a pitta, so she'll leave me alone, then took out a piece of paper from the side pocket of my bag and looked at it, contemplating about the events that brought me here.

After Anna left I didn't know what to do with myself; I was devastated and lost. We were so happy in those two weeks and the future looked so bright. Then suddenly, in one blow, it was all gone.

I was at a crossroads in my life, with a stack of cash, but nothing else. No love, no friends around to support. A blurred future; my career was over, and I needed to leave the city but didn't know where to go.

I tore the plane tickets and threw the pieces into the bin, thinking, "I don't want to go there without her, it will not be the same."

Eventually, I called the landlord and left a message that I'm leaving the flat, left the key in the post box and took the U-Bahn to the central train station. I decided to get on the first international train that leaves the station, no matter where it was heading. The first train went to Oslo, so I bought a one-way ticket and jumped on the train.

In Oslo, I tried to busk again on Karl Johan Street, the main pedestrian street in the city where thousands of tourists pass every day. The atmosphere was lively and vibrant, with many other acts in the street, and the air was full of happiness from the spring and the incoming summer. However, it wasn't for me anymore; I lost the interest and the fun of meeting and experiencing the crowd. I loathed all those people that were walking in the streets looking for entertainment. They all seemed so common and ignorant, and I couldn't stand doing this any longer.

So I took a train to Copenhagen, then to Prague, then a bus to Rome, then a train and a ferry to Athens. I spent between two days to two weeks in each of those cities, travelling and sightseeing, hoping for some inspiration or an answer to what I should do with my life from that point. Even though I visited some of the most incredible cities in the world, none of those places and no one excited or impressed me; the Colosseum in Rome looked like a bunch of ruins, Charles bridge in Prague looked to me like any of the hundreds of other bridges I saw in Europe, and the Parthenon in Athens was just a square building with pillars. All that month on the roads I was like a zombie, empty with a total lack of interest and care of my surroundings; I lost the meaning and the sense of purpose. An exception was the house of Franz Kafka, which I visited in Prague that impressed me deeply; maybe because of the existential maze I was trapped in, I identified with him and the characters in his stories. I don't have many memories left from that time.

The only thing left from that month was this poem that was written on this piece of paper, which I wrote while sitting by myself looking at the sunset on a beach in Ios, a small Greek island where young people from all over Europe come for drinking, partying and sex, and where I have finally given up and decided to go back home.

"The place is so beautiful,
even the cynical get hopeful of its sight.
The simple beauty of sea and sand,
white houses, smiley people and innocence.
But you are there, and I am here.
And you are there, and I am miserable.
Still trying to fight, but my strength is lost.
After a battle of thirty years, minus a tad.
And I'm small, only five feet six and a half.
And they are big and strong, and they are a lot.
They are an entire system where money and matter
are the motives, the tool, and all that is being sought.
I was ready to give up, disappear, become a dream.
Then you emerged and allowed me to breathe.
And I knew this is it, it is you.
I will not fight alone anymore, I will not fight.
But then I ran...
I ran because you couldn't be with me.
I ran because I couldn't be with you.
I ran because I couldn't...
I ran because I...
I ran because...
I ran...
And I'm running, I'm running around the world.
To Rome and Prague, to Oslo and Amsterdam.

Just to be afar, from there, you, us.
With no home, with no warm bed or a hot bath,
I have no solace; I have lost my path.
I want you to be here with the sea and the sand.
But you are there, and I am here, and you are there.
I want to return already, to you, to reality, to work.
But I can't.
Because you can't be with me.
Because I can't be with you.
Because I can't be with...
Because I can't be.
Because I can't...
Because I...
Because...
When we will be together, maybe in a week or a year,
I will kiss your lips and give you a flower.
Then I will hug you for at least an hour.
And I will make passionate love to you all night
until we both see the holy light.
Just let the day finally come before a passing dream
I will become.
So we could be together.
So we could be.
So we could.
So we.
So..."

When I returned home, my mum offered me to stay in her
house until I figured out what I wanted to do next.
After 2 weeks of living in her house, I felt that I'm losing my
mind. I was in such a bad place with myself; I couldn't stand
people around me, and everyone annoyed me. I was quite

unpleasant to my mum, who was thankfully so patient and supportive and gave me space. When friends or other family members offered to meet and hang out together, I waved them off and stayed in my room. I realised I need to find another meaning and sense in my life, to find a way to get over Anna, find a new challenge and interest, and build my life again before I'll do something stupid.

When a friend told me I'm becoming an arsehole, I made up my mind to take my backpack, go down south and head into the desert as I needed to get away from people, social codes and expectations. I hoped to ease my soul and find some answers. I didn't know how long I'm going to be there and what I'm going to do, but I had to get away from everything. So, I said goodbye to my mum and took a bus to Eilat, a holiday resort town on the Red Sea on the edge of the desert.

The first thing I had to do was to buy some gear and as I could not carry it all by myself, I decided to purchase a camel to carry my stuff. So, I asked around the town where I can buy a camel and someone referred me to the camel ranch that was situated about 20 miles out of town in the desert. I took a taxi to the ranch and asked the owner if he would sell me a camel.

I still had the money Anna's father's assistant gave me in Berlin, which was more than enough to buy a camel.

"We can do a deal, but you need to familiarise yourself with camels, their needs and behaviours before you own one." He said, "It's not a goat, they can be dangerous if you don't know how to handle them."

We agreed I will work on the ranch for a period, and in return, he will give me a place to sleep, food and teach me how to handle and take care of camels. When I'm ready, he will sell one to me.

A month later, I left the ranch toward the desert on a journey with my new silent friend.

I folded the paper and thought about the question that will always bother me:

"What did Anna's father say to her in the car to make her leave me and our happiness, and go back to the family that she resented? A family that clearly didn't show any love or care for her in the past."

I knew that we would never meet again, and this question will stay open until the day I die.

A Hungarian porn film

Every so often I need to go down to the beach to get supplies. I normally make it a day and a night, so I have some time to break my solitude and socialise with my species, which I normally try to avoid. Usually, I leave Nadya in a camel ranch that specialises in camel excursions for tourists and is located a few miles from the beach. I often stay there for a bit to have a coffee and a chat with the workers, as I used to work there for a short time before I bought Nadya from the owner and went on my journey. We are still on friendly terms. After a catch-up with the juicy news, I make my way down to the beach, where the closest grocery shop and pub are situated. The guy at the shop already knows what I need and prepares it quickly. I leave the pack with the supplies in the shop to collect in the morning and go to the pub which is open all night, where I sit at the bar, have a few beers and laughs with the bartender who is an old buddy of mine, and look at the beauties in minimal clothing. Once in a while, I chat up one of those lovelies and finish the night in her hotel room. In the morning, after fulfilling the emotional and physical needs for human company, I take the supplies from the shop, pick up Nadya from the ranch and head back to the mountains.

In one of those times not long after I began my desert journey, while I was on my way to drop Nadya off, about a mile from the camel ranch I saw a large marquee that was designed, unsuccessfully, to look like a Bedouin tent, popped up in the middle of the valley that leads to the beach. Men stood on the road on both sides of the camp to stop passers-by from getting close. Halfway up the mountain shoulder that looked over the valley, I saw Salah and Gill, two guys who work at the camel ranch, sitting and looking down. I tied Nadya to a tree and climbed toward them.

"What the fuck is going on down there, guys?"

They were laughing their ass off. "Just look down, mate, it's hilarious!" Gill answered and continued to laugh.

I looked down and saw the most bizarre and surreal sight that I've ever seen; in a tent in the middle of the desert, on mattresses and rugs, there were a bunch of men and women, some with traditional Bedouin clothes and others half-naked or completely naked. The girls were mainly blondes with large boobs that unnaturally defied gravity and a fake tan, and the guys were muscular, shaved chested and with larger than normal penises. Some of them were fucking, and others were preparing for the next scene or just chilling with plates of food and jars of drinks scattered around. A film crew was moving between them, filming all the variations and positions of sex that they could think of and could physically perform, while the director shouted instructions. Under another small shade, I saw other people who looked like the support; the producer, the makeup lady, and the props guys. It looked like a Roman orgy, the Desert-style; a cheap version of the film Caligula.

I turned back to the two chaps. "What the hell is that? Are they shooting a porn movie?"

"Shut up and enjoy!" Salah said, "It's a free show."

I sat with them for a while watching this real-life display of emotionless raw sex, staggered by the genital athleticism of the actors. It didn't titillate me even a bit; it was more like a circus freak show than a turn-on. It reminded me of the feeling I got a few years back when I went, only for the experience, to a live sex show in Amsterdam. The mechanical movements, the director's loud instructions to move from one position to another that often took the actors over the limits of what a normal human body can physically endure, the cameraman that tried to get as much close-up as possible to the private parts; the entire scene made me somewhat uncomfortable. It wasn't like watching a porn film that can arouse at times. Maybe the screen is a barrier that keeps the extreme sex only as a fantasy, and when the screen is absent, it becomes tangible and the participants become actual people.

The surreal setting of the serene, untouched virgin landscape disrupted by those sexual acrobats, reminded me of the hedonistic atmosphere in the paintings of Hieronymus Bosch. The whole situation was rather hilarious, but also unsettling, even repulsive.

We sat there for some time until the producer looked up and spotted us. He waved his hand in the air and shouted toward us; "Hey, you cannot be here! You need to go away!"

We stood up, looked at him, and waved back. We couldn't stop laughing.

Suddenly, Salah started to run downhill.

"What the hell are you doing?" Gill shouted to him.

"Don't worry! Just watch!" Salah answered without looking back.

When he got to the tent, he started to scream at the people, take head covers from the actors' heads and throw props on the floor. The actors, camera crew and director crowded in one corner, looking scared and in a bit of shock. The producer and security men took Salah to the side and talked to him. We couldn't understand what they said, but from their body language, we could see that they were trying to calm him down.

After ten minutes of heated conversation, they seemed to come to some understanding and Salah appeared to calm down. He shook their hands and walked back to us with an impish, full of himself expression on his face.

"Guys, I'm going back to the ranch! Ari, are you going back to your hermitting, or do you want to come to the ranch for coffee?"

"I'll come with you, I was on my way to the ranch anyway, to drop off Nadya for the day as I need to go down to the beach to get some supplies. Coffee sounds great!"

"Salah, you crazy Bedouin! What the fuck just happened down there?" Gill patted Salah on his back and asked, amusingly.

"I'll tell you after the coffee is ready."

When we got to the ranch, I released Nadya in the compound with the other camels to catch up with the latest gossip in the herd. It was feeding time, so she was pleased and content. Then I joined the lads in the sitting area near the kiosk for coffee and biscuits.

They told me about the day's events; apparently, a Hungarian porn film production company contacted Ron, the ranch owner's son, and offered a large sum of money to close the ranch for a day to shoot their film. The business was slow at the time because of a very low amount of tourists at that period, which naturally affected the ranch's revenue. So Ron thought it was a good deal and agreed to a date.

His father, who was an old-school man with conventional morality and had the last word regarding business, didn't know about the deal. Tal told him about it only a day before it was supposed to take place. So, he put his foot down and refused to allow them to shoot sex scenes at the ranch.

"Have you totally lost your mind, Ron?" he said. "This is a respectable business and I will not allow them to shoot this filth here! Even if the business is slow at the moment, it doesn't mean that we should lower ourselves to this level. The business will pick up eventually, we have enough cash aside to get through this period."

"But how come you allowed last year's Christmas party?" Ron tried his luck.

On Christmas Eve the previous year, at the time I worked in the ranch, a guy who owned most of the massage parlours and managed several call girls in the nearby resort town and went with Ron to the same high school, rented the ranch and arranged a meal and a party for all his girls. The party was only for the girls and was an evening off work for them where they could relax and have a fun night without giving service to anyone. The ranch was full of dozens of escort girls. However, we were not allowed to leave our caravans to join them.

"It was a bit different, Ron, the people on that Christmas didn't have an orgy and haven't been filmed fucking each other on the rugs; they had a meal and party like normal people. It wasn't my business what they were doing in their life outside the ranch."

After some convincing, he agreed for the Hungarians to film in the ranch the scenes that did not include sex and the main part of the film, the sex scenes, had to be filmed in the open desert outside the ranch.

"We couldn't miss this once in a lifetime opportunity to watch live the making of a porn film. We had a day off work as the ranch is closed on Sundays," said Gill, "So we sneaked quietly and watched it from the mountain."

He turned to Salah. " So what was it all about down there, mate?"

Salah looked smug and had a silly smile. "Well," he said, "when the guy spotted us and demanded that we leave, I decided to mess with them a little. So I ran down and shouted in anger at them about how they dare to disrespect my heritage and pretend to be Bedouin; how dare they disrespect our women and tradition by filming this obscenity in the desert? In my home. That's why I took off their head scarfs, the hijabs and keffiyeh, and messed up the props."

Salah was a Bedouin. His family, though, settled down and lived in a normal house in a village in the north of the country. They were not traditional nomads who lived in the desert.

"Guys, you should have seen their faces, they were quite terrified from this crazy angry native that appeared out of the blue. Then the producer apologised to me and said that they didn't mean to offend anyone, he even offered me money to let them finish the last scene, and then they would leave. I told him where he could shove his money, as he can't buy pride and respect with money, but I've agreed for them to finish the shooting as soon as possible and leave."

Gill poured another cup and said; "You're such a bastard, Salah! Though, it was certainly entertaining."

We chilled there for a while, drinking coffee, smoking and chatting about casual things. In the late afternoon, when I got ready to walk down to the beach, a small convoy of cars entered the ranch, 2 MPVs, a van and 2 private cars. Ron came out of his dad's office and told us that the film crew are here to shoot a few scenes at the ranch and instruct us to behave and be hospitable.

When the producer saw Salah and called him to the side, they had a quiet conversation. The producer then called two girls, put his arms around their shoulders and introduced them to Salah, who shook their hands and said something that we couldn't understand. When he came back to us and sat down, he seemed pleased and full of himself.

"What was this about?" I asked

"He apologised again and offered me, as a goodwill gift, to choose any or both of the girls for a private session in my room. He said that the girls will do whatever I'll ask them to do, and begged me not to make a fuss and let them complete the shooting."

Gill's eyes shone. "So, why the fuck you are still here? You moron! You can fulfil any fantasy you ever had."

"Are you crazy? I don't know which STDs they are carrying, I don't want my dick to fall off next week. Also, the boss is in the office and I don't want to lose my job. So I told him I appreciate the gesture, but I have to decline the offer and promised that I'll not disturb them."

I got up and said, "Well guys, it was an eventful and unusual afternoon, but I have to hit the road as the shop will close soon. Salah, you are my idol, man! I'll see you tomorrow morning when I pick up Nadya."

As I exited the gate of the ranch, a car came from behind and stopped next to me. It was the boss who had finished the working day and headed home. He offered to give me a ride and drop me at the beach. As it was a 2-mile walk, which I was happy to avoid, I gladly jumped into the car.

And people think a desert is a boring place where nothing ever happens...

A night to remember

Two months later, on the day of New Year's Eve, at the end of the century, at the turn of the millennium, I had to go to the camel ranch to repair a broken stripe from Nadya's saddle. I didn't plan to stay for long and intended to head back to the mountains as soon as the saddle was fixed. The guys from the ranch invited me to come with them to a millennium party at the Dolphin reef bar. At first, I was reluctant to go, as the noise and the party atmosphere didn't appeal to me at that time. They promised that the invitation to the party is by word of mouth only so it will not be overcrowded, and the music will not be a noisy rave as it's not the style there. The bar at the Dolphin reef is a cool place with a nice atmosphere and good music, and as they said:

"It is the fucking end of the Millennium, mate. It comes once in a thousand years! It's not a night to be alone by yourself."

So I decided to join them. I thought in the worst-case scenario; if the party would suck, I'd go back to the wilderness and celebrate with Nadya and mother nature.

The party wasn't too bad. People were dancing to 80s and 90s alternative rock; Red Hot Chilli Peppers, REM, Pixies, The Cranberries, Beastie Boys and others. Some people sat on the bar, and others lounged on Bedouin rags that covered the floor, leaning on palm tree logs that were laid horizontal and were also covered by rags, drinking or smoking Shisha; a traditional water-pipe with flavoured tobacco. The oasis-like venue was lovely; the beach, the palm trees, the design of the bar, the different swimming pools; a pool with hot water, a pool with cold water, a pool with saltwater and a pool with normal water. A wooden boardwalk led to the reef, where visitors in the daytime could gather to meet the dolphins at.

As the evening progressed, more and more guests became intoxicated by the alcohol or drugs that they've consumed, or just from life and the party's vibes. They were dancing everywhere; on the dance floor, on the bar, on the beach or between the tables.

I was sitting at the bar most of the time, drinking beer and observing the guests. I said hello to a few people that I knew and made short small talks of "Hi" and "How are you?" But not much more than that. I found it hard to engage in meaningless conversations and didn't feel the need to mingle with people.

It was only 21:30 when the DJ put "Killing in the name" of Rage Against the Machine, followed by "We gotta fight for the right" of Beastie Boys that got almost everybody on their feet dancing. The place was packed, and the cacophony of the music with the loud conversations started to make me feel uncomfortable and annoyed. When it became too much for me, I took my drink and stepped out. I went down to the beach and sat on the edge of the boardwalk with my feet in the water.

It was a bit nippy, so I put on the sweatshirt that was tied around my waist. The refreshing light breeze that came down from the mountains, and the gentle ripples of the sea brushing my feet, took the edge off from the intensity of the party.

"Hi!" A woman's voice came from behind and asked in English with a French accent, "Do you mind if I join you?"

I looked back to where the voice came from and saw a smiling brunette standing over me. She wore a white summer dress and as the light came from behind her, I could see the outlines of her body through the dress; she had a slim and athletic figure with very long legs. She wasn't pretty by the classic definition, but if I was describing her to another guy, I would say that "She is a bit of alright".

"Sure," I said, "I wouldn't mind the company."

She took her sandals off and sat next to me, paddling her feet in the water.

"It seems like we have at least one thing in common; we are both refugees from the party."

"Yeah, I was sure that I'm the only person who is uncool enough to abandon and walk away from this nifty party, shocking! Well, legs, I guess we should put our heads down in shame."

Both of us laughed.

"I'm Sophie, by the way, not legs." She pronounces her name in a cute French accent that puts a smile on my face.

"Nice to meet you, Sophie, I'm Ari."

We sat in silence for a while, enjoying the serenity. We didn't feel the need for a banal introductory conversation; just two strangers in paradise living the moment.

"Tell me, Sophie," I asked in a sudden poetic vibe, "If I would come in your dream with my hand reached out for you, and if you were not blind, and I would take your hand in mine and guide you through a shrouded yellow path to a garden flourishing with wildflowers. And it's autumn; the trees are in shades of red, brown and green, and the road crosses ponds and brooks until we get to the centre of the garden where a bench stands. And if we were alone in the hidden garden, sitting on the bench, the bird singing around us, and I would lean and kiss your lips, and you would respond by covering my shoulders with trembling arms and embracing me to your heart, and we stay like that forever. In the evening, I would take you back to your bed and you would wake up in the morning with me in your thoughts. For the rest of your life, then, you will look for me, but you'll never find me."

"Well," she said, "I would think you smoked too much weed, or you are a poet from the 19th century that was frozen in time for the last 150 years and just woke up."

"It could be both." I put on my sandals and stood up. "However, my lovely, I do enjoy your company, but I've exhausted all my efforts to rejoice at this party, and I'm ready to head back home. You seem adventurous, and I would like to invite you to join me for a once in a lifetime experience."

She shook her head and I could see on her face the anger that she tried to repress.

"Wow! You are so full of yourself and not beating around the bush, man! We hardly said a few sentences to each other, and you are already inviting me to your hotel room to sleep with you? Pardon Mon Ami, but I'm not normally going to the houses of strangers I've just met to sleep with them. Even if they are quoting romantic poems to me. I have a French accent, but it doesn't mean that I'll do 'The last tango in Paris' with you. By the way, I'm not even French, I'm Swiss."

I laughed. "Hold your horses, firecracker, you got me totally wrong. I'm not inviting you for a one-night stand to screw me in my hotel room. I don't even live in a hotel or a house; I live outside, in the desert. Me and my camel. The invitation is for something much better; a midnight stroll on a camel to the mountains on the millennium night. We'll see the fireworks from the top of a mountain and if you stay the entire night, you'll see the stunning sunrise and dawn of the new millennium. Don't worry, you'll be safe; I'm pretty harmless. I promise we won't do anything you don't want to do. With such feistiness, I wouldn't even dare... Anyway, I promise to bring you back to your hotel in the morning, safe and sound, but with an experience that you will not forget."

She calmed down but seemed to be in two minds.

"So, what do you say? We still need to get to the camel ranch and get Nadya, my camel. From there it's about an hour and a half walk to the peak. So we should hit the road now."

"You know what, Ari? What the heck! This party sucks anyway, and you seem like a decent guy... ok, Mr drifter, let's have a night to remember."

It was getting late, so we took a taxi to the ranch instead of walking there. The ranch was dark and quiet; most of the staff went to the party. The only person on the premises was Saji, the cleaner that never went anywhere and was almost part of the furniture. All he was doing was working and saving his money to send to his family in India. He did make a world-class curry and sticky rice, though.

I saddled Nadya and loaded all my stuff, then explained to Sophie how to sit comfortably and safely. A short scream when Nadya stood up, and we were on our way. The desert was dark, though, after the eyes adjusted, the deemed light which came from the sickle of the moon and the trillions of stars was bright enough to see the road and the landscape.

The monotonic sway, the silence, and the dark night make it easy to fall asleep on the back of a camel. So, I kept chatting to her to ensure that she was awake, and also to get to know her.

She lived in Geneva, and to make a living she worked in a travel agency selling holidays. She always wanted to see the Red Sea, so when she won the 'Employee of the month' with a reward of a plane ticket to anywhere she chooses up to 200 Swiss Francs, she chose to fly to Eilat.

However, the centre of her life was playing volleyball with a local team and singing in an amateur opera chorus supported by the Geneva opera house.

"Well, a volleyball player and an opera singer! This is a combination that I haven't seen yet. With legs like yours, I can see the volleyball players, but I can't see you as an opera singer. As far as I know and from what I've seen, opera singers are normally large women. Probably with the size comes the tone and the power."

"You are such an ignorant Middle-eastern bushman!" She laughed, "You probably saw Montserrat Caballe, the opera singer who sang with Freddie Mercury, who is a large woman, and decided that all the female opera singers are fat. It might surprise you, but many of the greats are actually slim. For example, Maria Callas or Renée Fleming."

"I guess I should put my head down in shame. You are right, I'm not really into opera; the only opera singer I've seen is this Montserrat with Freddie on the TV. Please accept my sincere apology for my unforgivable ignorance. I would love to hear you sing. Please sing something for me?"

"Do you want me to sing here in the desert? On a camel?"

"Yes, why not? It's only me and the night animals here."

So she sang.

There, in the desert, on the back of a camel, on the night of the end of the century, at the end of the millennium, she sang the "Un bel dì vedremo" from Madame Butterfly.

It was midnight when we arrived at the top of the mountain. She was singing the finale of the aria and was exactly in the emotional climax when the sky over the far sea suddenly illuminated with colourful explosions of the new year's fireworks. I'm still getting goosebumps every time I remember this powerful moment.

After the song ended, she asked in a casual tone, as she had just finished a rehearsal in the studio: "Did you like it?"

I was speechless; the whole scenery of the desert at night with the fireworks, together with what I felt at that moment to be the most beautiful music ever written, was overwhelming.

Then she added, "It is absolutely amazing up here! Can we stay here for a while?"

"This is the plan," I said when I could get my words together, "we are parking here, and I must say, girl, your voice is utterly mesmerising! Thank you."

"Thanks for the compliment, and you are welcome, it's no biggie. It's quite a regular thing for me; singing on the back of a camel that walks up a mountain at midnight."

I asked Nadya to sit down, and Sophie got off. Then I unfolded my thin mattress on the ground and unpacked the woods for a fire. She sat on the mattress and looked at the fireworks display.

To protect the fire from the wind, I placed the woods inside a circle of stones under the wall of a large granite rock. The rock, unlike the limestone which formed most of the stony and sandy terrain of the area, was not affected by the weathering and erosion and was standing tall in the middle of the mountaintop. I lit the fire, then after a few minutes, shoved embers to the side of the fire and put a kettle with tea on it. When the tea was ready, I poured two glasses and sat down next to her.

The mountain was the highest point in the area, and consequently; it was windy and fairly cold. So we wrapped ourselves with the only blanket I had and sat close to the fire. We could see miles away; the bare desert landscape of the mountains and valleys under the starlight, together with the sea and the silent fireworks above, were powerful and made both of us humble and intimate in this experience that only we were the witnesses to.

After about half an hour of sitting quietly, hypnotised by the scenery and drinking tea, she pinched my arm and said:

"I sang for you. Now it's your turn; can you tell me one of your romantic nomad's poems? It's just fair, don't you think?"

"Alright, let me think... hmm... ok, I have something for you."

"Laying on my back on a warm summer night.
A barefoot moon is strolling on the broken, shiny glass.
The dark-haired girl leans on my chest,
takes out one breast, then another one.
I'm not alone, I don't care about all the rest.
The wind moans between the trees around in a silent whisper.

She sends a caressing, gentle hand to my shaken body.
Her eyes shine with lust like two pearls in a blue sea.
My hand tours with joy between the mountains and craters of her warm body.
Sometimes stops to explore and dig in a canyon that is deep, soft, and sweet.

Cuddling and loving we are laying on a bed of green leaves.
Her tongue flickers in my ear words of love and giggles with lust.
Time disappears down her white breast and up a red nipple that looks like an old wine with a great taste.
A quiet sigh sewing the silence like a sharp knife.
Fireworks exploding around our small bubble.
Together we are getting to the big bright light only for this one single night."

"That's beautiful! It's about us, isn't it? Did you just make it up? You are cheeky! You told me you are not looking to sleep with me."
"Hey, you asked for a romantic poem." I moved a few inches away from her so she wouldn't feel threatened.
She moved closer to me and whispered in my ear: "Relax, It's alright if you do, you might get what you want tonight."
Then she swung her leg over my legs and sat on my lap, facing me, then leaned forward and kissed me.

We woke up at dawn. The fire died out sometimes during the night and we were cold, so we packed everything fast, loaded Nadya, and walked off the mountain. When we got to the valley at the bottom, where there was no wind and it wasn't so cold, I lit a small fire and brewed a kettle of coffee. I had a pack of biscuits, which we shared while we sipped the bitter coffee silently. When we finished, I put down the fire, and we started walking towards the south beach where her hotel was located. Although it was about a 2 hours walk from where we were, she preferred to walk next to me this time instead of riding the camel. We didn't have much to say, and most of the morning each one was within their own thoughts.

When we arrived at her hotel, she gave me a brief hug.

"It was wonderful! Thank you. It was no doubt the highlight of my holiday, and a night I wouldn't forget."

"You are more than welcome." I said, keeping cool.

"Au revoir, Desert-man." She said, then turned and walked away.

Both of us knew we wouldn't see each other again. We were two individuals that met at a specific point in time and shared experience. As much as it was an incredible experience, none of us wanted more than what it was; we weren't looking to be lovers, friends, or anything of the sort. So, we didn't feel the need to change phone numbers and addresses, or for a long embarrassing goodbye.

After she disappeared inside the hotel, I smiled and said to myself:

"Yeah, it was definitely a night to remember!"

Boy soldiers

"Hey! Wake up, buddy! Are you alright?"

I open my eyes and see a young soldier leaning toward me and slapping my cheek gently.

"What the fuck are you doing, man?" I push his hand away and sit up.

"Oh, sorry! You were lying here with no movement, so we thought you'd lost consciousness, or you were dead."

Behind him, I see a group of about 25 soldiers; they look very young and fresh, probably on their basic training. The sergeant, the one that woke me up, doesn't look much older, but his mannerism and body language demonstrate more confidence and authority.

"I'm fine, I was just meditating."

"Alright then, sorry for disturbing you. Do you mind if we have our lunch break here? It's the only shade for miles, and they are new recruits, they are not used to walking for long distances."

What is your name, Sargent?"

"It's Omer."

"Well Omer, I don't own the desert, you can have a break wherever you like, as long as you leave the area clean."

"Of course, they already know that if I'll find any rubbish before we leave they will run for it, a lot." He turns to go back to the platoon.

"Also, please tell them not to bother my camel."

"Sure." He says and walks away at a fast pace.

I can hear him shouting: "Ok everyone! On your feet! Gather around me in U shape, each one with full water canteens in your hand! Come on, hurry up!"

Looking at those 18 years old lads running to get in line; most of them just out of high school, just past the legal age to buy alcohol and drive cars, but were already given guns and been taught to kill, throws me back to my national service.

I was an average soldier; I've done what I've been asked or ordered to do, no more and no less. The highest position I've reached was a platoon sergeant for new recruits like those guys, though I was probably the worst platoon sergeant in the army, as I was lazy and didn't give a toss. I survived one month in this role before I'd fallen out with the lieutenant and was moved to another company to be responsible for the company's magazine, where the explosives were stored.

The memory is a funny thing; most of the memories from my time in the army are not from standard military activities or events, but from absurd episodes that look like a script for a parody film about army life.

For example, in my basic training, we learned how to crawl on the ground with all our kits and rifles; for an entire week, we had to flatten entire fields of thorny bushes with inch long razor sharp prickles.

One day after we finished the training day, before we headed back to the base, the section's corporal decided to add an extracurricular activity, only for volunteers. He pointed at a field where the weeds and bushes were still standing intact and announced a competition; the volunteers will jump head first to the bushes, and the winner will be the one that jumps the farthest. The price for the winner was to be off the kitchen duties for that evening.

Some guys wanted to impress the corporal, got excited and raised their hands. Those morons didn't bother to check the field if it's clear of stones and rocks before they started flying to the bushes one by one. I stood aside looking at the ludicrous display of idiocy of young men running as fast as they could and jumping star jumps like Olympic divers into a sea of sharp thorns, screaming their heart out, while all the rest of the section were standing on the side and cheering and clapping their hands. All I could think about was dinner and the cigarette afterwards that awaited me in the camp.

There was also the Navigation training week when we had to navigate in the desert every night. We walked in pairs, with only a map, a compass, and the stars to show us the way. We had to go to different landmarks during the night, and at the end of the night when returning to the camp, we had to show the lieutenant proof we'd been to those points; the proofs were normally different shapes and symbols that were marked on walls or rocks.

On Thursday night, my partner and I were fed up with walking night after night in the dark and the cold, so after the bus dropped us off, we waited until it drove away and the rest of the soldiers disappeared in the desert, then we put our thumbs up and hitchhiked to the nearby town. We went to a pub in the town centre with our combat gear and dirty clothes and spent the entire night there eating, drinking beer, and listening to music.

Just before the sun came out, we took a taxi to the gathering point. The driver dropped us off half a mile away. We dirtied our boots and clothes with mud as it was rainy in the night, and walked fast to the bus pretending to be knackered.

At the camp, we showed the lieutenant a list of marks we found in the landmarks which we supposedly visited. We wrote those symbols while sitting and drinking beer in the pub off the top of our heads. The preposterous thing in this anecdote is that we didn't get into trouble; the lieutenant accepted most of the marks we've shown him, even though he had the list of symbols for each landmark.

Another memory that could be a scene written by the "American pie" scriptwriter; I was stationed in a base on the border with Lebanon. One night I was on guard, standing on a watchtower to ensure that terrorists were not infiltrating the border fence. It was mid-winter, and it was freezing, so I wore a heavy thick jumpsuit. The shift was for six hours and I couldn't leave my post. About two hours into the shift, I needed to empty my bowels.

As I wasn't allowed to go to the toilet, I stepped off the tower and went behind a bush; I got my arms out of the jumpsuit and pulled it down below my knees. Then I squatted and relieved myself. When I finished, before I pulled back and wore the jumpsuit, I looked back and realised that I forgot to pull the hood between my legs.

I've literally taken a crap directly into the hood of the jumpsuit.

All I could do was take off and dispose of the jumpsuit by hiding it under a bush, and at the end of the shift, I was shivering from the cold. I preferred to freeze for the rest of the term then take the jumpsuit back to the base to be cleaned; If anyone in the platoon knew what happened, I would be an object of jokes and mockery for the rest of my army service.

Looking back at it, I wonder what the enemy would think if they saw me shitting in the hood of my suit, they would probably still be laughing today.

After a one-month stretch, guarding and patrolling the border, my CO gave me a long weekend break at home. I got a lift from the base to the nearest city, Haifa. The Jeep dropped me near the central bus station after midnight. I just missed the last bus, so I stood at the side of the main road and raised my thumb. It was midweek, and at this time of night there weren't many cars on the road, and those who passed by didn't stop.

I stood there for almost an hour until a car finally stopped and the driver offered me a lift. The man was in his early forties, with curly hair and a thick moustache; he looked like a nerdy teacher. He was going to Tel Aviv and was happy to drop me off at the junction near my kibbutz, where I grew up and where my family lived.

I thanked my good fortune, put my kitbag in the back seat, and sat in the front passenger seat with my rifle between my legs. The chap seemed like he needed company and was very chatty. He talked about himself and his life, then asked me questions about my life. I was quite tired and just wanted to close my eyes, so I gave him short answers of yes and no, hoping that he would understand the hint.

Halfway through the 45 minutes journey, I saw his right hand slowly crawling toward my leg, so I leaned my legs to the right closer to the door. Then he moved his hand back to the steering wheel. It happened a few times and his hand became more and more persistent and closer to my knee, but eventually, he gave up and stopped. I didn't want to miss this brilliant ride all the way home by getting out of the car or confronting him, as I didn't know for how long I'd have to stand outside with my thumb up. I remember thinking:

"Is he crazy, stupid, or just have a death wish? He's hitting on a guy that has a loaded rifle on his lap. What the fuck?"

When I saw the junction near my kibbutz, I asked him to stop for me. He stopped the car and said: "I think I'll take you home with me tonight."

I kept calm and said: "No, thanks, I'll get off here."

After he drove away, while I was walking to my house, I thought to myself how lucky this guy was that it was me in the car; any other man wouldn't keep cool and beat the shit out of him.

There are definitely weird people in this world.

For most of my military service, I felt detached from the patriotic goals, the pride, and the military banter. Although I've done my duties, I wasn't emotionally involved. I observed situations and sequences of events from the side with cynical eyes, ridiculing the stupidity and ignorance of people.

I remember the night when my section entered Lebanon to do an ambush after info about terrorists that will try to cross the border. We lay down the entire night in the bush; it was rainy and cold, and all I could do was to feel sorry for myself and think:

"What am I doing here? Lying in the mud, wet to the bone, waiting for people, so I can shoot them as soon as they appear. This is so senseless; Personally, I did nothing to them, and they didn't hurt me, so why do we need to kill each other? The night is time to sleep in a warm bed, not to lie in this stupid fucking mud."

Eventually, the terrorists didn't show up, and we returned to the base soaked and knackered, to the disappointment of the CO that wanted action.

I couldn't understand then, and I still can't understand how bricks that lay on top of other bricks can be sacred? It's only bloody bricks! Life is sacred, not bricks, stones, wood, or any other materials or monuments. Governments and organisations spend billions on the development, manufacture, and purchase of weapons that aim to end the lives of people in order to protect man-made structures, and when using those weapons, they often ruin other structures that took years to build. Really? What is the sense of this? What the hell is the difference between the gravel on one side of the border to the gravel on the other side of the fence? Those billions can be used to save and improve lives on both sides of the border and make everybody prosperous. This common sense is expected in the 21st century, isn't it?

Nonetheless, our nature does not evolve in line with the evolution of technology and, as a species, we are going in the opposite direction. As a result, we see the devolution of the culture; three main forces are empowered by technology and by our nature: Stupidity, Ignorance, and Covetousness. Through these forces, those who have the power, the charisma, or the talent can manipulate people through the media and direct the culture and civilisation to do a U-turn and head back to times of aristocracy and peasantry. This Neo-feudalism together with religion leads to wars.

It will not be long before those boy soldiers that are standing there, properly positioned in straight lines and erect posture, will face challenging moral dilemmas that many of them don't have the maturity and emotional tools to deal with.

I faced some of those dilemmas several times in my service; it was the first uprising in the West Bank and Gaza, and our assignment was to patrol the streets of Bethlehem and keep the order. The locals used to throw stones at us, and we used to chase and try to arrest them. I remember a time that a stone hit a mate of mine in the face and broke his teeth and jaw. He was standing right beside me. After a short chase, we caught the lads that threw the stones at us; they were only young teenagers. We were furious; it isn't fun to see your friend with a broken face. A few guys wanted to beat them up, although they were handcuffed. If the lieutenant hadn't stopped them, I'm not sure what would have happened to those boys. I, as usual, didn't get involved.

While we waited for the Jeep to return and take them to the base for integration, a soldier from another unit approached and asked me:

"Do you mind if I'll bite your prisoners? I've already bitten our prisoners."

I looked at him in disbelief. "What the hell is wrong with you, man? Those are people! Fuck off back to your unit, We are not abusing prisoners here!"

He uttered with an irritating snort: "Calm down, Arab lover, I'm just kidding. I didn't bite all our prisoners…" He burst out laughing and walked away.

Fear and power can make it easy to lose the moral compass in conflicting situations, especially for those who have the power.

Young children, often 10 years old or under, also joined the sport of throwing stones at us. Imagine the absurdity of a soldier with combat gear chasing little boys in the street of a city. I remember the day that I caught one of those boys; I grabbed his wrist and stopped him, my hand closed and closed around his wrist like there was nothing there; his arm was so thin. The boy was about nine years old but so small and slim that he looked six years old. The situation made me feel so stupid, so I let go of the arm and let him run away. While I walked back to my unit, all I could think was: "What is wrong with this world where soldiers need to chase and arrest little children?"

The locals also used to write inciting graffiti on the walls of the houses. We were ordered to wake up residents of houses with graffiti and make them erase it, even if it was in the middle of the night. It was an awful feeling to wake up a family with young children, often after midnight, and force the men to wash the writing off the walls while the women are screaming and children are crying. The residents were usually innocent families that wanted to live peacefully. It was the activists that wrote the graffiti on random houses, not the residents.

I did get the reason for those orders; extremists from their side slaughtered families with babies and bombed buses on our side, but I could also see why they hated us so much. I kept asking myself how abusing a family by waking them up in the middle of the night to wash the wall of their house helped stop the violence? Furthermore, I always believed that there is another way.

The soldiers finished their break. They are collecting the rubbish and standing in line to continue their daily activities. I hope they will complete their national service without the need to deal with the consequences of violence.

Green meadows

My desert journey is coming to its end. Lately, I often find myself wishing to see more shades of green and have people around me. The yellow/brown barren landscape and the Spartan solitary life, with all its beauty, start to smother me. I feel the need to be surrounded by life in the shape of people, vegetation, water, and culture. I think I'm ready to move on to the next chapter; the chapter of acceptance. It's time to live a normal life, find a place I can call home, work in a regular job, live in a normal house in a village or a small town, and maybe even have my own family. The big question is where?

When I worked on the camel ranch, I befriended an English guy who joined one of the excursions I've guided. He was over the moon with the experience. After the tour, we went for a drink and had a friendly chat. He was a lovely man in his late fifties, lived in a small town in Essex, and ran a local neighbourhood pub which he also owned. He was a divorcee with two grown-up children that had already left home and were doing their own thing. He planned to retire at 60, and he was looking for a trustworthy person to take over the daily running of the pub.

Before we said goodbye, he gave me his address and invited me to come to England. He said he would give me a job in the pub and pay me cash-in-hand until he could sort out the formal paperwork for me. The job will include free accommodation, as the pub had a small en suite room with a bed on the second floor.

It was over a year ago, but it wouldn't hurt to call him and see if the offer still applies. England seems rather enticing to me at the moment. I imagine the man's pub to be a vintage English pub; dark with wooden decor, but lively and loud, with a beer garden where the people sit on wooden picnic benches on sunny days. I can see the pub surrounded by green hilly meadows with sheep, horses, cows, and small water streams that divide the fields. Villages and large manor houses scattered in the greenery all the way to the horizon; a classic picturesque English countryside.

On my afternoons' reflection time, these days, instead of delving into the memories of the past, I more often turn the dial the other way and move in time to the future. As the future isn't set yet, I see only fragments of episodes that appear in different lengths and details; sometimes I see a very clear portrayal of events like in a video feed with narrative, and at other times I see only an abstract sketch of pictures, emotions, and intuitions.

I travel in my mind through time and space to the evening of the most important day in the world's history; the day she was born.

I'm lying down on the sofa in our living room with eyes open and a stupid smile on my face, daydreaming about the inconceivable, mind-blowing event I had witnessed earlier in the day; the birth of a living baby girl, my daughter.

At 7:30 that morning, my wife woke me up and said that it's time.

"Time for what, babe?" I asked, half asleep.

"To go to the hospital, silly, it's happening."

I instantly woke up, stood up, and put on my clothes as fast as I could.

"Are you alright? Do you need anything? What can I do?" I asked, trying not to be too panicky.

"I'm alright, relax, we still have time. My water just broke while I was in the bath and there is still a long time between contractions. Get yourself a quick cup of coffee and something to eat, I'll get my bag packed ready, then you can take me to the hospital. Just, please keep calm and don't stress me out. However, first, put on your shirt properly, you are wearing it upside down the wrong way. I don't want the staff in the hospital to think my husband is a slob."

Trying to stay calm, I made myself a cup of coffee and a cheese sandwich, but when I was halfway through, she came down and said that we should go as the pains are getting worse. I jumped off the chair, left the food on the table, and took the bag from her. Then got in the car and drove it as close as possible to the house, opened the car door, and offered to help her sit.

"I'm not disabled, I can sit by myself." She said impatiently and moved my hand.

We headed quickly to the hospital, which is 10 minutes from the house.

There wasn't much traffic, as it was Saturday morning. However, we succeeded in picking up all the red traffic lights, which slowed us down. Her contractions became stronger and more frequent, so my stress level rocketed; I shouted and swore at the traffic lights: "God-damned! Come on, you fucking machine! Turn to bloody green already!"

I could hear her breathing heavily from the back seat.

"Are you alright, babe?"

"I'm fine, let's just get there."

Finally, we got to the hospital and parked the car. There are two automatic doors at the entrance to the maternity ward and the second one did not open. We had to ring the bell and ask them to open the door for us. We were stuck between the two doors for what seemed forever. She was already in intense pain, and there was nothing I could do to help.

I hammered on the door, screaming for someone to come. Eventually, after a long 10 minutes, a nurse came with a wheelchair and took us to the first floor where the maternity ward was.

The birth itself wasn't as I imagined; there was no shouting and swearing at the midwife, at me, or at God. She didn't exaggerate like the women in labour in American films. Except for some groans, a few tears from pain, and nails being dug in my arm, the birth was relatively easy; no complications, she didn't need an epidural, and the baby slipped out in no time.

The baby was a little ugly thing, but again, not how I imagined a newborn would look; in my mind, I pictured her coming out red, wet, bald, and wrinkled. However, to my surprise, she came out covered with white stuff, which I was told later is natural moisture, and a head full of thick dark hair. In my eyes, though, she was the most beautiful thing I've ever seen. The nurse laid this little creature on her stomach, on her mother's lap. She lifted her head, opened huge brown eyes and looked at us, her parents. She didn't cry, she just looked curious and wary about the surreal new world that was revealed to her, craving for guidance from the peculiar beings with big teeth in front of her, who were crying and laughing at the same time.

I realised, then, that I have just witnessed the most divine wonder in this universe and my best ever creation, my masterpiece; a birth of a new life, a life which I was a part of creating. When I saw those big eyes looking at me, our souls bonded forever. I knew that I'll always be there for her; if required, I will protect her with my life. I knew she would grow up to be wonderful.

We called the baby Ella. For no particular reason, we just agreed that we want a short name that is easy to pronounce, and both of us like the sound of it.

At noon, Laney, my wife, said she needed to rest and asked me to go home and come back after dinner, so she could sleep and shower.

Now, I'm lying down on the sofa with a big grin on my face, counting the minutes until I can go back to the hospital, hold my baby and hug my beautiful brave wife.

I know life as I knew it had ended; I'm no longer number one. The world changed now since she is here, and all the existential insights that I comprehended on my peregrination in the desert, which emphasise that our lives and actions are insignificant and don't make any difference to the grand scheme of things, are now redundant. I accept that I'm not able to make a world's peace or have input on fixing climate change, yet I ought to make a difference and be significant in her life. The question that will be in the back of my mind for the next 18 years is:

"What can I do to ensure my daughter has a happy childhood and gains the tools to choose and live the life she wants as an adult?"

I'm not anxious or apprehensive about raising my first child. I know I'll do a good job, we will do a good job. Naturally,

I'm a bit concerned about handling this tiny, fragile baby. "How can I hold her safely? What if she rolls out of my arms? Am I going to hurt her with my stiff man hands?"

Anyway, Laney used to babysit for her sisters' kids until they relocated to Dubai following her husband's job as a civil engineer. So, although Ella is Laney's first child, she is experienced in caring for babies. I'm sure I'll also get the hang of it after a while.

I'm thinking about the last two-and-a-half years since I landed on this green island.

The aeroplane landed at Stansted Airport. Pete, my host and my future boss, was waiting at the Arrivals' exit. He shook my hand and seemed genuinely happy to see me.

"Alright, mate? Did you have a good fight? Where is your luggage? Did the airline lose it? They lost my suitcase a few years ago when I went on a holiday to Spain. Eventually, they found it and brought it a day later. Since then, I always put a pair of pants, socks, a toothbrush, and body spray in my hand luggage."

"Hey Pete, thanks for picking me up. The flight was fine, and that's all my luggage." I pointed to my small backpack that contained two Jeans, a few T-shirts, a sweatshirt, and some pants and socks; that was all I owned and needed. I planned to buy whatever I'll need with my first salary.

"Alright then, I guess we can go, young man. Welcome to sunny England! It's almost rush hour, so it will take us about 25-30 minutes to get to your new home. I hope you'll like it here; it's not as exotic as the desert, but we have rain, sarcasm, and roast dinners. You might find your place here."

Because of the horrendous traffic as a result of a car accident between the airport and the M11, the trip took us almost an hour. Finally, just before the sun started to set, we arrived at Saffron Walden, my new home. I wasn't disappointed. The town was exactly what I had pictured in my mind that England would look like; a small rural market town with an old and cosy appearance, medieval churches, a river that runs between the streets, old pubs, and a market square. The town was surrounded by lush green meadows and cultivated fields, woodlands, and large country houses. I loved it.

Pete's pub, "The stable", was an old horses' stable at the edge of the west side of town.

He was a military man most of his adult life and served in the Royal Air Force as a logistics and supply officer. For most of his career, he was stationed in RAF Chicksands, with occasional short periods overseas. He was careful with his money and after two years of service; he saved enough money for a deposit on a house in Saffron Walden. It was a wedding surprise for his wife to be.

In retrospect, buying a house there was a smart move; in the following years, the house prices in the town had a substantial surge as a result of a migration of well-heeled posh Londoners out of the city.

At 45, after 25 years of service and a divorce, he decided he had enough of the military life. A day after his wife moved with their kids out of the house, he retired from the service, looking forward to following his dream to be a pub owner.

He used his connections to buy, from the army for a bargain price, an old empty stable that had been deserted since the war. After a year of work, which was mainly done by himself, the abandoned old stable was converted into a pub.

It was a small venue; only 10 tables, a bar, a small stage for live performances, and a beer garden with four picnic tables. The bar was in a U shape; the main area with the majority of the tables and the little stage was in front of the bar. On the right side were two small tables for people who wanted quiet and privacy. On the left side of the bar were a pool table and a dartboard. Shelves at a chest height had been built around the wooden pillars that held the ceiling and on the walls, for those who prefer to drink while standing. A large TV screen was hanging on the wall in the corner, as sports and beer are unseparated for most of the pub-goers in this country. The front of the bar was covered with hundreds of coasters from beer brands from over the world that Pete collected during the years, and the wooden walls were decorated with covers of whisky barrels from different distilleries and old pictures of the town in the 40s and 50s. Although it was a relatively new establishment compared to most of the rural pubs in the country, Pete designed the decor as a traditional old English boozer. Also, as I've seen in my mind, from the beer garden you could see green meadows and fields crossed by the Rivers Cam and The Slade. I fell in love with the place as soon as I saw it.

My room was on the second floor. It was originally the storeroom for the equestrian and stable equipment, which Pete converted to be a living unit. It had a double bed, a wardrobe, a small fridge, a kettle, and a bathroom with a shower and toilet; everything a person needs to live comfortably.

"I hope the room is alright for you, mate. It's not much, but it's free, no rent. There is no washing machine, but there is a laundromat a couple of streets away, and for cooking, you can use the pub's kitchen." He said while showing me in.

"It's perfect! Much better than what I've had lately." I said and shook his hand. "Thanks for everything, Pete."

"It's alright, it's my pleasure. You are probably knackered from the flight and I need to open the pub, so I'll let you sort yourself out and rest. If you want to join me for a pint later, I'll be behind the bar. Tomorrow, you'll start your new job."

I put the clothes in the wardrobe and jumped in the shower. The flight was only five hours, and I wasn't tired at all, so I went down to the pub and sat at the bar. It was midweek, early evening, the pub was rather empty, only four guests; two middle-aged blokes who looked like builders that came for a few pints after work stood at the bar sipping ales and watching horse racing on the large screen that was on mute, and a young couple sat at a table in the corner, drinking wine and chatting quietly. Pete was behind the bar sorting out the bottles and wiping the glasses.

"This is a lovely place you got here, Pete."

"Thanks, mate. It was hard work to turn the old stable into this. It is my pride and joy. What would you like to drink?"

"I'll have a Lager, please."

"I hope you understand; I didn't bring you here just to work behind the bar; I'm planning to retire and move to Cyprus in a year or so, and I'm looking for someone to run the pub for me."

"I'm ready, and won't let you down. I just wonder why me? Why not someone local? I'll need to get to know the culture and customs here, which will take some time. And, you can't pay me cash forever, I will need to have a working visa sooner or later."

He took a large sip from his glass, then poured crisps into a bowl and offered me some.

"Well, I don't trust the younger generation that grew up here, I think most of them are spoiled cunts who only look for the easy way, and expect everything to be handed to them. I'm looking for someone that I can trust to do the work, and I was really impressed by you on the camel tour and what you have done in your life. To be responsible for the health and safety of 25 people and 25 camels, and at the same time to guide, and cook, while still being funny and creating a relaxed and fun atmosphere; it's not a simple thing to do. The excursion was an unforgettable experience for me, and the main reason for it was the way you led it. I've been on camel tours in the past in Tunisia and Jordan, but they were not even close to the tour you guided. Also, you were in the military, which means you know what discipline is and how to get things done."

"I'm not retiring yet, and we have some time to see if you're fit to take care of my baby, and for you to see if life here in the cold and the rain is what you want. Don't worry about the working visa, I'll sort it out in a few weeks."

I learned the job fast and enjoyed every minute. For the first few weeks, I worked mostly behind the bar, pouring drinks and chatting with the customers. Then Pete started to teach me the other aspects of running a pub; dealing with suppliers, dealing with the bank, pricing the food and drinks, and planning promotional events like quiz nights, performances of local bands, and dart tournaments. He also wanted me to start managing the small pub crew that comprised a waitress, a cook, and a morning cleaner.

After two months, I got my working visa; one day Pete asked me for my passport and took it with him to London. When he returned, he handed me back the passport; it was stamped with a working visa for three years. He never told me directly how he succeeded in getting me the visa. From what I could put together from different conversations we had, I gathered he had an old buddy from the RAF who was working in the Home office in a high position and owed Pete big time for something he had done for him during their military service, so Pete called in a favour.

I enjoyed my new life and where I lived. Despite the perception of Brits, especially the English, around the world, as being cold and distant, I found them mostly to be warm, friendly and welcoming. The harmless sarcasm and ability to laugh at yourself alongside laughing at others spiced most of the social interactions with light banter and fun. I found it refreshing and enjoyable compared to conversations with Germans in Berlin, for example, that were normally deep and intellectual but lacked humour, or the mannerism of Israelis that had humour, but cynical and arrogant, or other Europeans that I have encountered that just didn't have the oomph.

It took me some time, though, to get used to certain cultural aspects and traditions that the English wouldn't divert from. However, after a while, I got used to the quirks and felt that maybe I have found my place here. Then I met Laney and I knew I found my home.

The first time I met Laney was in the pub, though, I can't call it a meet as I just served her drinks. She came one Saturday evening with a guy and sat at a corner table. From their body language, I could see that they were on a date. She seemed quite relaxed, but from his hesitance and discomfort, I guessed it was their first date. He ordered two glasses of red wine from the bar, and when he turned to take the drinks to the table, I looked at her, our eyes crossed for the first time. Something happened at that brief second; a tension, electricity in the air. Then she turned her eyes and smiled at him. During the evening, I glanced at her every so often and could see that she was getting bored. The chap was talking most of the time, probably trying to impress her, and all she was doing was nodding her head and smiling politely. When I collected their empty glasses, I asked if they wanted another drink. He put his hand on hers and asked:

"Should we have another drink? The evening is still young."

She moved her hand off the table, looked at me with a silent cry for help, trying not to roll her eyes, then looked at him and said:

"Thanks, but I have a lot to do tomorrow. I should go home and have an early night."

He was clearly disappointed, but as he was just a bit of a knob, not an arsehole, he took it on the chin and stayed polite. When he opened the door for her, she looked back at me and smiled. I smiled back and raised my glass.

I didn't think I'd see her again, but she showed up in the pub three weeks later with a group of friends on a ladies' night. They were five women in their early thirties, none of them was bad looking, yet I noticed her among the group as soon as she came through the door. Unlike her mates, who were overdressed and covered with heavy makeup, she wore a simple and elegant outfit with minimal makeup; a black skirt almost knee-length, a simple thin cream jumper, black boots, and a grey beret hat. She had the French chic that I find attractive and sexy.

They sat around a table near the wall the entire evening, drinking wine and vodka with Red Bull. As the evening continued, they became tipsier and louder. It was a Saturday night, and we had a band playing Irish songs which naturally created a cheerful atmosphere, so no one minded the noise.

Every time I looked in their direction, I saw her looking at me. When it was her turn to buy drinks, she came to the bar and ordered another round of vodka with Red Bull.

"I hope we are not making too much noise? Some of the girls are getting a bit merry. It's Aimee's 30th birthday today." She pointed at the loudest woman in the group. "The tall sexy girl on the right."

"Oh, well, tell her happy birthday from me."

I poured the drinks and put the glasses on a tray, so she could take them in one go.

"I'm Laney, do you remember me? I came here on a date a few weeks ago."

"I'm Ari," I answered, "I remember you. How is the poor fella? He hoped to end the night in your knickers, and you just waved him off. I found it rather entertaining."

"Oh, please, don't remind me about that dickhead. It was the first and last date I had with him. He bored me to death; I had to listen the whole evening to stories about his success at work, his car, and his house."

"Well, you win some, and you lose some. I like your name, it's unusual."

"Yeah, it's actually short for Lalena. My parents were teenagers in the late 60s and had their first kiss during the song "Lalena" at a Deep Purple concert. So they decided to call their first daughter after the song. I'm not sure how true the story is, but I love my name."

"It's nice to meet you Lalena, but you better go back to your friends, they're waving for you. By the way, you are much sexier than Aimee."

"Well, thanks." A big smile spread across her face as she walked back to the table.

I could hear the girls teasing her: "Laney, you naughty mare! we are dying from thirst here, and you are flirting with the bartender... He is fit, girl!... Can we share him? We are your best mates."

When the band finished the session, the girls got up and put on their coats, ready to go.

"I'm going to stay a bit. Happy birthday, Aimee!" Laney said and gave goodbye hugs to the others.

The girls winded her up while walking out giggling:

"Don't do anything I wouldn't do, girl!"

"Make sure you use protection, Laney!"

"Hey, let us know how it was!"

"You are such a slut! Leave some for us, you lucky sod!"

She stood there looking at them until the pub's door closed behind them, then came and sat at the right corner of the bar.

"Hi again, sorry for that, they had a bit too much to drink." She looked a bit embarrassed by their remarks.

"It's alright," I said. "What can I get you?"

"I'll have a glass of red wine, please. So, where are you from? You are clearly not local."

"Me? I'm from here, can't you hear my posh accent?" I said jokingly.

"Yeah, right, if your accent is posh, I'm the queen. Really, where are you from?"

From there, the conversation flowed. She stayed and chatted with me even after I rang the bell for the last orders, and after I closed the pub when everybody left. We talked about ourselves, about our journeys in life, in love, about our beliefs, expectations. I found her fun and easy to talk to. She was 31 years old and grew up in a village nearby. Her dad owned a real-estate agency in town. At 23, she married her university sweetheart, and they moved up north to Leeds, where he came from. The marriage didn't work out, and they broke it off after four years. They didn't have children or their own house, so they separated on good terms with no complications. She moved back to her parent's house, where she had her own 2-bedroom living unit in the back garden. It was comfortable, and she could save money on rent. She had a teaching diploma from uni and worked as a teacher for year 1 in a primary school when she lived in Leeds, but didn't enjoy teaching and decided to give it up. When she returned to the south, she started to work at her dad's agency; first as an admin assistant, then as an agent; selling houses. Since her marriage broke down, she didn't have a serious relationship. She dated here and there but found most of the guys on the dating sites to be creeps, wankers, or just knobs like the chap on the date in the pub a few weeks ago.

After I closed the pub, we played pool and darts. I showed her how to pour drinks, then I put on some music, and we danced.

She stayed the night with me in my room, and we haven't separated since.

We got married a year later in the registration office, with Pete as my best man, and had a small wedding reception in the pub with only immediate family, close friends, and some of the regular pub-goers.

Both of us had a bit of money saved, which we used for a deposit on the house. We couldn't afford the houses in Saffron Walden, so we looked outside of town. Laney's dad found for us an old 3-bedroom house in the outskirts of Cambridge, not far from Addenbrooke hospital, that was cheap and affordable. It was neglected for years and needed a lot of work to be done, hence the low price. With Pete's help and guidance, as he is handy and had experience in renovating his pub, I turned the house from a dump into a house suitable for a small family.

Two months after we moved to our new home, Laney informed me she was pregnant. We were so happy and looked forward to being parents.

We started to plan and prepare for the new addition in our lives. But as the old Yiddish proverb says: "Der mentsh tracht un Got lacht" ("Man makes plans and God laughs"); one morning, two months into the pregnancy, she came out of the bathroom looking distressed.

"I think I just had a miscarriage." She said with tears in her eyes.

I could see that she was trying to hold herself together.

"What are you talking about?" I said in disbelief. "Sit down and tell me what happened."

She sat on a chair in the kitchen and I made her a cup of tea, then sat next to her.

"I went to the toilet to have a wee, but then I felt a sharp pain and something came out, and I bled a bit. I think I lost the baby."

I took a deep breath and held her hand. "Are you still in pain? You sure it was a miscarriage?"

"I have minor pain in the stomach, not too bad. I'm quite positive it's a miscarriage, but I'm not sure, it could be something else."

"OK, let's not jump to conclusions, babe. Finish your tea, and I'll take you to the hospital."

When she went to wash her cup, I stopped her and gave her a big hug and said:

"Leave the dishes, babe. Come on, you need to be checked. Whatever it is, we will go through it together."

The doctor in the hospital confirmed that Laney had a miscarriage.

We were gutted. She held it in all the time in the hospital, but as soon as we entered the car she burst into tears. I had nothing to say to make her feel better, so I just put my arm around her shoulder until she calmed down.

"I really need a drink now." She said and wiped her tears.

"There is a pub around the corner, let's have a drink and go home."

At the pub, we sat drinking in silence, each one in our own thoughts. Then she looked at me.

"I wanted this baby so much, Ari! The doctor said that most miscarriages are the way for the body to tell us that something was wrong with the pregnancy. But maybe I've done something wrong that triggered it, or maybe there is something wrong with my body and I'll never be able to have a baby?"

"Hey, come on, you've done nothing wrong, and nothing is wrong with your body. These things happen, and it's not your fault. We will try again soon. I promise you we will have a baby. You know I love you so much."

"I love you too. I'll be fine, I just need time."

"Let me take you home. I'll call Pete and tell him I'm not coming to work today, he will understand."

"Don't be silly, babe! I'm alright, Pete is moving to Cyprus next week, and I'm sure he has a lot to do and needs you at the pub. You should go to work. I'll be fine, I need time alone anyway."

In the car on my way to work, I couldn't stop myself; tears ran down my cheeks, and I cried for the first time since I could remember. I was quite surprised how it affected me, as I was level-headed and realistic about the whole thing. However, the frustration from the universe and the worry for Laney's emotional well-being got to me, eventually.

Life continued. Laney had a rare ability to overcome the curveballs that life throws at her and come back on top as a fighter. We concentrated on our jobs and carried on trying for a baby. On Easter Sunday, five months after the miscarriage, Laney woke me up with a hug and said how much she loved me, then informed me she was pregnant again.

The next nine months went well. This time we kept quiet about the pregnancy and told our families and friends only when the bump was visible. Laney was glowing and looked happy most of the time, except for the last few weeks, when she struggled with daily tasks.

I'm relieved, thanking destiny that everyone was healthy and nothing went wrong with the birth. Having my own family after so many years alone seems almost inconceivable, but it is my reality now, and it looks promising.

It ain't fair!

An obnoxious fly walks on my lips and wakes me up. I wave my hand and swear at it, but it is stubborn and keeps coming back until I get up and take my notebook from the bag, then squash it on a stone with one blow. Flies are probably the most annoying thing in the desert. They are always around; they wake you up in the morning as soon as the sun shines and never let you have a good afternoon nap. I became quite skilled in killing them, though; it doesn't matter how many you kill, others will come to haunt you.

After I get rid of the nuisance, I'm closing my eyes again and surfing the timeline back to the future. This time to an outdoor gathering in a large open space scattered with stones in different forms that are standing up out of the ground and flowers between them.

Little Ella is standing on wet green grass holding an umbrella in the shape of a mushroom. She looks so small and lost next to all the adults that surround her. She doesn't know what to do or what to say, so she clings to the umbrella with two hands and looks down at her feet. I'm standing next to her looking at the pile of heavy red soil in front of me, and all I can think is: "Life ain't bloody fair! What the hell am I supposed to do now?"

Penny, Laney's mum, gives me a big long hug.

"Take your time, Ari, we will be in the pub; Pete arranged the wake to be held in the pub for friends and family. Do you want us to take the little one with us?"

"Thanks, Penny, but I want us to say our goodbyes together."

"Alright sweetheart, see you at the pub."

Arthur, Laney's dad, shakes my hand firmly.

"We are here for you, son, don't forget it."

He puts his arm around Penny's shoulders, and they are heading towards their car.

"Why are we staying here, Daddy?" Ella is looking at me with her big brown eyes, confused.

"We are staying here, so we can say goodbye to Mummy together, just us. You can say to her whatever you want."

"But Daddy, how can she hear us under all this sand?"

"Well, Leeloo, Mummy is not there anymore." I put my hand on her chest. "She is here, inside us, and she can hear you. It's only her body buried here. Mummy loves you and will always be with you. Do you remember what she told you before she went away? All you need to do is close your eyes and think of her."

We had a good run for almost six years, Ella, Laney, and I; we were happy in our little family. I loved every minute of being a dad, and Laney bloomed; motherhood suited her like a glove to a hand. Ella was the sweetest baby and toddler; I prepared myself for sleepless nights with endless cries and for annoying paddies if she didn't get what she wanted. However, we were very lucky as she had such a lovely nature. As a baby, she normally woke up only one time a night to feed. As a toddler, she often used to wake up in the middle of the night, come quietly to our bedroom and crawl under the duvet between us, seeking comfort. In the morning we found ourselves on the two edges of the bed, almost falling off, while she lay with spread arms in the middle. She cried at times, but only when she didn't feel well or if she was upset, and occasionally when she wanted attention. It was more cute than annoying, though.

We loved to spend time together; playing at home or sitting in the park watching her play with the children in the playground. Both of us ensured we had a good work/home life balance; Laney went back to work part-time at her dad's real estate office, and as she was brilliant at her job, although she worked only four hours a day, she earned good bonuses from sales and brought home a decent salary at the end of each month. As I managed the pub, I had to work long hours. Most of the time off work, though, I spent with the girls. I also hired a young lad to cover me, so I could have two rest days a week and have more time at home. However, we knew that being in each other's pockets most of the time can be a relationship breaker, so we made sure we had time away from each other to hang out with mates.

We were lucky to have Laney's parents close by; they were delighted to have Ella occasionally for a night, or even for an entire weekend. It was convenient and allowed us to have an adult's time and not neglect our relationship like it often happens to many couples with children. They were relatively young grandparents, only in their late fifties, so they had the energy to have all their three grandchildren at the same time.

On my time-surfing, I hovered over those years fast and could see only fragments of vague pictures, no clear events, just feelings. What I could tell by connecting the pieces is that we were happy; those years concluded a normal pleasant routine. Although it lacked the mind-blowing peaks and the turbulence that I had in the previous life, it was accompanied by a sublime sense of achievement and peace.

Only when you become a parent, you understand that to put someone else in front of yourself with all the inconvenience, the worries, and the frustrations, is the highest form of happiness; to sit on a bench in the playground for hours bored to your core while your daughter plays, to run for hours after your son when he first learns to ride a bike, to sit with your crying baby in your arm for long nights when she has teething pains, and you cannot do anything to help except trying to comfort her, to have your heart stop every time you hear a baby cry in the street or in a shop as you worry it's your baby. This is the happiness of a parent, as with the inconveniences and frustrations, you are experiencing your daughter's happy screams and laughs while playing in the park, your son's smile with a sense of achievement and pride after succeeding to ride by himself without your help, your baby sleep peacefully in your arms after an eventful night, and the relief when you spot the crying baby in the shop and see that she is not your baby, and she is not in pain, just wants her bottle of milk.

Also, the sense of togetherness, of a unit, a home, that a family gives you; the warm feeling inside of caring for someone else but yourself, and having someone else truly care for you, with all the bickering and the arguments of the routine family life, beats any other endorphins fuelled cheap thrills.

However, to show us our place in the big picture; how insignificant we are, and how random and ruthless nature is. My sweet Lalena was gone.

Two months before Ella's sixth birthday, Laney woke up one morning with excruciating pain in her lower stomach. We thought it was something bad that she had eaten, so I called her dad to tell him she would not be coming to work, and got her painkillers from the corner shop. The pills didn't work and in the evening the pains worsened, so I called her mum to come and stay with Ella, and took her to the hospital.

They kept Laney in the hospital for tests; the doctor said that it looks like her bowels are inflamed, which is probably nothing major, but it could also be one of several conditions like Crohn's, Colitis, or something else. Hence, they had to conduct a series of unpleasant tests to eliminate those illnesses. They also gave her something to help relieve the pain.

After two days of testing, just before lunch, the doctor invited us to his office to tell us the results.

"Good afternoon, Mr and Mrs Klein, please sit down."

He looked like he was trying to find the right words.

Laney was tired and impatient.

"What is it, doctor? Is it Crohn's?"

The doctor took a deep breath. "I'm sorry, Mrs Klein, it is not Crohn's disease; you have cancer, pancreatic cancer."

He stopped to let us digest the news. I felt her fingers squeezing my hand.

"What do you mean by cancer, doctor? Two days ago, she was perfectly fine. How can she suddenly, out of the blue, have cancer? You didn't tell us you are testing her for cancer?" I said abruptly in disbelief.

Laney stayed calm and said: "It's not the doctor's fault, Ari, let him explain, he is here to help"

She always had a way to put me back in my place before I said things I could regret.

"You're right. I'm sorry, Doc, It's just a bit of a shock."

"I understand, Mr Klein. Look, the symptoms could have been from a number of conditions and illnesses, so we had to check by elimination. Unfortunately, the diagnosis is not what we've hoped for."

I looked at my wife, and she looked back at me, then I squeezed her hand under the table for reassurance that I'm here for her. Then I turned back to the doctor.

"So what now, doctor? There is a treatment for it, right?. Laney is young and strong, and I'm sure that with the treatment we can beat it."

"Well, Mr and Mrs Klein," he paused for a moment to find the correct words, "Pancreatic cancer often doesn't show symptoms until a later stage. Unfortunately, in Mrs Klein's case, the cancer is in stage 3, which means it has spread to nearby organs. We don't think it has spread to the large organs yet, like the liver or colon, but it is spreading."

"What does it mean? Is it going to be a long recovery?" I asked.

The doctor kept calm and answered clearly and professionally. He'd been there before and understood the emotional blow of the news on us.

"When the cancer is in this stage, it's too late for an operation, and it's normally terminal. Nevertheless, Mrs Klein is young and strong, and if she starts chemotherapy now, we might have a chance to slow it down to give you more time. I don't want to give you false hopes, but the human body is full of wonders; with the medical treatment together with alternative therapy which I can recommend, I know about cases in this stage where the cancer was beaten, and the person lived for years later. Just to make you aware, the chemotherapy treatment has unpleasant side effects. The other option is to give you a support treatment until the inevitable."

He stood up and said: "Again, I'm so sorry. I'll leave you alone now to digest and discuss what you want to do."

A million things ran through my head; I wanted to scream, to throw the chair, to smash the computer that sat on the doctor's desk. I was angry; at the doctor, the hospital, the health system that doesn't have a cure, at nature, at bloody God. But I knew I had to be strong and support Laney, so I blocked the negative selfish feelings, held both her hands and looked her in the eyes.

"We are going to beat this, babe! We'll do the treatment, and together we will beat this fucking cancer! You are not going anywhere; we are going to get old together."

She burst into tears and dug her head in my shoulder.

"The side effects of the chemo are horrible." She said after she calmed down. "I had an aunt that had lung cancer and had chemo. She lost all her hair and felt awful for days after every treatment. I'm not sure if I want to go through all of this and make you and Ella go through it with me. You heard the doctor; the chances to stop it with chemo are slim."

"We cannot give up, babe. I will be by your side all the time. I don't think you are aware, but the universe needs you, not only me and Ella; the world will not be the same without you, it will not allow you to go without a fight."

"You know, babe, I'm going to lose all my hair. Are you still going to love me then? bald without eyebrows."

I caressed her hair and kissed her mouth gently.

"Lalena Klein, I will always love you! With or without hair. Please, don't doubt it again. I'm here for you, and I'm not going anywhere."

"I love you so much too, Ari. Ok, let's tell the doctor to go forward with the chemo."

Our life changed. Chemotherapy is a horrible experience. At the beginning of the treatment, Laney tried to act normally; go to work, play with Ella, do the housework. However, under the smiley face, I could see how she was struggling, although she was proud and stubborn, and refused any offer of my help. When I suggested cutting my hours in the pub, so I can do the housework and cook to allow her to rest more, she snapped at me.

"I'm not disabled, Ari, I'm not feeling 100%, but I can still look after my home and our daughter."

After a while, the pains, nausea, and fatigue after every treatment were taking their toll on her. She had diarrhoea or constipation regularly; she didn't sleep well and found it hard to concentrate for a long time. Laney was quite confident in her appearance, so losing her hair didn't bother her too much.

"At least we save some money on a hairdresser." She said with her typical sarcasm.

Pete came back from Cyprus to look after the pub, as I had to be absent more frequently.

"Go and take care of your wife, mate, don't worry about the pub. Take as much time off as you need, I'll pay you a full salary."

I've insisted on coming to work for at least a few hours a day while Ella was in school or if Laney had a good day, as I don't like to get charity, even from a good friend like Pete.

After three months of treatments, she started to feel better.

On the weekly appointment with our doctor, he informed us that the chemo seems to work, and the tests showed remission of the cancerous area. He paused, and we looked at each other in disbelief. I wrapped my arms around her and whispered in her ear, "You beat it! You are so amazing!"

Tears trickled down her cheeks. She was speechless, but I could see the light in her eyes, the light that dwindled since she started the treatment, was back.

The doctor looked genuinely happy.

"It is excellent news, Mrs Klein, but we are not out of the woods yet, and you still need to continue with the chemo, though, we will reduce the frequency of the treatments."

Unfortunately, the universe had a different plan.

A couple of weeks after the meeting with the doctor that gave us a lot of strength and belief that we are on the right path to beat the illness, Laney collapsed while shopping in Sainsbury's.

I was in the pub checking the inventory when I received a phone call from the hospital. Before the lady finished her sentence, I dropped the phone and everything I had in my hand and ran to my car in a panic. I drove as fast as I could to the hospital. On the way, I called Laney's mum.

"Hi sweetheart, this is a surprise! I'm sorry for the wait; I was outside watering the plants and didn't hear the phone ring. Is everything alright?"

"Not really, Penny, I'm on my way to the hospital; Laney collapsed in Sainsbury's and was rushed to the hospital in an ambulance." I tried to calm my voice, to hide my stress.

"Dear god! Is she alright?"

"I don't know, the hospital didn't give me many details. the only this they said is that she has collapsed and lost consciousness for a few minutes. They only said that she is awake now."

"Oh, god! I thought she was getting better…"

"I'll call you as soon as I know more, Penny. Can you please pick up Ella from school at 3:30?"

"Of course I can. Ari, please take care of my daughter and let us know what is happening?"

"I will. I'm entering the hospital parking now, so I have to finish now."

I ended the conversation and parked the car near the A&E entrance and ran through the automated doors to the lobby. I asked the receptionist where I could find Laney. She checked the computer, then looked at me.

"She is in the recovery room, Mr Klein, let me check with the doctor if you can see her."

She picked the phone up and talked for a few minutes, then put the phone down and smiled at me

"The doctor said you can see her now; she is awake but needs to rest, so it will need to be short. She is in Recovery room 3."

"Thank you very much." I turned toward the sliding doors with a sign: "Recovery rooms".

"Mr Klein!" I heard the receptionist behind me, "Please don't run in the hospital."

I looked through the door's window before I entered the room; a young doctor was with Laney, checking the paperwork on a clipboard. I knocked on the door. She looked at me and signed with his hand to wait, then wrote something on the clipboard, and came out.

"You are probably Mr Klein, the husband." She said and shook my hand. "I'm Dr O'Neil"

"Yes, I'm Laney's husband. How is she?"

"She is better now, but still has a headache and dizziness, which is typical after fainting. She needs to rest. We will need to do further tests, though, because of her condition. Who is dealing with your wife's cancer treatment? Is it Dr Kumar?"

"Yes. Is the cancer getting worse, Doctor? Just two weeks ago, Dr Kumar informed us that the tumour shows regression."

"We can't say until we see the tests' results, it doesn't have to be cancer, there could be numerous reasons that caused your wife to faint; a sudden drop in blood pressure, or maybe she didn't eat or drink enough this morning, heat, anxiety. You can see her now. She needs to rest for a few hours, and then you can take her home. I will talk to Dr Kumar, and he will contact you regarding further tests."

"Thanks, Doc."

Laney was sitting on the bed when I entered the room.

"Hey babe, how do you feel? You scared me." I sat and caressed her cheek.

"I'm alright, babe, I feel better now. I was doing the shopping, and suddenly I saw black and found myself in an ambulance. Can we go home now? This hospital depresses me." She stood up, then sat again. "Can you help me, please? I'm a bit dizzy."

"Whoa, slow down, Laney! The doctor said that you need to rest for a few hours before she'll discharge you. I'll stay here with you."

She muttered, "Bloody doctor! I feel fine! I just didn't eat much in the morning." And lay down unwillingly. "What about Ella? Someone needs to pick her up from school."

"I already spoke to your mum, she will pick her up and take her to their house."

"Oh, that's alright then. Can you please get me something to drink from the vending machine?"

"Sure, babe." I covered her with the duvet and went to look for a vending machine.

When I came back with a can of diet Coke, she was asleep.

Laney wasn't discharged from the hospital that evening; she woke up in agony from stomach pains and headache, with dizzy spells that didn't go away until she was given morphine to numb the pains. She was moved to an oncology ward until the doctors will diagnose what is wrong.

The next few days Laney had to endure again a series of unpleasant tests, which, together with the constant pains and nausea, left her disheartened and in a low spirit.

On Friday afternoon, she had a brief phase when she felt better and was able to walk by herself. Dr Kumar invited us to his office to discuss the diagnosis.

He had a sombre expression when we came to the office. We looked at each other worriedly, as he was normally cheerful and smiley.

"Good morning, Mr and Mrs Klein, please sit down." He paused for a while, trying to find the right words. "I'm so sorry, but apparently the cancer sent metastases which now formed tumours in the liver and the brain. It..."

I barged in the middle of his sentence in anger, "You told us that the cancer is shrinking, Doctor, how come it suddenly did a U-turn and is spreading now?"

"Well, the tumour in the pancreas did shrink. However, cancer cells often break away from the original tumour and travel through the blood or the lymph system, and develop new tumours in other organs in the body. It is often hard to spot a new tumour before it is large enough to affect the body. With treatments like Chemo, we try to kill the original tumour before it sends metastases. In Mrs Klein's case, we clearly didn't start with the chemo early enough."

"Ok, so what now, Doctor?"

"I'm sorry, but the cancer progressed too much now, and there isn't much we can do in this advanced phase. We will stop the chemo treatment immediately, as it will just continue to give you the side effect but will not improve your condition. At this stage, we can only give you care and support to relieve your symptoms and improve your quality of life. Again, I'm so sorry."

I stood up and walked around the office.

"I can't believe there is nothing you can do. Are you saying that she is going to die? Laney is only 36 years old; I'm sure that there is something we can do. Come on, babe, let's go. We can find hospitals or doctors who are more positive. We have to fight it!"

Laney grabbed my hand firmly and forced me to stop.

"Sit down, Ari! Please! We have to come to terms with the situation. Dr Kumar and the hospital have done the best they could do, and I'm not going to go to some witch doctor or through an experimental treatment."

"But, Laney, we can't just give up," I said.

"There is no but, Ari! It is my decision. Now, please sit down and let's hear the doctor." She turned back to the doctor, who waited patiently; it was not the first time he had to tell a family bad news.

"I'm sorry for my husband's behaviour, Dr Kumar. How long do I have?"

"With the rapid and wide speed of the metastases, and as it, unfortunately, reached the brain, I believe that you have a couple of months. We will do as much as we can to make you feel comfortable here; this ward is known in the country to be one of the best wards for end-of-life patients."

I heard her struggling to breathe, so I covered her with my arms.

"Only two months?" she cried and buried her head against my chest.

Dr Kumar stood up, walked around the table, and put his hand on Laney's shoulder. "I'm aware it's overwhelming, so I'll let you be alone now, so you can talk and digest the bad news. Please, take your time."

Laney was a fighter; she fought for her life like a lioness that protects her cubs, but the illness was stronger. She pulled through for 3 more months before it defeated her. During this period I saw her withering; from a colourful flower that won against the unseen enemy, she turned to a wilted pale plant. She lost a lot of weight, and every day faded more into the void.

I sat next to her bed most of the time and witnessed the unbearable pains and suffering that she'd endured. The frustration of not being able to do a damn thing to help her and make the pain go away drove me down. However, I had to be strong for her, so I repressed the negative feelings and supported her as much as I could.

The last two weeks Laney was not responsive, in a catatonic state; She didn't recognise the surrounding people anymore, including Ella, her parents, or me, as the cancer spread more and more in her brain. The doctors said that she is going to pass away any day, and we should be ready.

I still sat and talked to her every day, hoping for a miracle.

On her last day, she suddenly sat in her bed, looked at me and asked for a glass of water. My heart was pounding when I handed the glass to her; I thought my prayers came true.

She looked around and asked, "Where is Leeloo?"

"She is with your parents, babe."

"I want to see her. Can you please call and ask them to bring her here?"

I called their house and Arthur answered. I was so excited and almost shouted at the phone.

"Arthur, Laney woke up. She is asking for Ella. Please come immediately."

Arthur was a bit confused.

"What do you mean, woke up? Are you sure? Penny and Ella are making cupcakes now."

"Yes," I answered. "I just spoke to her; she is asking to see Ella. Please hurry."

20 minutes later, they came to the room. Laney smiled a tired smile toward them.

"Hi, Mum and Dad!" Then she saw Ella. "Hey Leeloo, I missed you! Come here, Munchkin, give me a hug."

Ella ran and threw herself in Laney's arms.

"Mummy, look, Nana and I made you cupcakes."

She screamed and grabbed the basket from Penny's hand.

"Thank you, sweetie! Put it here on the side, I'll eat it later."

Then she looked at us. "Guys, can you please go to have a coffee or something? I want to talk to Ella alone."

When we came back to the room, Laney asked me to take Ella and wait outside for a few minutes, as she wanted to talk to her parents.

We sat in the small chapel that the hospital provided to the religious visitors.

"What did you talk about with Mummy, Leeloo?"

"She told me she needs to go away for a long time, and I'm going to be able to see her only when I close my eyes, but she will always be with me here, in my heart." She put her little hand on her chest, "And she said that I can always talk to her when I miss her or when I feel lonely."

My eyes became misted from tears.

"You know that Mummy loves you very much, right?"

"I know that, Daddy! She also told me some secrets that I'm not supposed to tell anyone; even you." She paused for a moment, then asked with a serious expression on her face, "Daddy, do you think Mummy will feel better in the place she is going to? It makes me sad to see her poorly all the time."

"Yes, baby, she will feel much better; like she was before she got sick. This is how you should remember and see her when you close your eyes."

"That's good. Can we go back to Mummy's room now, I want to say goodbye to her?"

When we returned to Laney's room, I saw Penny wiping her eyes; she didn't want Ella to see that she was crying. She took Ella's coat and said:

"Come here, sweetie, let's put on your coat, then give Mummy a big hug and a kiss. She is tired and needs her beauty sleep, and we need to go home and get the dinner ready."

Ella put her coat on, then jumped on Laney with a big hug, giggling. Just like a child with no worry in the world.

"I hope you'll have a lovely trip, Mummy. Every time I will miss you, I will close my eyes and call you."

Laney held her firmly for a few minutes, not wanting to let go. Then pushed her off, so they could look at each other, then put her hands on Ella's cheeks.

"Munchkin, I love you so much, and I will always be with you! Please don't forget it."

She looked at Penny and Arthur and nodded her head. Penny took Ella's hand, and they left the room.

"Ari, please sit. I need to talk to you."

I sat on the bed, and she held my hand in hers.

"Ari, I want you to promise me two things."

"Sure, babe, anything you want."

"I want you to promise me you will do everything in your power to ensure that our daughter has a happy childhood. I will not be here to help you, and it's going to be hard, but I made my parents promise me they will always be here to support you. I want Ella to grow up and be a strong independent woman with happy memories from her childhood."

I looked into her eyes, held both of her hands, and said:

"I love our daughter more than life itself, and I will do my best to make her happy, babe. You just need to concentrate on your recovery now."

She put her finger on my lips to shut me off.

"Shush! I didn't finish. The second thing I want you to promise is to find a woman that will love you and share your life with her. You can mourn and grieve on me for a while, but then I want you to get on with your life and find a woman that makes you happy."

"Come on, babe! Stop worrying about me! Just concentrate on getting better, you are not going anywhere."

"Please promise me, Ari."

"Ok, I promise."

"Good. Now, can you please go home, Love? I'm exhausted, and need to sleep."

I kissed her on her lips and got up. "Sure, I'll come to see you tomorrow morning. It's so good to see you feeling better. I love you."

I didn't want to come to terms with it then, but that was her goodbye.

She died in the early hours of the following morning.

"Daddy, can I ask you a question?" Ella asks while we are making our way to the pub.

"Of course you can, Short stuff."

"Why Mummy and you are calling me Leeloo? It doesn't sound like Ella at all."

"Well, Leeloo is the name of the perfect human in a movie that Mummy and I loved to watch. When you were born, we looked at you and saw how perfect you are, so Mummy gave you this nickname."

"What is human?"

"A human is a person. In the movie, it was a young woman."

"Can I watch this movie, Daddy?"

"It's a grown-ups' movie, you can watch it when you are older."

The pub is already full when we arrive; family, friends, work colleagues, schoolmates. It was a surprise for me that Laney knew so many people; although she was friendly and loved meeting new people, she preferred intimate times with 3-4 friends in a pub or a restaurant rather than parties or large events.

Donna, Laney's sister, is waving to me, signalling to come and sit next to her.

She came on the first flight from Dubai after Laney passed away and is staying in our house, in the guest room, for the last two weeks, helping me to cope. Her daughters are still young and there was no point in bringing them to a grieving environment, so they stayed with their dad in Dubai.

Ella sees a familiar face amongst all the people and pulls my arm.

"Daddy, Daddy, aunty Donna is there, let's go and sit with her."

I let her run to Donna while I pour a pint of beer for myself and a glass of squash for Ella from the bar, then sit next to Donna.

"How are you hanging on, mate?"

Ella sits on her lap, dangling her legs and looking at the stage; good old Pete used his contacts again and brought a band that performs covers of classic rock ballads. They are preparing their instruments on the stage.

"Well, I've been better. Thank you for staying with us for the last two weeks. Ella needs a woman figure in this period, she is crazy about you." I'm pausing for a moment, trying to find the right words. "It also helped me... without your company I would probably sink to self-pity."

"Hey, Laney was my sister, and Ella and you are my family. I was happy to stay for a while and help you. It was also an opportunity to bond with my niece, which I don't see enough; she is absolutely drop-dead gorgeous! I'm going to miss her so much..."

A noise of a tinkling glass stops her in the middle of the sentence.

Liz, Laney's best mate, stands up and taps on her glass with a fork until everyone is silent.

"Good afternoon, everyone! We all knew Laney and loved her. She would want us to celebrate her life, not mourn her death." She raises her glass, "The next songs are for you Laney, You've been an inspiration for all of us."

The band plays "Lalena", followed by "She" from Elvis Costello. By the time the second song ends, there is not one dry eye in the room.

Liz stands up again. "Now, after we all got it out of the way and cried, let's drink and have a great evening! Most of you don't know it, but it was Laney who put this evening together, with the help of Pete. When she realised she would not make it, she refused to allow all of us to be miserable farts (those are her words) and wanted us to celebrate. The next song she dedicated to you, Ari.",

The band is starting to play "Don't cry" by Guns N' roses. It was Laney's favourite song. I put my arms around Ella, who moved to sit on my lap, and Donna put her arm on my shoulders.

Some people are singing along, and others are only swaying with the rhythm. All I want is to go home because without Laney sitting beside me, it's all a bunch of bullocks!

The evening goes by; people standing one by one reminiscing about Laney with anecdotes and funny stories, and between the stories, the band plays songs she loved. I had no clue that she had such an effect on so many people. It just makes me love and misses her more.

We leave the pub before the evening ends; Ella is tired, and it's also enough for me. Many of the people are following

Laney's request; getting pissed and having a good time. But I can't and don't want to enjoy the evening without her.

When I finally lie down on my bed after the long day, I'm looking at Laney's empty side of the bed, and the realisation strikes me:

"Laney is gone! She is not coming back! The funeral and the wake are finished. Donna is flying back to Dubai Tomorrow; it will be only Ella and me from now and on."

I need to pick myself up and start planning our life without Laney. Penny and Arthur will help as much as they can, but it's my responsibility to raise Ella.

My mum fell and broke her pelvis a couple of years ago. She can't walk properly anymore and uses a mobility scooter, so she hardly goes out of the Kibbutz where she lives. For this reason, she didn't come to the funeral and just called twice to check on us. Ella and her see each other only once a year when we come to visit, so they are not very close. Anyway, she is busy with her issues and getting old. One of my brothers lives in Australia; he married a local and lives in a cattle ranch in the outback, and my other brother has four young children and a "She-devil bitch" as a wife. My few old childhood friends and I have drifted away since I moved here. Hence, I can't rely on my family and old friends for emotional or material support.

I have to be strong for Ella.

Eventually, after 3 hours of tossing and turning, I'm falling asleep with a solid decision that no matter what I feel or the hardships I'll endure; I will make up as much as I can for the absence of her mum and ensure that Ella has a happy childhood. I will try to give her the tools and strength she needs to deal with what the world will throw at her when she grows up.

Life goes on

I continue my journey, hovering over the thread of time that weaves the fabric of my life.

The stuff that fills memories is mainly events or moments which are out of the ordinary. Life goes on between those moments in an endless routine. The genuine happiness is the feeling of contentment and joy that comes in those little moments within this routine; when you lounge on the sofa watching TV in the evening with your partner after a day of work and the kids are in bed, your hand caresses her leg and her head leans on your shoulder. Or when you put on music and dance with your daughter on a midweek afternoon for no specific reason. Or the smile and gratitude from an old neighbour after you helped carry her groceries to her door. Or when you sit in the pub catching up with friends who you didn't see for a while.

People often confuse happiness with excitement like adrenaline-fuelled activities, parties, holidays, trips. Big events, which are the building blocks of our memories. Happiness, on the other hand, creeps in small doses to everyday moments for a short time and disappears before we can get a hold and keep it.

I couldn't afford to pay the mortgage repayments on the house by myself with only my salary. I also needed help in looking after Ella in the evenings when I was in the pub, so I accepted Arthur and Penny's offer to sell the house and move with Ella into their guest house.

I was a bit reluctant at first, but Arthur was adamant; we were sitting in his garden one evening when I was off work, having a few pints while Ella and Penny were preparing dinner.

"Listen, buddy," he said, "Ella is our granddaughter, and you are part of the family. We'll be very happy if you sell the house and move here. The guest house is empty, anyway. You'll have your privacy over there; there is the garden entrance, so you don't need to come through our house. We are happy to babysit Ella when you are at work or when you need time for yourself to see friends or date women; Laney wouldn't want you to stay celibate forever."

Eventually, after some convincing, I agreed. I wanted to pay the rent, but Arthur refused.

"This is the minimum we can do. Our mortgage is paid off, and the guest house is empty. Laney will never forgive us if we take money from you. We are quite comfortable financially and don't need your money. You'll be able to save money for Ella's future."

I insisted on paying, as I don't like to feel like a charity case, but he kept refusing. When we finished the second pint, Penny shouted that dinner was ready. Before we got in, we came to an agreement that I won't pay rent, but I'll pay for the utilities that we use.

We moved to the guest house, and Arthur put my house up for sale through his real-estate Agency. It was sold quickly due to the popularity of the area in which it was located.

The work that Pete and I had done in the house raised its value significantly, so I made some profit on the sale. The money which was left after paying back the mortgage, I put aside in a savings account. The plan was to use this money to buy a small house for us when Ella will be a bit older and able to stay in the house by herself.

Time went by, and we got used to life without Laney. Pete went back to Cyprus and I continue to run the pub. However, I didn't spend more time than necessary at work, and as soon as I could, I went home to have quality time with Ella.

She grew up to be a beautiful girl, happy and full of life and joy. At school, she wasn't the smartest girl in a class and wasn't a straight A's student, but at parent's evenings and in the end-of-year certificates, the teachers always praised her for being friendly, hard-working, pleasant to work with, and adamant to do the best she can. She wasn't the most popular girl in her year, but she had a couple of friends with who she used to hang out. Her teacher approached me one morning after I dropped Ella in school; she was a bit worried as she often sees Ella sitting alone and talking to herself. When I asked Ella about it, she said that when she feels lonely or confused; she talks to her mum. As she grew up, these one-sided conversations with her mother happened more seldom, until they completely stopped.

When Ella was about 8 years old, she came to my bed one Saturday morning and woke me up excited.

"Daddy, I know what I want to be when I grow up."

"What is it, baby girl?"

"I want to be a doctor, I want to find a cure for cancer, so other kids' mums won't die."

"That's great, Leeloo, I hope you will find the cure."

I thought it was only a quirk of a child, but I was so wrong. She became obsessed with being a doctor; she started to watch hospital programs on TV like Holby City and Casualty and was reading books about human anatomy. A day after her 10th birthday, she joined St John's ambulance's Cadet unit that gives first aid skills and experience in the field for children who seek a future in health care.

Ella was adamant to go to a university that is in the top 10 best Med schools list. So, from year 10 until she finished Sixth-form, she prioritised her studies over everything else. She sat in her room for hours revising; after school, on weekends, on school holidays. Her efforts paid off; on her GCSEs and A-levels, she achieved A's and B's. On the relevant subjects, she achieved A*'s and A's. Eventually, she found a slot and was accepted to Swansea university, which has a very good Med school.

When she told me the news about being accepted to the university, I wasn't overly happy about it; I preferred her to go to a more local uni and live at home. I knew, though, I was being selfish, and it was time to let her go to find her place in the world. So I took her out to celebrate in her favourite Pizzeria in Cambridge.

As soon as Ella was mature and sensible enough to stay at home by herself, I said to myself it was time to move away to our own place. So I bought a small house. It wasn't fancy, but it was within walking distance from the pub, from Ella's school, and it suited our needs. I saved enough money by then, to pay for it in full, and I got it freehold without the need for a mortgage.

Arthur and Penny weren't thrilled about us moving away; they loved having their granddaughter around, but they understood my need for privacy and independence. We visited them regularly and rarely missed Penny's fabulous Sunday roast dinner. Ella also went there often in the middle of the week.

Both Ella and Penny, and also some of my mates in the pub, kept pestering me about starting to date again:

"Ari, it's been years since Laney passed. I'm sure she would want you to find someone to share your life with."

"Dad, I'm growing up. I like to spend time with my friends, not just with my old dad. Sooner or later I will move away, and you need a woman to take care of you. You are not bad looking for an old man, I'm sure there are plenty of women that will be happy to date you."

"Hey, mate, you can't live like a monk for the rest of your life. Half of the birds who come here to drink are looking for a chance to wrap their legs around you. It's not natural to ignore all this good."

Eventually, only to stop the budgeting, I started dating.

I had some casual hookups and even some brief affairs, but I never settled down again and didn't have a serious long-term relationship. They didn't have a chance; I compared every woman that was getting close to me to Laney, and none of them matched her. I couldn't get any relationship to work, as Laney's light was still so bright and didn't fade in time. It blinded me from seeing the light of other women. None of them was good enough. Something was broken inside me, and the only person who could mend it had left me.

Pete got killed in a road accident in Cyprus in the summer of Ella's graduation from Sixth-form. A group of 4 drunk young Italian lads drove their rented car out of a party at 5:30 in the morning. Pete was crossing the road toward the beach for his morning swim when they crashed into him at a high speed. He didn't have a chance; he was killed instantly. They were so drunk and didn't even realise they hit him, so they drove off. There were several witnesses to the accident, so it didn't take long for the local police to catch the bastards. It didn't bring Pete back to life, though.

A couple of days after his funeral, I received a call from a solicitor's firm. The woman on the other side of the line identified herself as Mrs Foster and asked me if we could arrange a meeting regarding Pete's will, as she was the solicitor that was dealing with the execution of the will. I was surprised but agreed to come the next day after lunch.

We met in her office, shook hands, and she invited me to sit down. She opened a file that was sitting on the desk in front of her.

"Mr Klein, I invited you here to inform you that according to Peter Griffith's will, you are the beneficiary of the pub "The stable" that is located here in Saffron Walden."

I was gobsmacked for a moment.

"What do you mean?" I asked.

"It means that after you sign the legal documents, you'll be the owner of the pub."

"But...but I'm not family-related."

"Well, apparently Mr Griffith considered you as his family."

"Oh, ok, so what do I need to do?"

"You just need to sign a few documents here, and the pub is yours."

After I signed all the papers, Mrs Foster handed me an envelope.

"Mr Griffith attached this letter to his will and asked to give it to you after you signed the deed to the pub."

"Thanks." I took the letter and put it in my pocket. "Anything else I need to do?"

"No." she put the paperwork in the file. "You are now the legal owner of the Stable. Congratulations!"

The meeting was over. We stood up, shook hands, and I left the office.

I was somewhat muddled up after this unexpected event. I sat on a public bench in the street, took the envelope out of my pocket, opened it carefully, so it wouldn't rip, and looked at the letter that was folded neatly inside. Then I took a big breath and opened the letter carefully.

It was a short letter; Pete was always a man of few words:

Hey, buddy!

If you read this letter, I presume you signed the papers, and the pub is yours. I bet you had quite a surprise when the solicitor called you.

I thought about it long and hard, and although my sons are not in contact with me, they are still my sons and I want to leave them something.

I decided to split the money I have(which is not much) and the house in Cyprus between both of them.

However, during the years you and Ella became like a family to me, so I want you to have the pub after I'm gone. It is my legacy and I know you'll continue to keep it running successfully.

Cheers

Pete

"Cheers to you, and thanks! Mate. I hope you can have as many pints as you want up there." I said quietly and raised my hand for cheers, pretending to hold a glass.

After graduation, Ella worked in the pub behind the bar for the summer. She wanted to have some spending money while she was at uni. It was the last time we spent together before she moved away, and I loved every second.

At the end of the summer, she started her studies to become a medical doctor at the University of Swansea. I drove her with the suitcases in my car to the university campus. She rented a room for herself, with no roommates in the campus accommodations, as she wanted to concentrate on the school work and avoid distractions. It was dearer than a shared room, but I was happy to pay a bit more if it would help her with her studies. When I drove away, I looked at her through the mirror standing on the pavement, smiling from excitement and waving me goodbye. All I could think was:

"She has grown up now! My baby has left me to find her place and put her mark on this world. I'm so proud of her and I know she will not stop until she gets to where she wants to be, but I'm going to miss her so much. I hope she will not forget her old-man when she'll be on the top of the world."

Somehow I knew she won't be back after her studies, so I treasured every time she returned home for the school holiday and tried to spend as much time with her as I could.

I was right; following her achievements at the university, and her tenacity and determination, she was accepted for an internship at Memorial Sloan Kettering Cancer Center in New York. According to her, it is one of the best cancer care and research centres in the world.

As soon as she graduated, she packed a suitcase and flew to New York.

Arthur contacted his former partner, who relocated to the Big-apple 20 years ago. He sold to Arthur his share in their firm, and with this money, he opened a successful real-estate agency over there. Arthur asked him a favour for old times; to find an affordable flat in the city for Ella.

With the flat ready for her and a fair amount of money I've transferred to her account which I saved all those years, I knew she'll be fine. Though, I wasn't sure I'll be fine with my daughter going further and further away from me.

After a year as an intern, the management offered her a position in the research department. She was over the moon; It was what she worked for all those years. She also fell in love with a colleague that year that was also on the intern program. He was also offered a position at the end of the year, but in another hospital in the city. They decided to get married and settle down in New York.

I was so happy that things turned out exactly as she had planned and worked for since she was eight years old. The rest of her life she'll dedicate to the last piece of the puzzle, a cure for cancer.

The years passed in an endless routine, although a pub owner routine doesn't lack drama, buzz, or joy. After Ella left, I put all my energy into the pub; it became the centre of my life. I still went on Sundays to see Arthur and Penny, but it wasn't the same without Ella.

Ella and Chris, her husband, decided not to have children; they felt their work is more important and needs their full attention.

"How can I be busy changing nappies or going to parents' evenings in school when I can save people's lives in that time?" Ella used to say when I tried to convince her about the joy of having children in our weekly conversation on the phone.

Even though I wasn't happy with their decision, I had to come to terms with it.

"She is happy with her choice in life, and I should accept and respect this choice. It's not that she is wasting her life on shallow, self-indulgent pleasures. What is driving her is altruism; helping other people. For her, having children is a selfish act." I said to Penny at dinner. As it was inconceivable to Penny that Ella doesn't want to have children. "I'm proud of this girl, even if I wouldn't have grandchildren."

Penny put her hand on mine. "You've done a wonderful job raising her by yourself, Ari. You should also give yourself a credit."

"Thanks, Penny, I appreciate it, but I had a lot of help and support from the people in this room." I got up and kissed her cheek. "Thanks for everything. Dinner was divine as usual! See you next week."

The world kept changing; technology, globalisation, pandemics, and conflicts changed the fabric of society and the economy. The sense and meaning of community changed from togetherness to forums and groups in the social networks, especially for the young generation. You didn't have to leave your house to see and talk to people; you could choose to communicate through video calls, talk on the phone, or just to text. People didn't need to dress up and put make-up on, then go out, often in the cold and rain, to meet with their mates or family. When you got fed up with the interaction, without the need for apologies and long goodbyes, you could end the conversation with one stroke on the screen. Many people preferred only to text instead of talking. And some people, to avoid actual conversation, used to record themselves then send it to their mates who also recorded their answer and sent it back. It could be agoraphobia with the help of the advancing technology that lifted its head in many people, following the pandemics, terrorism, or only the fear of how one looks like, as physical appearance became the most important thing for the young adults. I believed, though, the main reason for the slow death of face-to-face communication was laziness, and the addiction to the legal drug called the internet. High-street was dying, cinemas disappeared gradually, and the young generation was fading from the streets.

The pub scene didn't change much, though. Fewer people attended pubs on regular days, but apart from that, it stayed the same as in the past. It was part of the culture that many people embraced and didn't let go of; watching football with a bunch of strangers drinking beer and cheering, weekend lunches in a pub on sunny days, first dates, pub quizzes or karaoke. The traditional pub was a part of the British identity, which thankfully still kept its head above the water.

Most people still preferred the traditional pubs to the "trendy" fancy-schmancy pubs/wine bars/cocktail bars with their shiny chrome and glass decor. Therefore, I kept the Stable as Pete originally designed; I tried to maintain an establishment where people can socialise with each other like in the old times when a pub was called a "public house". The staff I hired had to have the good nature with the resilience to deal with the pub goers' banter. During the years I extended the menu to attract more families, but I didn't fall into culinary adventures and kept it as a simple traditional English pub food.

My mum passed away the same year Ella moved to New York. I didn't feel the need to visit Israel once a year anymore since she was gone; my home country stopped being home years earlier. The people, culture, and landscape totally changed since I moved to the UK, and I felt like a tourist every time my feet got off the plane. With my brother over there, I spoke every few months on the phone; it was enough to catch up, as we had little to say to each other. During the years later, even those conversations stopped, as we didn't feel the need to pretend we have anything in common anymore after our mum died. The last time I saw my other brother who lives Down-under was at the funeral. For a couple of years after the funeral, he kept inviting me to come to Australia for a holiday, and I kept declining with the excuse that I couldn't leave the pub for so long. We had a good bond as children, my Aussie brother and I, but because of the physical distance and the paths that life led us to, we eventually lost touch.

The rest of my life passed like a dream; swift and unmemorable.
When my body started to deteriorate and the age-related ill-health emerged, I had no one to take care of me; Arthur and Penny were already six feet under, and Ella had her life in New York. She did try to persuade me to come and live with her and Chris, but I couldn't bear the thought of leaving my pub and the surroundings and moving to the noisy big city. Eventually, after endless arguments, she convinced me to sell my house and move to sheltered housing, which is another name for a home for elderly people who are still independent but can benefit from supervision.

It was a lovely retirement complex at the edge of town; expensive, but with nice residents and many facilities and activities. At first, I was bitter and acted like a dick to the staff and other residents, but after I accepted that I'm getting old and require help at times, I was happy to live there for the rest of my time in this world.

So I retired.

I left the pub to be run by the capable hand of Martin, who was working for me for 20 years. He was in his mid-twenties when we met, married plus two children, without a penny in his pocket. He opened a restaurant with a partner a few years back, which was successful for two years until his partner embezzled all the money from the account and disappeared. He left Martin with a huge debt to the bank and suppliers, and only his dick in his hand. When I met Martin, he was drinking spirits in the middle of the day as he didn't know what to do; if he wouldn't pay the money off, he could end up in prison. He had to close the restaurant and was ready to sell his house.

My senses told me that he is a sound lad who is just down on his luck. I decided to help him, so I paid enough of his debts to keep the bank and suppliers off his back, and in return, he came to work for me in the pub. Over the 20 years, he slowly paid me the money back.

Martin didn't know it, but I decided to follow my mentor and friend Pete and put him in my will to have the pub after I'm gone. I saved a nice sum in the bank to bequeath to Ella. She never had an interest in the pub anyway.

life in my new home was pleasant and relaxed, as it is supposed to be in the last chapter of life. A journalist from a local newspaper came one day and asked me if he could interview me, as he was writing an article about The Stable that became through the years a local institution.

at the end of the interview, he asked me:

"If you could come back to have another life, would you come back here? to Israel, where you grew up? To America, where your daughter lives? Or anywhere else?"

"I will tell you what my late nan said when she was asked the same question.". I said.

"I do not want to live again at all. One life is enough. I hope this current incarnation is the last one. There were ups and there were downs. Life was pretty hard. Like for any other human being; Lots of worries and lots of trouble. but also a lot of beautiful things, many experiences, many achievements, and a lot of love. But to come back again? No! I hope there is no life after death."

Epilogue

The walls are closing on me like the giant claws of a two-thousand-year-old crab.

My life passes before my eyes on a green screen of old leaves.

The ancient ticker beats heavily in my chest like hot lava in the heart of a young mountain.

My friends left me forever. They went with him, all of them.

Only I left here, only I survived; very old, but alive.

Soon he will come and take me to the big blue peace; a peace which no one alive ever witnessed.

I'm lying on the bed of my grave, no one in the world I have but you, and you are gone. You went away beyond the mountains, beyond the sea, beyond my reach, beyond my love.

You left me no word, no note, and I've been waiting since.

For 50 years I've been waiting by the phone; with every ring, every knock on the door, I thought maybe you came home.

You are the only one. You always were.

I'm longing for your beautiful smile, for the bells of your voice when you were laughing out loud, for your soft lips kissing me goodnight.

I'm old now, I'm going to die. My last breath I'm giving to you, babe, You are the only one.

I'm lying in my tomb now, I see our daughter above, tears in her eyes and flowers in her hand.
"Go away from the grave!" I shout with no sound. "You are a little bit late. Go back to your life, Love, to the light. Maybe we'll meet beyond. Eternity can't keep our family apart."

I close my eyes slowly, then open them, thinking: "No! It's not the time."
A bright light dazzles me. I sit up, rubbing my eyes until they get used to the sunlight. The endless desert lies in front of me with all its glory. Nadya is munching a tree branch. She lifts her head and looks at me with a silly smile. She walks towards me, push me with her nose, then she opens her mouth and says:
"Come on, stop being a lazy bum! Let's hit the road, mate."

The Old Garden Bench

1

Nothing about this house was familiar anymore. The wind was whispering through the bushes and trees that grew wild, attacked and swallowed the white walls and the red roof that once used to be home. He touched the wall trying to feel the excitement he imagined he would feel on his entire journey, but nothing changed inside, just memories left, and they are not in this house. "There are no memories or roots in bricks and wood piled on top of each other," he thought, "They are inside me all the time." He looked around; most of the tarmac on the road leading to the house was covered with plants, and the slabs in the garden were hardly seen. "Nature takes back what she owned before we violently conquered the land," he thought, "plants are like people; When there is no stronger obstacle or enemy they will spread, taking over any available space and strangling the weak and the small. As people, the plants will continue to spread until they have faced a stronger force. They can't act differently; they have been programmed to behave this way, to grow as much as they can, with no mercy, no morals, no right or wrong, no conscience, and no future. In a few years, nothing will be visible to hint that a family once lived here; my family." It was supposed to be a depressing thought, but he realised that he didn't care what would happen to this house.

He sat on the old wooden bench that was still standing on what used to be the lawn he played on with his brother at another time, another life when the world made sense. On this bench, his mum used to sit on sunny days watching the kids and getting a tan while his dad was gardening. He had his first kiss at the age of thirteen on this bench when she came to visit while he was grounded for a week after swearing at his teacher and got suspended from school for two days. He proposed to his wife on this bench, and she sat there a few years later looking at their son and him playing football on the grass. Now it was just an old wooden bench in a neglected garden. What was he looking to find here? Maybe he thought the pieces of his shattered life would bond together and some answers to how to continue would appear, or maybe he hoped that the last few years were a dream, and he would find everything as it was; smells of dinner in the oven, mum with a smiling face giving him a wet kiss and dad inviting him for a beer and a cigarette in the garden. But his father was long gone, and his mother was disappearing into a hollow shadow of her younger self and she couldn't recognise him anymore. There is nobody here to guide him or even just to give him advice on where to go from here, there is no one that will put a hand on his shoulder and say, "Everything will be alright." This house was not his childhood home anymore. It used to be the only place except for his own flat where he didn't need to knock on the door or announce himself before he came to visit. He was always welcome without interrogations or complaints; his parents knew that if he had anything to tell them he would not hesitate and when he needed any advice or help, he would ask. His wife and son loved to visit on the weekends, the easy-going atmosphere, warmth, and space were a normal climate here it was a blessing to his small family, compared to the modern stressful life in the city and his pushy cold in-laws. It's all gone now, and will never come back; just a crumbling house and an overgrown garden with an old wooden bench in the middle are all that remain.

His mind went back to his first kiss, just before puberty, when everything was simple and innocent. They used to spend long hours together; he never understood what attracted him to her. He was shy, a bit of a geeky boy that preferred to sit and read a book than run around with the other boys. She, on the other hand, was a loud energetic tomboyish girl that hated to be indoors. She never hesitated to start a fight or to climb the big oak tree in the school playground, playing football or causing trouble. For some reason that he never understood she preferred to hang out with him after school instead of the popular kids, during school days, especially at playtime, she was in the centre of the attention; laughing with the girls, teasing and challenging the boys for arm-wrestling or a race, and being cheeky to the teachers. After school, though, she blew off all the arse lickers and the "cool" kids and chose to hang out with him. Maybe his introverted character and relaxed nature calmed down the fire in her belly and kept her balanced.

The river was their favourite hangout place; they used to go for long rides on their bikes in the woods eventually stopping on the river bank where they fished, swam in the water in the summertime or just sat and chatted. She always teased and dared him to do crazy things like jumping from the little waterfall, eat raw fish or doing "a wheelie" on the bike. He used to act annoyed, as he just wanted to chill out and enjoy the freedom. Nevertheless, he actually enjoyed the attention and her constant enthusiasm. She called him Ziggy and said that he reminds her of the character from the comics. He didn't mind, though, he saw himself more like Ziggy Stardust. Now he feels more like Major Tom that's floating in space and can't come back down to earth. He called her Pippi, after the Swedish children's book character Pippi Longstocking, with her ginger hair and strength it was obvious why he chose this nickname.

One evening, a week after the summer holidays began, they sat on the bench in the garden after a long day in the woods and a swim in the river. They had been tired and enjoyed the quiet twilight time before she had to go home. Suddenly she looked at him with a strange grin. "Close your eyes for a second."

"Why?" He asked with suspicion.

"Ziggy," she pinched him, "just, trust me, I want to try something...I'm not going to hurt you."

He closed his eyes wondering what mischief she had planned for him this time. Then he felt her soft, wet lips covering his lips, it was the first time he had been kissed. It was a strange sensation; he wasn't sure if he liked it, but he didn't dare move, then their lips separated, when he opened his eyes she had already taken her bike and rode home. Although it was just a clumsy kiss of two kids, he never felt, with any girl or woman, even his wife, the intimacy that he felt with her in those few seconds.

Two weeks later she changed; she went for a week to visit her dad who lived in the city and came back as a different person.

On the outside, she looked and acted the same, but he could feel and see in her eyes that something was gone, something happened to her during that week away. He tried to ask her what happened in the city, and if he could help? She said that everything was fine, and she'd had a great time, but he didn't believe her.

She started to avoid him and stopped coming to his house on her bike. He missed her dragging him from his books to go to the woods or to the river, to play on the lawn or just to sit with her on the bench badgering and tickling each other until one was running away into the house. He called her a few times and even went to her house to knock for her, something that he normally avoided as her mother was not very hospitable to him; she thought he was a strange geeky kid, and she preferred her daughter

167

hanging out with the popular kids. However, every time he called for her, after that week at her dad's, she found different excuses not to hang out together. She refused even to chat saying that her mother wouldn't let her out or excused herself saying she was feeling unwell. When he came to her house, after the start of the school year, she said she had to do homework and then shut the door in his face. He knew that she was avoiding him; her mother never stopped her going out before, she was very rarely ill and homework was the last thing on her mind, he used to help her with that normally.

After a while, he gave up.

2

The house was never put up for sale, at first, after his mum's dementia worsened, and she had to be put into a nursing home, he believed that he would be able to convince his wife to move back here, but she was a city girl who needed the noise and speed to function, even when they came to visit, by the second day she became restless and ready to go back home.

His Brother moved to another country many years before and had no interest in the house or the family anymore. Hence, the house had stood unattended for a few years now.

"This house and the memories are all I have left now." He thought, "I had everything I wanted, but I threw it away."

Many questions popped into his mind:

"Did I really want it all?"

"Did I ever really love my wife and son?"

"Did I enjoy my job?"

"Did the company of our friends, her friends mostly, the house parties and nights out give me joy?"

"Were the holidays abroad more than just a stressful burden?"

"Why did I try to hold on to those things so hard until it nearly destroyed me?"

He knew the answers; he fought to keep these things because it gave purpose to his life, it wasn't always a joy ride, and he never really felt satisfied, but the family, job, friends and social life gave meaning to his life, a path to walk through, and a sense of direction. Nonetheless, it was a compromise, she, Pippi, was always with him, hiding deep, but shadowing every relationship he'd ever had, he wasn't aware of it, but for the last three decades, every person in his life, except his parents, he compared with her, his wife, son, friends, or work colleagues. He hadn't consciously thought about her for years, however, when he sat on this old bench he realised that the last time he was happy was that summer twenty-nine years ago.

The dusk started to come down and he decided to head to the village pub that had a B&B, to have dinner and see if they had a spare bed for the night. But first, he had to find the only thing he wanted to take from the house, he found it in a book in his old room, not touched since he hid it there all those years ago; it was a piece of paper with a poem written on it, a poem that he wrote for her, though she never received it as he was too embarrassed to give it to her. He wrote the poem after that awful scene that he witnessed in the back office of the village hall during a school party.

He opened the paper carefully; inside with his untidy handwriting was the last thing relating to her in his life.

She is dancing alone in a blue velvet cloud.
She is inside her world, a world of ecstasy and fear.
She is dancing alone, dancing her past, afraid of a look, from a touch.
She is dancing alone, then me from the side, giving her my hand.
I want to say, "I'm here, I want to."
But she is on her own, dancing alone, ignoring it all, me, the world.
I want to get close, but I can't.
I want to say, but I don't dare.
Just to myself, I'm whispering, "I love you."
I want to find refuge in the shadows of your little castle.
To integrate with your beautiful eyes.

To grow in your heart that beats with strength inside
perfect breasts.
I want to laugh, to be naughty, to embrace, to be close.
I want to shout aloud, "I love."
But you're on your own, dancing alone.

Slowly she opened the doors of my heart until it was wide
open for her,
but entered she not.
There was always the old black cloud that clouded over
her life,
a fatherly protective cloud that got her heart.
I went far and then I was back, hoping that the cloud is
gone with the
winds of change, releasing her from chains.
She was my lady Godiva, my Lorelai.
I wanted to give her, to take, to share the love.
I felt my second half I found but unlucky for me, she was
still bound.
The night came down, and I looked deep into her eyes,
no words from my mouth, no sound.
"I don't think so," said Lorelai, "it's better from far".
"I hope you are not offended." She shouted from up there
while I walked down the stairs.
"No," I said while crying inside, while the sword of pain
cut my chest to half.
The pillow of darkness gladly surrounded me with a smile
when I stepped out the door, out of her life.

After he had written it, he had erased her from his life and
hadn't thought about her until now.
He read it a few times. It was actually two poems, he was
surprised by the intensity of the feelings that he had
towards her back then, and the mature lyrics for a
seventeen-year-old.

He wasn't in a hurry, so he started to walk instead of waiting for the bus. The road led him through the main street that crossed the village; the pub was at the far end next to the big road sign which marked the end of the local parish.

It seemed like time had stopped still in the village since he left, everything looked familiar, the village's old church, the Indian restaurant with the chip shop opposite it, the village hall which he passed quickly before the picture of that night at the party will come back and haunt him, his old upper school, the park with the children's playground; he could almost hear the kids screaming with joy and the mothers telling them off, the small lovely water fountain that comes out from a statue of the village's famous hero and teacher from the 15th century, that still standing sentinel with his sword and book. He felt that he was sucked into an episode of the twilight zone as nothing changed but himself, he couldn't see new pubs or restaurants and none of the houses had been renovated, there were no scaffolds or roadworks at all. He recognised the few people he crossed paths with; they were older but had the same walk, the same clothes, with the inhospitable, suspicions and dull expression that he remembered from his early life. The only different thing was the merchandise in the windows of the few shops that were left.

He never liked the mentality of the residents of the village; he found them generally snobbish, small-minded and even ignorant in a way. He preferred the cosiness of his home and the freedom of the outdoors where he could do and be himself without being judged constantly. As a child he always felt happy that his parents' house was located on the edge of the village, bordering woodland with a small river that runs through.

Unwillingly the picture of that night crept into his thoughts; it was the prom night at the village hall when he was seventeen years old, around 23:30 he was on his way out to get a bit of fresh air as he'd had a bit too much to drink. When he passed near the offices at the back, he heard laughing, so he looked through the glass window of the door and saw a horrid sight; two guys from his school year, one with his back towards him, and the other guy faced him, she, his Pippy, was on her knees in the middle, giving oral sex to one of them while the other taking to her from behind.

He couldn't move for a few seconds due to the shock, and then she looked up... They had looked at each other for a second before he pulled away and ran home.

The sadness in her eyes that almost shouted for help didn't leave him for years after, he could not stop beating himself up for his helplessness until years later when he succeeded to repress the memory. Even now when it came back he thought to himself that if he had come into the room to take her away, his whole life would look different. But he didn't have the courage and at the time he thought to himself, "Those guys are not forcing her, and she will refuse to come with me anyway."

Since then, they could never look at each other again, every time they bumped into each other they would look down. Then they went their separate ways; he went to university and she took a job opportunity as far away as possible from the village.

The pub was just in front of him; he stopped, shook his head to push the memory away, and entered. It was midweek so the pub wasn't full, a few men were sitting at the bar and a few couples at the tables, the barman told him that there is a room available for the night and the breakfast time then he sat at one of the tables in the corner and checked the menu.

"Hello Ziggy"

He froze; the smoky voice that sounded like there was sandpaper in the vocal cords was not familiar, but then again, there was only one person that called him by that name…

He slowly looked back and there she was standing with a notepad in one hand and a pen in the other.

His mouth was open, but he couldn't say a word, he just sat there and stared at her.

She was older and heavier than the slim athletic girl that he remembered, but still quite attractive; the age marks did not take away but maybe even added to her beauty. However, something was missing; it seems that her vitality, the exciting life force that defined her in her youth was gone, the light in her eyes was not there anymore.

"You can close your mouth now it's only me." She said after a few seconds of staring at each other. "Can I take your order?"

"What are you doing here?" was all he could finally say.

"I work here." She started to look impatient, "Are you going to order? Other clients are waiting for me."

He ordered sausages & mash with a pint of lager, and then looked at her trying to find what to say.

"It is good to see you," she said, then walked away to the kitchen.

Rambling thoughts and feelings went through his mind and body; the surprise of suddenly meeting her after all those years totally threw him off-balance, leaving him dizzy and shaking. He felt that he couldn't stay there and face her again, so he grabbed his coat, left a twenty-pound note on the table and walked away towards his room, on the way out he looked back and saw her coming out of the kitchen with a plate and a pint of beer in her hands, their looks crossed before he closed the door, he was sure that he saw some disappointment in her eyes.

The cosy room above the pub was a refuge from all the mixed feelings and emotional storms of that day, but he hadn't had anything to eat since the morning and the hunger started to bother him, so he went out looking for a corner shop. He remembered that there was a shop behind the old church that was owned by the family of one of his school classmates. As the rest of the village, the shop was still there, looking exactly the same as he remembered it. Behind the till there was a bald heavy man with a goatee, in his late thirties or early forties talking on his mobile, the man glanced at him for a second when he entered and nodded his head.

The man looked familiar, he couldn't point out exactly where from, then suddenly the memory of conceited, mean laughter struck him, he remembered the man; it was the guy from his school year that was receiving a blowjob from Pippi in the Village hall office on prom night. The guy looked at him again for a second like he was trying to remember where he knew him, then gave up and looked back at the till.

"I cannot face this man now," he thought to himself, so he put his head down, took a sandwich, a bag of crisps and a six-pack of beer then put a tenner on the counter and left without waiting for the change.

The rage that built inside of him almost forced him to turn back and smash a can of beer on the guy's face; he could almost see the despair in Pippi's eyes in the village hall's office almost twenty-five years ago while this man and his friend used her body to satisfy their primeval compulsions for domination and sexual accomplishment. He took a big breath and continued to walk, almost running away, squeezing the items in his arms and ignoring the urge.

"Why did she do it?"

"They were arseholes, but she did it willingly, and they didn't force themselves on her."

"What was going on in her head when she went from the party to the back room with them?"

"What happened to her during that summer at her dad's place in the city that changed her so much?"

"What the hell is she still doing in the village?"

"What should I do now?"

All those thoughts rushed through his head at the speed of light while he walked back and by the time he got to his room he had such a headache that he felt like his head was going to burst. He lay on the bed, opened a can of beer, drank all of it in a few seconds then opened another one. He was totally knackered from the eventful day and by the fifth can he felt his eyes closing and his mind shutting down, then he drifted into a deep but restless sleep.

3

It was almost noon when he woke up with an excruciating headache; he had never been a big drinker, even when he was a young lad he could never keep up with his mates at the weekly pub crawl. Therefore, the beers from last night with the day's events drained him mentally and physically. His lips were very dry and he was extremely thirsty. After three glasses of tap water, he felt a bit better and ready to face the world. Though, he pondered, "Where should I go from here?"

"I cannot go back to my family and my life, even though my wife would take me back," she did love him in her own way, "She is probably a bit worried by now if she has realised that I wasn't around, I didn't even notify my boss that I'd left."

The previous morning he left his house as usual at 8 am, but instead of going to work, he went to the ATM and drew out all that he had in his current account; he wasn't worried about his family as his wife had her own bank account that has been topped-up monthly by her wealthy parents with a generous lump sum, then he went to the train station, bought a ticket for the first train that headed to the closest town to the village, and left his life behind. He didn't plan or think it through for long, when he woke up he felt that if he stayed a minute longer in his present life, he would explode.

The last few years he was like a zombie, his son became a teenager and didn't need his constant attention, he went every morning to a job that didn't challenge or satisfy him anymore, or did it ever? His work colleagues, friends, wife and son bored him to death. The evenings were an endless routine; Wednesdays, cinema or theatre evening with his wife with a meal after. Fridays, poker evenings with the lads that had the same conversations for the last ten years; about work, their wives or lovers, new cars or houses, and the last holiday. Even Saturday's weekly sex with his wife didn't turn him on anymore, the other evenings he spent staring at the telly. He felt hollow inside; nothing excited him anymore, and emptiness has taken over his soul. Even the holidays were a burden, the preparation, the stress at the airport and the boredom in the holiday resorts, which his wife loved so much, were unbearable now. At the beginning of their relationship, he tried to persuade her to go for road trips, camping holidays or just go to different places in the world, but she refused; she didn't like adventures; a holiday for her was the beach, the sun, cocktails, and shopping. She could laze on the beach chair in the sun, roasting herself and sipping Tequila sunrise or Mojitos for days.

He couldn't find a common language with his son anymore, when he was a kid they would go to the park when the weather permitted them to play footy, to throw Frisbee or to ride their push-bikes when it was cold and damp they played board games and worked on models of ships or aeroplanes, and in holidays they used to go for long walks or played on the beach while his wife sacrificed herself to the sun god.

The past few years his son became an obnoxious teenager that all his time outside school-time was spent in front of screens; his mobile phone, tablet, laptop or telly, or out with his mates until late evenings after he scrounged money from his mum who spoiled him and never said no. When he tried to put limitations or had a go at his son for being late or disrespectful, she always defended the son, an argument usually followed in which she always won.

She wouldn't even ask the boy to do any chores in the house; as long as he did his homework and got good grades in school, he was free to do almost anything.

Eventually, he gave up trying to educate and support his son, and they drifted apart. They ended saying hello to each other when meeting after school or workday but not more than that. On holidays he travelled to see site scenes by himself as his son stayed in the room chatting to his mates on the social networks.

His mobile phone sat on the chest of drawers next to him, he glanced at it for a second then grabbed it and sent a short text message to his wife; "I'm OK, left the house, I can't live like that anymore, not coming back, please don't try to look for me, everything is yours."

He put the phone on silent mode yesterday, so there were eight missed calls and two messages from his wife and from work. He ignored it, turned the phone off, banged the screen on a drawer's wooden knob until it broke and then chucked it to the bin at the side of the bed. His stomach was rumbling from hunger, so he went down to the pub for breakfast. He stopped for a second in front of the main door, praying to all the gods that had ever been worshipped by mankind, that she is not at work at the moment, then opened the door and looked around, when he was convinced that she wasn't there he snuck in and sat at a side table. Although it was already lunchtime the young smiley waitress agreed to talk to the cook and came back after 10 minutes with a large fry-up and a large cup of warm coffee. Between the bites of bacon and sausage and sips of coffee, he came to a decision to stay for a while at his parents' house until he figured out what to do with the rest of his life, and how he would fill the emptiness inside. He also wanted some time to deal with the sudden appearance or maybe even of Pippi in his life.

The meal was very tasty, and the waitress was lovely, so he paid for the bed and breakfast and left a large tip, then went to the village groceries shop that was opened by the family that owned the Indian restaurant a couple of years before he graduated. The pretty woman behind the till greeted him with a smile, he remembered her; she was a couple of years under him at school and always seemed very shy, walking with her head down trying not to look into anybody's eyes. He remembered that her modesty and reserved nature was mysterious in a way that attracted him, he never had the guts to actually approach her and start a conversation, though. If she recognised him, she wouldn't show it. He forced himself not to stand and stare at her beauty, pathetically he still didn't have the courage to start a conversation with her, so he filled the basket with few ready-made meals, fruits, bread, cheese and ham, and most importantly, coffee. Then he paid the lady, thanked her with the silliest smile on his face and left the store rushing to his parents' house.

It was a typical autumn day; grim and windy, the colours almost merged together and differed only in shades of grey, the sky was covered with a blanket of light grey clouds, the leafless trees stood and waited in silence for a gleam of sunlight that didn't come. While he walked up the high street back to the house he came across very few people out in the streets or in the park, hardly any children, which surprised him as it was a school holiday that week.

"I guess the activities that involve screens and require being indoors and usually alone are more attractive than outdoors activities with others to present-day children." He thought to himself.

The song Ghost Town from a popular Ska band from the Seventies started to play in his head as he passed the park with the statue, even the chip shop that used to be full of teenagers and mothers with young kids on the school holiday's afternoons was almost empty.

Although he wasn't an outdoors boy as a child, a wave of nostalgia went through him; the village's daily life was definitely livelier 20 years ago, "It seems like the existence of children these days is very lonely, they are living almost a solitary life in their room and communicating mainly by electronic pulses through an abstract virtual network, or having fake adventures and experiencing life with consoles that connected to screens, and binges of films or series."

When he was a kid, they did have TVs, computer games, and phones at home, which were fun and exciting even though they were more basic. They were not, though, the centre of their life, the physical communication; talk in person, shout, laugh, play together, run around, fight, was much more exciting to most kids.

However, nostalgia is a deceiving feeling; it causes you to look back and remember only the good things and events. It paints the past in vivid colours and paints the present in dull shades. Being nostalgic makes all the unpleasant elements of your bygone days forgotten.

The house appeared ahead and interrupted the melancholic contemplations, so he said to himself, "there is a lot to do in the house, so I'd better start."

The rest of the afternoon he concentrated on cleaning the house and made it suitable for the accommodation again. It wasn't as bad from the beginning as all the furniture had been covered by cloths, hence, the dust didn't get to them. His mother always had plenty of cleaning materials in the utility room, so he took off the white cloths from the furniture in the living room and his old room; he hasn't felt comfortable yet sleeping in his parents' bedroom, although it had a large king-size bed, the material was filthy with dust, so he left it out for later, then mopped all the laminated floors on the first four rooms, and vacuumed his bedroom as it had a carpet, then wiped down all the windowsills, cupboards, shelves and other surfaces that gathered dust. All this time he focused on the tasks and cleared his head from any reflective thoughts of the past or future.

Just before dusk he finished, grabbed a bottle of beer from the fridge and assembled himself on the bench in the garden. He sipped his beer slowly, then the wind cleared the sky for a short time, exactly at the right time for him to enjoy the rare sunset. It was almost perfect, until they started to crawl in again, the thoughts...

"I'm quite successful in my job, my house has been paid off, I have some savings in the bank and I obtain a pretty comfortable life."

"I have a beautiful wife with a successful career of her own, that still loves me and has parents that are loaded. And I have a son that is fairly successful in school."

"I also have a reasonable social life with a circle of long-term friends."

"I'm a great example of the cliché of the successful upper-middle-class representative, a bourgeois who achieved a well-balanced life and brought pride to his parents."

Then he looked up and shouted to the bleak windy sky; "SO WHAT THE FUCK IS MISSING AND WHAT THE HELL DO I WANT?"

No help came from the sky; no voice of God answered the questions and pointed him in the right direction, the wind was just howling and taking no notice of the shouting man on the bench.

A few hours passed, he just sat there looking at the garden fence trying to figure out his next move, then he heard the chime of the church bell from the village, and suddenly everything was clear to him, he knew what he needed to do. He got up, had a nice long bath and went to bed excited and a bit unsettled by the thought that tomorrow might be the first day of his new life.

An unusual lovely day welcomed him when he stepped out the front door that morning; it was bright and fresh, a bit nippy, though, he wore a light jacket and put on a pair of work gloves, then, as he had a couple of hours until it was time to go, he started to clear and tidy up the shed and the back garden. Around 10:30 he put the tools back, looked briefly in the mirror to ensure that he did not look like a slob, then headed down to the village.

He didn't know where she lived, so he decided to try to check at her mum's house, although she never really liked him as a child; adolescence was the highest peak in her life as she fell pregnant just before the end of her last school year, where she was one of the popular girls. She married the father of her baby, who was only a year older, a few weeks before the birth. They gave up all the career prospects and the plans of the gap year trip in the Far East after uni to start a family life. He joined a local bricklaying gang that paid quite well, and she became a stay-at-home mum. Pippi came out to the world a couple of years later, then, a few months after her youngest boy was born, when Pippi was 3 years old, her father suddenly left the house and moved to live in the city; he did love his children, but the young love with his wife naturally faded and the envy of the free worries and "exciting" life of his single mates eventually made him do the deed and leave.

She found herself by the age of 23 with three young children to care for, and no man to support and share the burden. Subsequently, she became somewhat frustrated and bitter from her own life and was looking to live again the glory of her teenage years through her second daughter. For that reason, she wanted Pippi to hang out with the "cool" kids and was quite resentful when she realised that her daughter is choosing to spend time with a bookworm nerd such as himself. Her conventional and narrow-minded outlook on life that was driven by her situation and past choices was the reason that her oldest daughter chose to move out on her 14th birthday and live with her dad that had settled down and remarried with an older childless woman a few years earlier.

The mother's house was a mid-terrace house that was situated in the east part of the village where the "newish" neighbourhood had been built. When the housing prices started to surge and the traditional village houses becoming too dear for the younger generation, the council decided on an affordable housing project that was aimed to stop young families from leaving and to attract families that wanted to move to the countryside.

The project stopped after a couple of terrace houses had been built due to budget problems. Her mum and dad were lucky to be within the group of a few families that purchased a house in the neighbourhood before the project stopped.

It was only ten minutes' walk from his house but felt like a decade, a few people that he crossed paths with looked at him like he was a madman as he was talking to himself trying to decide what to say to her and with which tone and facial expression.

At the front of the house, he stopped, hesitated for a second then knocked on the door, he did have a tiny hope that nobody's at home, no one answered. When he lifted his hand to knock again the door opened, and she stood there staring at him while drying her hair with a towel.

"Hi", was the only thing he could say, he prepared himself to meet her mum, and not her... he was gobsmacked.

"Hi", she answered looking at him with her big blue eyes, "what are you doing here?" she just came out of the shower and was still in her dressing gown slightly shivering from the outside chill.

"I'm not sure… I… I thought… Can we talk? Can I invite you for a coffee somewhere? Of course, if you are not busy now."

She looked at him with a piercing gaze for a couple of seconds, then her expression softened, "sure, as long as you will not do your vanishing trick like yesterday and leave me sitting there by myself." The old mischievous spark glinted in her eyes, and she looked as if she was going to smile, but just kept an indifferent face.

"There is a little café behind the church; their cookies are second to none, we can meet there in half an hour, I just need to put some clothes on and sort myself out."

"OK, great, I'll see you there." He said trying to keep cool without too much enthusiasm.

4

She closed the door but looked at him through the curtained window, while he walked away, she smiled to herself thinking; "He still has the same goofy walk that he had as a kid."

Seeing him yesterday in the pub after all those years overwhelmed her, she had to gather all her willpower to stay professional and not burst into tears, hug him, or run away. When she went to the kitchen with his order, she had to lean on the sink for a few minutes so her legs would not collapse under her.

The cook looked at her worried, "Are you alright?"

"I'm fine; I was just a bit dizzy, I just need to sit down for a minute while you prepare this order if you don't mind." She handed him the piece of paper with the order and sat down.

"What the hell is he doing here?" she said to herself without a sound, "did you come to haunt me Zigs?" "You bastard!"

In the last few months, she finally found a bit of peace within herself after an unsettled life, to say the least, and now he sits there with this untrendy accountant's suit and a bewildered look on his face, reawaken the past with his presence.

Since they were young kids, he was the balance in her life, the demons inside her always, since she was a toddler, urged her to challenge conventions and confront her surroundings. She loved her mother but resented her provincial disposition and the small village mentality, her mum and the teachers in school tried to force her to follow the rules and comply with the unwritten protocol like the rest of the children, all she wanted was to experience everything, spread her wings and make her own choices. Although the other children looked up to her for her free spirit and audacity it was on many occasions, a veneer or smokescreens to cover the fear of ending up like her mother. With Ziggy she could just be herself without being judged, she still had the energy and cheekiness around him as it was in her nature, but his introverted personality calmed her down and gave her a break from the daily battle against the world. Ziggy was to her like Ritalin is to a kid with ADHD.

She used to love coming to his parent's house, they were always welcoming to her and the house, unlike her mum's house, was charged with warm vibes. Her mother was constantly busy with what other folks were thinking about her and her children; she always wore make-up and was well-dressed, before leaving the house she had to check that the kids looked tip-top and there are no creases on the clothes so no one will think that she was neglecting her kids. She religiously followed all the expected social behaviours and became much stressed when one of her children stepped out of the norms. She believed that by following what she thought were the public expectations and by saying what she thought that people wanted to hear she will be respected and valued. Pippi's mum was a people pleaser which was the total opposite of her daughters that their individuality craved to burst out. This clash of personalities created a perpetual tension in the house; consequently, Ziggy's house, his parents, and his company were a breath of fresh air for her, until that week at her dad's...

When she came back, she was so ashamed, she felt that she disappointed him; she wasn't worthy to enjoy his company anymore, so she shut herself away from him. In her eyes, she was a dirty scum that needed to be punished.

She had been punishing herself ever since. Only a couple of years ago after her mum passed away she moved back to the village and started to forgive herself, "Fuck you Zigs!"

It was hard for her to block him back then, but she was adamant, he tried for a while to approach her, he knocked on her door a few times, in time, after she didn't respond, he gave up. In school, though, she often felt that he was looking at her from a distance, sometimes with yearning and other times with pity.

Her popularity among other kids didn't change; she hid her shame and acted as cheerful as normal around people, but inside she has torn apart, "I'm just a useless piece of shit that's good for one thing," she kept saying to herself, "To make others feel good about themselves."

The boys loved her; she was daring and exciting and didn't hold back. Boys always surrounded her, and she changed boyfriends frequently. She gave them what they wanted; fun, confidence, sex, a carefree approach to life, but she ended up hating herself after every date. They were all "cool" boys, although she didn't really like any of them, she felt that she would contaminate the decent and worthy guys if she would pursue them.

The relationship with her mum and her grades in school deteriorated, but no one seemed to care or see her desolation; her mum was busy with herself and did not reflect more than on her own desire to be accepted, and she succeeded in charm and convinces most of the teachers to pass her.

Then the dreadful prom night episode took place; she was dancing with a couple of guys and had a bit to drink, not too much but enough to loosen her up, one of them was her boyfriend at the time and the other one was his best mate. The boyfriend kept badgering her to come with him to the back office whispering in her ear how horny he was, eventually after teasing him for a couple of hours she agreed to come with him.

They started to make out when she felt another pair of hands on her. She opened her eyes and saw his mate with a stupid smirk on his face grabbing her boobs, "I hope you don't mind if he joins us?"

"Yeah, whatever." She uttered and closed her eyes again while they peeled off her clothes. Then her boyfriend lay on the desk, grabbed her head and shoved his penis in her mouth and at the same time his friend entered her from behind, she started to suck him praying that both will come fast. Then a light breeze of cold air stroked her face like someone opened the door, so she opened her eyes... standing next to the door she saw Ziggy looking at her with dismay, for a second their eyes crossed, then he closed the door.

She was mortified and humiliated, "Why did it have to be him?"

When the boys finished their business, they high five each other and got dressed. Then her boyfriend said, "We are going to get a drink, do you want something? You were absolutely great!" He kissed her on her cheek and smacked her bottom.

"We should do it again," said the other guy

She put on her best smile, "Yes, definitely chaps, you were also great... Both of you, thanks but I don't want a drink; don't wait for me I'll be out in a minute."

After they left, she put on her clothes and ran home, got into the bath and scrubbed every inch of her body until it hurt.

As soon as she graduated, she found a job working for a holiday deals provider as a Holiday Rep at one of the Mediterranean islands that specialise in young people, where the focal point is the night-time activity; parties, pubs, alcohol and sex. The job didn't require any qualifications, and the only thing that it entailed was the aptitude to inspire others to have fun and spend money during that time.

Working there was the dream of any youngster that just finished school; the pay was very low, but she didn't pay for accommodation and used to get free drinks at bars and clubs as she brought them many customers. She met all kinds of people from all over the world, had the sea and the sun in the afternoon then alcohol and parties at night. The nights, or to be precise in the early mornings, she normally ended with the chosen man or woman that were lucky enough to turn her on.

She did hate every minute there, though...

The late mornings were the hardest time in the day with the hangovers and the loneliness as no one really cared about her, everybody on that island including her colleagues were busy with themselves and their own fun. Although she slept with every Tom, Dick, Harry...and Mary, none of them became more than a passing fling.

The island's lifestyle of decadence and self-indulgence almost killed her; after 3 years of almost daily binge drinking and partying she collapsed one night and had to be taken to the A&E. The doctor said that her body got to a point that it could not take more alcohol, smoke and noise, and she must have a break and stay in bed for at least a week.

As soon as she was able to stand on her feet, she packed her bag and called her boss to give her notice. He tried to convince her to stay at least until the end of the season as she was his best Rep, he even offered to increase her salary and give her an additional bonus, but her mind was made up, she couldn't stay one more day on the island.

She said goodbye to everyone then bought a ticket for the same day back home.

At first, she relished the sense of home; the pastoral and tranquil ambience was exactly what she needed. Her mum was extremely happy to have her and was sensible enough to give her space to patch herself up. She was quite lonely as her younger son moved to the city to study fashion design as soon as he graduated from school, so except the weekly bingo night in the community centre and the odd quiz night in the pub the only thing that kept her company was the TV and above all the reality TV programs that became almost an addiction, and so, Pippi's "homecoming" gave her a certain energy boost and positive frame of mind that lasted a week before it was smothered by the bitterness of her existence.

To be pampered and spoiled was a refreshing joyful change; the home-cooked meals, the laundry that had been washed for her and at first even to lounge on the sofa and watch TV with her mum. Nevertheless, as a week passed she realised that her mum is so fixed in her little life and could not see anything and anyone beyond. She had only three subjects for a conversation; the weather, TV programs, and gossip from the village, she never asked Pippi to tell her about the years away nor how she felt at the moment, not even politics or the news interested her, though, an exceptional topic was the royal family, especially the princess who she adored and saw as a role model and could talk about her for hours. Their chats became minimal, and they often sat at dinner in total silence each one in their own thoughts. It started to drive her mental, every so often she had the urge to grab her mum by the shoulders, shake her and shout to her ear to wake up and see outside of the little bubble she lives in. The combination of her mum mindset together with the fact that most of her old friends left the village convinced her that she cannot stay there for long. So after 3 weeks, she couldn't hack it anymore, so she packed her suitcase, kissed her mother goodbye and jumped on the first train that headed to the capital city.

5

The café was small and not very trendy, but it had a nice atmosphere. The church opened it a few years ago as a non-profit place for the community to be a quiet alternative for villagers that wanted to get out and socialise without alcohol, it was run voluntarily by a lovely retired couple that made the place warm and intimate. They served coffee, tea and on hot days a cold lemonade and homemade cookies. The prices were very cheap compared to the overpriced cafés in the city and the small profit went for church events.

There were only five tables in the café; two elderly ladies were sitting at the right table next to the window sipping tea and chatting about gardening and politics, a young man with old fashion glasses and a heavy beard sat at the back tables, he was working on a laptop with a cup of coffee next to it. "It is a strange hangout for a hipster," He thought, a bit amused. Behind the counter there was a tiny woman in her sixties with kind eyes that smiled at him, then with a surprisingly loud voice; "Good afternoon young man, sit down please, what can I get you?" he remembered her vaguely; she was a teaching assistant in his primary school, she was much younger back then, though.

"Black coffee no sugar please," he said, then, before he sat in the left corner next to the window he leaned over her ear and said quietly, "I heard that you make the best cookies in the region, do you think I could try one?"

"Of course you can my dear; you can have more than one." her face shone and her smile widened, "by the way: the best in the region you heard? They are the best in the country, laddy!"

"Amen to that." He laughed.

While he was waiting for the coffee, he tried to make his mind up on how to start a conversation with her, and then as the lady was putting the coffee cup and the cookies on the table he saw her on the other side of the street heading towards him.

She wore skinny denim jeans, low heeled black boots and a long white jumper, "she is still an attractive woman," he thought, "Although it seems as she lost her "joie de vivre", and the vitality in her movement still gives me a tingling sensation."

"Hi," she said as soon as she stepped in.

"Hi, I'm sorry, but I didn't order for you, I wasn't sure what you would like…can I order you a drink?" He uttered.

"Don't worry about it." She waved to the nice lady, "Morning! Oh, sorry, it's already afternoon…may I please have my regular?"

"Certainly my love, should I put in my special secret ingredient?"

"You know I cannot say no to the secret ingredient." She sat opposite him and whispered, "She put a bit of vanilla in my coffee and confident that I can't tell what it is, just watch…"

The old lady came holding a tray with a mug of white coffee and a small plate of cookies, she put them on the table and kept standing there looking impatiently at Pippi who took a small sip from the coffee.

"That is so good!" Pippi said, "When are you going to tell me what is the secret ingredient?"

A big smile spread across the lady's face, "If I'll tell you it will not be a secret anymore." She said, then turned and walked back to the kitchen.

"She is lovely, isn't she?"

"Yeah, she seems great."

They looked at each other not ambiguous on how to start and how to get rid of the elephant in the room. After a few silent minutes he decided to take the plunge and start; "I'm really sorry for walking away yesterday, seeing you there all of a sudden after all this time took me by surprise and totally bowled me over."

"It's ok, I was also quite shaken." She looked at him with one of her smiles that immediately calmed his nerves.

"She still has the talent to make you feel like the most important man in the world." He thought.

"How are you? When did you come back? I didn't think you'd ever come back here."

"Well, it's been over twenty years and people change, my mum passed away three years ago, my brother and sister are financially comfortable and since I didn't have my own home they decided to waive their rights to her house. At the time I was between jobs and at the end of a lease on the flat, so I decided to move back." She stopped, it seemed like she was making a decision about something, then she raised her eyes and looked directly into his, "You know what? I don't want to lie anymore, to myself or to anyone else, and I could never lie to you, you always saw the bullshit; my life didn't really flourish since school and when my mum died, it was just after a very unhealthy and troubling time in my life, so I decided to move back here and finally face my demons."

"I'm sorry," was all he could say, "I didn't know."

"What are you sorry about? We haven't talked to each other since year nine in school, I haven't seen you since prom night." she paused for a second looking down, and then continued, "Anyway; I'm feeling better now."

He felt the urge to embrace her but just sat looking at his hands and said in a low voice, "I should have intervened and taken you out of there…"

"What do you mean to take me out of there? Take me from where?"

"On prom night, I saw you with the two guys in the back office… I saw the look in your eyes… I should have taken you out, but I was a coward." He sipped his coffee slowly.

"It was a long time ago, all water under the bridge, you couldn't save me anyway. I didn't want to be saved at the time and wouldn't have gone with you." She said softly, "So don't beat yourself up for that. I was messed up at the time, in fact; I was messed up before and for many years after." She took a cookie from the plate and smiled at him, "I'm much better now and not looking for anyone to take pity on me so stop looking so apologetic. Try the cookies; they are absolutely delicious!"

For a few minutes, they sat drinking their coffee and eating cookies quietly, and then she broke the awkward silence, "What about you? I heard you've done well with yourself… What brings you back here?"

"I've done ok with my life, accomplished everything they wrote in the "book of success, but I don't really feel accomplished or successful. So, I left my family and my job yesterday and came here to take the time to decide what to do with my life. Then I met you in the pub… God and I are not best mates, to say the least, but it was almost like a sign from him. You know, I have never forgotten you, since we were thirteen you've always been in the back of my mind, I think I have unconsciously compared every woman I've ever met, including my wife and also some men, to you. I had been thinking about you for the first time in years before I came to the pub; I was thinking how I actually have missed you for the last twenty-nine years, even if I wasn't aware of it, and how different my life would have been if you didn't cut our friendship off back then. I guess I needed some closure... and then you showed up! Pardon my French, but it is un-fucking-believable, don't you think?"

She seemed a bit unsettled, looked into her handbag then closed it with disappointment, "I've quit smoking last year but still crave a fag from time to time."

"I remember that you used to sneak out with your friends on breaks to the maintenance shed behind the drama hall to smoke, the deputy headteacher caught you and put you on detention for a week." He smiled.

"Yeah, it was the longest and most boring week in school," she laughed, "I did have my revenge, though."

"Revenge is an understatement Pip; you turned the whole school against him until he gave up and took early retirement."

"Well, he was an old tosser; someone had to put him out of his misery. The school was better without him; I bet that even the teachers were happy when he left."

The tension eased a bit, and they both laughed.

"You know," she said after a while, "it was such a long time ago, we were kids back then, the girl that you remember is gone, if she ever really existed."

"Well, she definitely existed, she was my best friend." He said softly, "Anyway, tell me what you've done since school, the last thing I heard was that as soon as you graduated you got a job on a Caribbean island. Everybody was so envious of you; they talked about your dream job for weeks."

"I'm sorry Z, do you mind if we take a rain check on that? It is a long story, and I still have a few things to sort out before my shift starts."

"It's fine; if you need to go we can meet some other time, if you would like to, of course, I'll be residing in the village for the time being."

"Are you still staying at the pub's B&B?" she asked while taking her purse out of her handbag.

He shook his head, "No, I'm staying at my parents' house; I cleaned and tidied it up today so it is reasonably liveable now. Don't worry about the coffee, it's on me."

"Thanks," She said and put back the purse, she hesitated for a second, "Oh, I forgot to say, I was so sorry to hear about your parents, your dad was such a great guy, a man as men should be, not like the fluffy so-called men of our generation, the youngsters are even worse. And your mum was the sweetest woman ever, I really loved them." She put her hand over his hand and pressed gently.

"Thanks, Pip, it means so much coming from you, my mum is still alive though, but dementia has completely taken over her mind now, and she doesn't even recognise me anymore, she lives in a home not far from here, it's expensive but it's one of the best in the country, and she can have visitors at any time until 9 pm." He said with an encouraging smile.

"I would really like to go and visit her one day... if it's ok."

"Definitely, I'm sure she would love that; she doesn't get many visitors these days, even I'm not going there as often as I used to."

She looked at the clock on the wall, "I'm sorry but I really need to go now my shift starts soon, can I come tomorrow to the house, so we can continue the conversation?"

"I would like that; we have twenty-five years to catch up on, what about breakfast? My cooking skills are not great, but I'll do my best"

"All right, but I like my sleep so let's make it a brunch, 11 am then."

She stood up and waved goodbye to the old woman, then looked at him, "It was nice seeing you again Ziggy." She headed for the door then stopped, turned back and bent over towards him, her lips fluttered gently on his cheek in a quick kiss, and then she turned away and walked out of the café without looking back.

His eyes accompanied her until she disappeared between the houses. Mixed emotions ran through him; there was a deep sadness in her eyes and it seemed that she has been through a lot, and he felt a strong compulsion to hold her in his arms. On the other hand, she was somewhat distant and almost hard, which said without words "Stay away! Don't get closer!"

6

After the conversation he suddenly felt an intense need to see his mother, he looked at his watch then outside, "There is at least an hour and a half of daylight left, if I call a taxi now I can get there just before dark and leave before she goes for her tea." He went to the lady behind the counter and gave her a tenner, "Keep the change, the cookies are indeed delicious, thanks I will definitely be back for more."

"You're most welcome, I'm happy to hear that." She leaned towards him, "You know young man, I have never seen her like that, she normally comes here and sits with a book, having her coffee while reading quietly at the side table, doesn't talk to many people outside of work and doesn't really have friends in the village, she is so different from the chatty energy bomb she was as a kid. Her face always seems a bit tense now, like all the pressure of life is on her shoulders. But today her face brightened up, she looked almost happy. I remember both of you as young kids, after school hours you were thick as thieves, and then you weren't anymore. You better not disappear now, after showing up in her life again, if you will, I'll find you and knock your head off."

He laughed, "I promise, thanks again."

While exiting the café he searched for his mobile in his pockets then remembered that he broke it, he recalled that he saw a public phone box near the statue in the park yesterday; he remembered thinking that it is a symbol of how anachronistic is this village for keeping a phone box in this mobile phone's era. "Well, maybe I was too judgemental; the public phone does have its use." He thought and hurried to call the taxi.

The nursing home was a large estate hidden from the road by evergreen trees, it was situated a quarter of a mile off the main road, halfway to the nearby town. It was built in the mid-19th century by a wealthy businessman as a country house for weekends. Part of the main building was bombed in error during the war and the house was evacuated, it had been abandoned for fifty years until the descendants sold it to a large real estate company that owns and operates a number of nursing homes across the country who renovated it and restored the house to its original glory.

At the reception, he was told that his mum was in the activity room. Before he headed there he asked one of the nurses how his mum was getting on; the nurse replied that her good days when she would conduct herself as almost normal, recognise the staff and remember things, are becoming fewer and most of the time she is in her own world not aware of when and where she is. He found her sitting and doing a puzzle, he stood at the door for a few minutes watching her, she looked so beautiful, even in her condition she always looked immaculate with no creases on her clothes and with full make-up on her face. A strong sense of guilt and shame crept in for not visiting her regularly, "I love this woman to bits, she has done so much for me and now she loses a part of herself day by day, I was so self-absorbed lately and couldn't even bother to come and see her more often, shame on me!" He thought, then entered the room and stood in front of her.

"Hi, mum!"

She didn't seem to acknowledge him being there and continued with the puzzle, so he put his hand gently on hers,

"Hi, mum!"

She looked up at him slowly, "Oh, hello, sorry but I wasn't aware that you were standing there, are you a new doctor here? You are very handsome, would you like me to make you a cupper my dear?"

"It's me; your son. Remember?"

She seemed confused, and then the light of a memory glinted in her eyes briefly but faded as soon as it appeared, and she went back to the puzzle, oblivious to his presence.

"I'm sorry I didn't come to see you much lately, I promise it will not happen again." He sat next to her quietly helping to complete the puzzle, "I left my family, mum; I couldn't take it anymore, so I left and moved back home to the village. I also met her today; do you remember the ginger girl that used to come to our house often when I was a kid? You used to call her Match Stick, remember? I hadn't seen her since school and suddenly met her in the pub yesterday, she has also moved back to the village recently."

She stopped, raised her eyes and smiled, "Match Stick? Of course, I remember her; she hasn't come here for a while. You can invite her here for Sunday tea, she loves my roast and I'll make her favourite pudding. You were inseparable, but lately, she stopped coming here, did you have a fight? If you did, just make it up with her and invite her here, I love this girl." She hesitated for a second, "You know, she doesn't have it easy, there is a dark cloud over her head, you are the best thing in her life and I'm afraid she will be lost without you."

He looked at her with empathy, "Mum, it was thirty years ago, we are not kids anymore."

Then, in a moment of clarity, she grabbed his hand forcefully and looked directly into his eyes, "Good things in life always have a price tag and you always need to struggle, mainly with yourself, to keep them, the benefits though, are priceless. Don't let misunderstandings and poor communications take it all away. Your father used to say, "Before you act, stop and think as you might regret it for the rest of your life." He was a smart man."

Then she regressed back to the void.

They sat together in silence for a few minutes more before the nurse came to take her to dinner, he gave her a kiss on her cheek and promised to come and visit the following week.

It was heart-breaking to see her gradual decline that escalated in the last year, he had two people in his life that he looked up to; his dad was a pillar of strength that no one could break down, and his mum was a pillar of hope that saw the best in everything and everyone. Side by side they were the foundations that held together the building blocks of his life, in this cynical world they were a reminder of what is real and that life doesn't have to be complicated, although he failed to adopt it in his everyday life, they showed him that happiness comes from what you do with yourself and what you give to others, then cancer had eaten his dad from within.

"And now this horrible Illness is consuming her... It's time for me to support her, time for me to be the pillar of strength and hope for her as she was to me." He decided, "All my difficulties and frustrations are so trivial compared to hers, it's all bollocks." He was determined to embrace a different perspective about his issues, nonetheless, he was in the same mood and made the same decision after every visit, and he knew that he is not as strong as his parents, the doubts and dissatisfaction will crawl back in sooner or later.

After the receptionist called a taxi for him he stepped outside to wait for it and sat on the bench in front of the large strip of lawn that was intersected by the long driveway to the estate.

The last words of his mum bothered him, "What did she mean? Was it about his family or about Pippi?" He thought she was never really fond of his wife; always kind and polite to her, but they didn't click or form a bond between them for some reason. Pippi, on the other hand, was almost like the daughter that she never had, but then again, almost thirty years have passed since she last came to his mum's house.

"Should I call my wife? Just to tell her that I'm fine… But then she will want to talk, and I'm not ready for that yet."

The taxi emerged from the woods driving slowly towards him cutting off his heavy contemplations. He needed some groceries, so he decided to go to the supermarket in town and to catch the eight o'clock bus back to the village. If there will be enough time after shopping, he might stop at a pub for a pint.

The taxi driver was a friendly and chatty chap; he was a welcome distraction from the state of mind he had after the visit; the small talk gave him a short and fun break from the existential dilemmas that kept haunting him. They talked about the current football series; he was never a big football fan but succeeded to hold the conversation and keep up with the driver without looking like an ignorant nerd, then they talked about the recent sex scandal in parliament, the driver was an entertaining geezer that made him truly laugh for the first time in months.

When they finally got to the supermarket, he shook his hand firmly and gave him double the normal fare. "Thanks mate; I enjoyed our conversation, and have a nice evening mate." The driver shouted while driving away.

Pippi said that she would come tomorrow morning to the house; he decided to make her a nice breakfast or brunch, depending on when she will show up, so he bought bacon, eggs, cheese and vegetables. When he got to the bus station, it was only 19:15, "time for a pint or two." He thought and went to the nearby pub.

As he stepped on the bus back to the village he felt a tap on his shoulder followed by a voice from the past, "Is that you? I can't believe it!" He turned and saw a tiny vivacious woman in her forties smiling at him, she was somewhat familiar. "Don't you remember me?" She said in a squeaky voice. He looked at her intently and delved into his memory, then, the image of a short and chubby girl with glasses that had a crush on him in the last two years of school formed in his mind, "Button? Is that you?" he asked with some reservation in his voice. Button was a nickname she got in primary school because she was small and round. The attractive woman that stood in front of him, though, was definitely not round, she was blonde with a thin but well-defined body, she wore trendy skinny jeans, a short designer's leather jacket and black stilettos.

"Nobody's called me that since school but yes, it's me, not looking like a button anymore, hey!" She giggled.

"Wow, you are looking great!" He uttered.

"Well, after my romantic and social failures in school, I decided to turn my life around, so I've done a total makeover, changed my eating habits and started to do Yoga and Pilates, the results are in front of you. Come on, give us a squeeze for old time sake, it's great to see you again."

He gave her a quick hug, "It's lovely to see you to Button."

"Are you coming on? I need to leave." The bus driver hurried them up.

"Yes, sorry... Keep your knickers on; we are coming." She muttered, then turned back to him smiling, "miserable sod, let's get on, we can catch up on the bus."

They sat together in one of the back seats as most of the passengers were sitting in the front, and they didn't want to disturb them with a loud chit-chat. The next half an hour they caught up with each other's life; apparently, she had a rather successful career as a solicitor in the city; she represented several blue-chip companies, and her speciality was mergers and acquisitions. She also managed in those twenty years to raise two kids and maintained a healthy marriage to the head of a faculty in a private college.

"You hit the jackpot," He said, "It seems like you built a great life for yourself, I'm very happy that everything worked out for you."

"Well," she said, "the makeover wasn't only for the physical appearance...my life is not always great, especially my marriage, it needs constant work, but I try not to let regrets lead and portray my time in this world, it's too short and precious to waste on being negative and look at the half-empty glass."

"You are definitely not the chubby nerdy girl from school." He said, "So, what are you doing back here?"

"My dad is not well; he can't walk anymore and needs caring round the clock, he has a Carer on the weekdays but on weekends my sisters and I are looking after him, we are doing rotation, so every fourth weekend I need to come down here."

"What about your mum?" He wondered.

"She is fine, they got divorced almost twenty years ago when I was at uni, they didn't get along for years and stayed together only for us girls. So as soon as all the daughters grew up and left home my mum moved out and went to live with an old high school sweetheart that she accidentally bumped into, on a girl's weekend a couple of years earlier, they still together living down south on the coast."

"Anyway, we are just talking about me; tell me a bit about how you've done since school?"

He opened his mouth to answer, but she continued. "You know," she said, "I always remember you as "The one that got away". For two years I tried to strike your fancy and catch your attention, but you were utterly resilient to my magnetic charms." She laughed, "I thought then that as I didn't have a slight chance with the cool guys, I might be more successful with a geek like me. Nonetheless, I didn't have a chance; the crazy ginger got you by her hook since primary school, you never talked to each other but I saw how you used to stare at her from distance in anguish, you know I actually saw her looking at you with a similar look a couple of times."

"You know how teenagers are. Always desire what they cannot have, and we weren't different, anyway, a lot of water passed under the bridge since, and looking at you now I'm almost sorry for turning my back on your attempts back then." He didn't tell her that Pippi was also back in the village.

"Well, thank Mr charming. I heard you've done quite well for yourself, with your rich and pretty wife." then whispered, "You still together aren't you?" She opened her bag and took out a sandwich,

"I haven't eaten anything since this morning and I'm starving. Do you want half?"

"I'm fine thanks. I had a bite to eat earlier, and yes, we are still married." He answered.

"That's good, so what are you doing down here in this gloomy time of the year? Did you move back here?"

He didn't think that his family situation and personal problems were her business, so he said that he came to clean and sort out his parent's house as nobody lived there for a while, and he is looking to sell it as his mum needs the money to pay for the nursing home. It was not all lies, His mother had enough savings to pay for the nursing home, yet he did think about selling the house sooner or later.

The bus arrived in the village and stopped near the church, "This is my stop," She said, "It was lovely to see you again, my first and only unrequited love." She laughed, "Maybe we'll see each other around." She put her hand on his shoulder in a friendly gesture then walked off the bus.

"That was an unexpected encounter," he thought as the bus moved again, "this week is getting weirder by the day, first Pippi and that guy from the prom, and now Button…who will come next, my first shag from the first year at uni?"

He got off the bus at the next stop and started to walk home, then changed his mind; it was like a force that turned him around and pulled him to the pub. When he got there he didn't enter and just stood out in the dark and looked at Pippi through the glass window for twenty minutes before his hunger led him to his mum's kitchen, he heated a ready meal of Spaghetti Bolognese in the microwave, as he was so hungry he devoured and enjoyed it like it was a Michelin star dish.

After dinner, he made a cup of tea then sat in the living room and flipped through old photo albums for a while, letting the memories of his family and childhood fill him before his eyes shut into a dreamless sleep.

7

When the door of the café closed behind her, she was relieved; she almost felt his eyes looking at her walking up the road. There were still over two hours until her shift at the pub was due to start, and she didn't really have much to do until then, but she had to make up something without being rude. All sorts of feelings gushed inside her, it made her uncomfortable and vulnerable; even though she hadn't talked to him for almost thirty years his presence calmed her and gave her the assurance that she can be herself near him, without pretence, that she was not alone in the world. Even when they didn't talk in the upper school, she still felt that he was always there, like a guardian angel, although she rebelled against those feelings by distancing herself from him as she didn't think she deserved such a caring and gentle friend.

On the other hand, she felt ultimately exposed around him; in the café, his openness about his sentiments towards her all those years ago made her really uneasy, if he had known what she had done since he last saw her, how a self-destructive journey wasted most of her life, he would be disappointed again like the let-downs she caused him in their teen years. She wasn't ready to tell him about the last twenty years, despite the fact that she has done so much work on herself since the move back to the village, and felt much more confident and worthy within herself, she was still ashamed and regretful of the past choices and behaviours. So when he asked her to tell him about herself, she couldn't hack it and had to make an excuse to get out.

Her life in the city was like one big multi-car crash.

After running away from the dispiriting reality of living in her mum's house she called a colleague who worked with her at the island, he invited her to stay at his flat and crash on the sofa until she found a job and a place to stay.

She contacted her ex-employer and asked about a job as an agent in their travel agency. She was told that she would need to obtain a Travel & Tourism diploma before applying for that role, and they recommended courses online to study at home that will allow her to work for a living at the same time. Unfortunately, they didn't have any position for unskilled staff, and her charms didn't have an effect in this case.

Eventually, after two days of looking at job ads in newspapers and job sites on the internet, she got a job as a hostess in one of the few gentlemen's clubs that was left in the city, where the wealthy and privileged men come for business meetings or to socialise with other wealthy and privileged men, drink, smoke cigars, talk about money or sports, or just to flirt with the hostesses without their wives around.

The job did not entail her being a sexual substitute for the wives; the requirements were quite similar to her previous job on the island, but for an older and richer clientele. All she needed to do was to dress nice and presentable, serve drinks, chat with the customers, and make sure the members are comfortable and content. Basically, the expectations of her were to ensure that they had a good time. She wasn't allowed to flirt back or to get personally involved with the members, but she was allowed to keep the tips which were very generous due to her bursting vigorous magnetism that fascinated the suited knobs that spent most of their life in meeting rooms. The financial remuneration of the salary and tips were fairly considerable for a job that doesn't require a specific study or training, and as the club's policy was to close at 22:00

to avoid dealing with drunks, the working hours were convenient for a young sociable woman in a big city. She felt extremely lucky to find this job and was adamant to hold on to it until she decided which direction to take in her life.

In less than two weeks, she found a loft to rent in an old industrial area that started to become hip among the twenty-something that was looking for cheap accommodation near the city centre. The small workshops and tradesmen that could not compete with the low prices of the large global companies were closing their businesses and started to leave the area, and agile forward-thinking entrepreneurs began to turn the commercial estates into residential accommodations. The area attracted young artists, designers, and nonconformists that were fed up with the pop culture fashion and the celebrity's idolisation. They also resented the hipster style and their way of life. A new subculture started to develop in this area of the city that undervalued technology and the modern beauty concept; mobile phones, computer and telly's that been dumped out in the street next to the rubbish skips were not an uncommon sight, and asymmetric, untraditional colours contrast style in fashion, art and architecture emerged from these old brown industrial buildings. After several years, this new philosophy and style dwindled and eventually disappeared; as soon as the city captains saw a beginning of an influx of people to the area and the potential, they poured out large sums of money for a face-lift of the old buildings, many new establishments for entertainment, food and culture have opened, and the in-crowd started to move in, prices surged and forced the eccentric artists to move out to cheaper areas. The alternative cultures that arose just a few years earlier lost once again to the popular lifestyle, the art, and the design that cultivated from human primary inclinations for sex, proportional beauty, indolence and comfort. It died out like many other cultural movements in history.

The loft she rented was small but did suit a young single woman, and the best thing was; it was all hers. She didn't need to live in a shared house with other tenants, which she was extremely happy about as she couldn't stand the idea of sharing a bathroom, toilet and kitchen with strangers.

City life's prospect seemed promising; the day she moved in was the first time in years that she felt positive about the future. Unfortunately, life had different plans for her...

By moving to the city she turned her back again and ignored the root causes of her pain and lack of self-esteem that paved the way for most of her choices and behaviours until then. She thought that by ignoring and running away from problems they would disappear, she didn't grasp back then that you can't run away from problems that are inside yourself as they will come with you. If you don't identify the reasons and confront the source, if it's you or someone else, the problems will remain and grow in time. Only years later, just before she sank into oblivion, she realised that if she wants to break the destructive cycle of dismissing oneself — fulfilling other's gratifications — indulging in self-pity — escaping to start again, she'll have to go back and start to do the work of peeling layer after layer of her masks until she'll expose and meet head-to-head the essence of her dejection. At that time she was in the "Escaping to start again" phase. The first nine months were exactly what she had imagined a city life should be; she thrived on the stimulation of meeting new people, new places open and another close, variety of markets, arts, concerts, clubs and restaurants, the constant movement and anticipation for the next thing to happen. It was a young single's paradise.

In the early evening, a day before Easter weekend, a young man walked into the club, he sat at the bar and ordered an expensive whisky. He wasn't much older than her but looked very wealthy; the designer's suit, prestige wristwatch, and the confidence spiced with a bit of arrogance that oozed from him could only come from old money; the new successful hi-tech whizz-kids don't rate much on smart appearance and a show-off of their wealth. She was chatting with a couple of elderly guests and sneaked a quick look at him thinking to herself, "A silver spoon is stuck so deep in his arse; he probably suffers from everlasting constipation. However, he is without a doubt a strikingly handsome man."

The two old farts have been rather entertaining with their posh twang and the old-fashioned manners, but the conversation about the incoming Black-tie party and the results of the weekend's horse races started to bore her. Then, while laughing politely to a punch-line that they found hilarious, she glanced at him once again and saw that he was staring at her while talking on his mobile. She often found herself as a subject of men captivation, but usually, they sneaked peeks or came and talked to her; he didn't just stare, he was clearly checking her out from top to bottom. Instead of being uncomfortable or even infuriated by his almost rude indiscretion, she felt a tingling sensation, the lack of embarrassment of this ravishing man excited her; she had an impulse to take her clothes off there and then and allow him to watch. Suddenly the magic was gone; he turned back to the bar and ordered another shot of single malt and drank it in one sip, he had a few words with the barmen and then walked out of the club.

The rest of the shift seemed like forever, she couldn't wait to get home, change outfits and go to the pub to mingle with people her own age. She thanked all the gods when the last guest had left, grabbed her coat, waved goodbye to her colleagues and walked out. As soon as she stepped out in the street a fancy convertible stopped next to her. "Can I give you a ride home, gorgeous?" The bloke lounged behind the wheel in an inviting position and gazed at her boobs; his confidence together with his looks allured and aroused her, nevertheless, men used to be wrapped around her little finger, not the opposite. So, she managed to keep cool and said indifferently, "I'm sorry mister, but I'm not allowed to have a relationship with clients." She walked off and sat at the bus stop. He waited for a couple of seconds, looking at her, processing the unexpected rejection, then pressed the acceleration pedal to the floor and drove away with squealing tyres.

The following evening, again, as soon as she stepped out of the club a heavy motorcycle stopped next to her, he took off his helmet and with a charming smile said, "I have cancelled my annual membership this morning, and I'm not a client anymore." He took out another helmet from the back storage and threw it to her. "Hop on love, I'll take you home."

She couldn't find any more excuses, so she stood there looking at him to give him the impression that she is in two minds, and after a moment she put on the helmet without a word, lifted the skirt above her knee, and sat behind him and hugged his torso firmly. He was fit; she felt his solid muscles under the leather jacket and thought, "What's the worst that can happen?" Then she let one hand drop down to his crotch and grabbed his package; it was hard as a rock. "Well well." She shouted in his ear against the wind and the engine's noise, "You are definitely geared up and equipped with a powerful machine between your legs."

"It definitely is, especially if a sexy girl is sitting on it" he shouted back. "So, where are we going yours or mine?"

"You're a cheeky sod you know that? Of course your place, but let's stop at a pub first and have a couple of pints, I'm not allowed to drink alcohol at work, and after mingling with those stuffed stick-in-the-mud old fogeys the whole day, I need a drink"

"You want to stop in a pub for a couple of pints? Who do you think I am, babe? I have a bottle of champagne at home that costs more than your monthly salary and that has your name on it."

"You are an arrogant, condescending and snobbish piece of work, you know that?" she answered. "But what the heck, you only live once, and you look extremely tasty…you better be in action like you are on the package, Mr wonderful."

He looked at her with a haughty smile and Instead of answering; he accelerated and crossed the city at 100mph.

8

She never came back to her loft or to the club; a day after that night she quit her job and moved into his penthouse that was situated in one of the exclusive new towers on the river bank. He sent his beck and call assistant to pick up a few personal items from her flat, paid the landlord for three months' rent and informed him that he can look for a new tenant immediately.

The penthouse was a mixture between the ultimate man-cave and a bachelor pad of a young single with excessive means and no responsibilities. It looks like he developed the elegant debauchery into a lifestyle. It contained only one single massive room that took over the whole floor. The entrance to the penthouse was from a lift in the centre of the room. To the right of the lift's door was the toilet which was the only closed space in the flat, farther to the right, 5 feet from the windows was the bathroom that was basically three walls planted in the middle of the room with a lowered square floor for drainage, a built-in shower and a bathtub. Left of the entrance was the kitchen and dining table with an elegant modern design of black stone surfaces and grey/white cupboards. In front of the lift's door was the living space; it had a well-equipped bar, poker table, 60-inch TV with the most recent games consoles, a stereo system with speakers scattered all around the flat, and sofas to sink in. At the back were a huge king-size bed, a wardrobe, another TV, soft lights and remote-controlled blinds on the windows. The walls of the penthouse were covered with large artworks of contemporary artists. The main themes of the artworks were femininity and sex; it was tasteful and classy, not vulgar or degrading as some single men's flats. A lovely balcony surrounded the flat; it included a fat Jacuzzi with space for six adults and a stunning view that looked over the whole city. Only in her wildest dreams, she fantasizes that a small village girl like her could live in this place.

He was the son of a real-estate mogul that owned a large part of the commercial land and properties in the city, and some luxury hotels and shopping centres around the world. He lived off a large trust fund that his father opened for him when he graduated from university, hence, he didn't need to work for the rest of his life. The charming articulate playboyish flair blew her away. He was the male version of her; mysterious, cheeky and challenging. On top of it, he spoiled and pampered her; holidays, weekends away, nights out, expensive clothes and jewellery, and the cherry on the cake; mingling with the rich and famous. She was in love and felt like she had won the jackpot, but life can be so deceitful.

The difference between being in love with someone and loving someone is like the difference between a decadent hedonistic lifestyle that pursues a physical and "on the surface" emotional stimulations, compared to a self-fulfilling life that on top of the shallow thrills, one seeks meaning in accomplishment, altruism, and sharing. It's the content and essence that one adds to the grey areas and times in life, that distinguish between the two, in love or in lifestyle.

They had fun and played like two kids for four years; the world was like a giant playground, no responsibility, answering to no one, "La dolce vita". Got up and went to sleep whenever they wanted, caught flights to the other side of the world in a split-second decision, parties, cruises on yachts, gallery openings, award nights, she had friends from the young aristocracy, film stars, and pop singers.

They got married after two months together, it was a small wedding in Vegas with an Elvis impersonator as the registrar and a few of his friends, his snotty condescending parents were not happy that the bride came from a much lower level in the social ladder, so he preferred to have a low-profile wedding. He did insist that they signed on a prenup, though, which stated that in case of a divorce, she would only be entitled to the property and money that was in her name at that time. She was euphoric, overjoyed and in love, and didn't think about the future at the time, so she agreed to sign without hesitation. In retrospect, she understood, too late, that in all those years they have been married, he always made sure that except a small car and some money in her bank account for spending, which he topped up every month, no properties or funds were ever in her name. Years later after moving back to the village to reflect on her life and reconcile with herself, she realised that all those years with him she only experienced things; she didn't do, create, and accomplish anything. She did not have any sense of fulfilment or achievement as her life was centred on pleasure and love for her husband.

Then, a tiny blood clot in a small blood vessel in the brain changed their lives.

His father passed away from a sudden brain aneurysm, which forced her husband to grow up overnight and take his father's place as the managing director of the company. He wanted to be taken seriously by the board of directors, the clients, and his subordinates. The wild flamboyant image had to be changed; he wanted to build a reputation as a consequential businessman. Accordingly, he sold the penthouse, and they moved to a large house in a posh suburb, a few miles south of the city. The undomesticated outrageous life ended.

The life of a suburban rich housewife was not glamorous and exciting as she had seen on films and on TV; his workday contained at least twelve hours, when he came back home he was still busy with endless phone calls, by the time he was finally free, on the late evenings, all he wanted is to lounge in front the TV to watch football or just zap between channels. She filled her days with yoga and Pilates classes, spa days, shopping sprees, and sitting in cafés gossiping with other rich housewives that she had met in the neighbourhood. The rest of the time she was at home waiting for him to come back from work. It was a lonely and rather meaningless existence. When she mentioned to him that she was thinking about looking for a job, he dismissed it immediately, "I make enough money so you don't have to go out and work babe, just enjoy what we have, most of the women in the world only dream of having your life. Anyway, I want to start to try for a baby...right now!" He looked at her with his most charming smile, pulled her toward him and started to undress her.

As she didn't have the power to confront him about it, she accepted her new life and concentrated on supporting and making him happy as much as possible. Nevertheless, due to her childhood experiences at home, she believed that she would be a horrible mother and made up her mind not to bring any children into the world, the thought of her children growing up and becoming like her was unbearable. She didn't tell him about this decision, though, and pretended in public to yearn for children, but, she had secretly continued to take contraceptive pills.

As the years went by the frustration from the boredom and the life without a real purpose crept into her soul, she started to use antidepressants and painkillers, soon the pills took over, and she needed more and more of them to function normally. Her husband was too busy with himself and with the business to see her decline, and anyway, in front of him, she always tried to show a cheerful face. On the outside; when they were alone, around people at events, or when she hosted events for friends at home, she was always her usual enchanting and delightful self, but inside she became a wreck. During the days at home, she sat for hours staring at the TV, waiting for her husband to come back from work. She continued to do all her usual activities, but they were done on an auto-mode for the intention of looking good to the eyes of the beholder. When he was at home it was all about him, she was hovering around him non-stop, craving for any bit of attention. But their worlds went apart; naturally, their subject of interests became fewer and fewer, he went forward, and she regressed. Even in bed, where they were so compatible in the past, the fire was no more. As much as she tried to turn him on, when they made love, he used to come inside of her as soon as possible, and then he would turn away and fall asleep.

He did, though keep talking about having children.

After a few years when nothing happened, he became more and more frustrated and agitated, and they started to have almost a daily barney about it. She even faked a fertility doctor's report showing that she is not barren and kept telling him that it is not uncommon and can take time to conceive a baby; he did not imagine that she was still taking the pills. Then one day she forgot the pills near the bathroom sink when she was high on painkillers, they were left there while she went out for a facial. It turned out that on this exact day he came home early and found the pills. When she came back home, she found him sitting on the sofa with a glass of whisky in his hand.

"Can you please explain this?" He held the pills pack up in front of her face.

She turned pale and felt that the blood had been sucked out of her body, and she had to hold the sofa to keep her balance.

"You don't understand, it's not…"

"I don't understand? What is there to understand? Are you taking these pills or not?"

"Yes, but… I wanted to tell you but I couldn't…"

"How long have you been taking them?"

"Well, I never stopped, but..."

He raised his hand and said calmly. "Stop, I don't want to hear anymore!"

He pointed nonchalantly at three suitcases that sat beside the door, "I took the liberty to pack your clothes, I want you out of this house right now, you can keep your car and the money in your account, text me the address that you will be staying at, and I will arrange for the divorce papers to be sent to you."

He then turned away, took out his mobile phone and started a business call like nothing had happened, leaving her standing, paralysed, too stunned to move. After a couple of minutes of confusion, she opened her mouth to explain and to try to change the inevitable, but before she was able to say anything he shut her up by raising his finger and pointed to the door. Having no choice, she picked up the suitcases, put them in the boot of her car and sat in the driver's seat, shaking all over her body.

Almost an hour passed before she could calm herself down and was able to think clearly, the thoughts scrambled through her head, "what should I do now? I have nothing! No job, no profession, there is a bit of money in my account, enough to last for a few weeks, and this little car that I can sell, but what then? Where should I go now?" She had to force herself not to go back to the house and beg him to take her back, she knew that he would never forgive her, it would only add to her humiliation. Although she had hundreds of acquaintances from the past years with her husband, she couldn't think of even one good friend that she could call. Her husband was the centre of her life for so long, she didn't nurture any real relationship beyond him, the relations with the other people that crossed her path have been all only superficial, "hi and goodbye", some gossip, fake smiles and small talk, without any emotional attachment. She didn't dare call her brother or sister to ask if she could stay there for a while as they lost touch since she moved out of the city and started to use the prescription medications on a daily basis. She knew that they would take her in without any hesitation, but she didn't want them to see her as a failure and to muddle up their perfect lives and perfect families. So, she took a couple of pills to sort out her head, started up the engine and drove off. She stopped near a cheap hotel, just off the motorway, and paid for a single room for two nights.

"Stupid bitch!" She thought to herself while lying on the bumpy mattress trying to look back at the day's events, "I'm a stupid bitch! How could I forget to hide the pills? I had everything a woman could ask for; a gorgeous husband, plenty of money, a big house, status, I had everything and I blew it because of one careless slip-up." Years later, when she started to look back on her life and patch up herself, she recognised that it was written on the wall, if she wouldn't forget the pills, something else would have happened sooner or later. Perpetual lies have a habit of bubbling up to the surface; close relationships that are not based on honesty are doomed to fail. That night in the small hotel room, which reeked from old carpets and damp walls, while lying under the cheap sheets, she vowed to stop with the medication and clean her body and mind. With the hope of a fresh start, she finally fell into a deep sleep. She succeeded in sticking to the vow for a whole twelve hours…

The miserable rainy morning agreed with the gloomy mood she had woken up with; the future which seemed bright last night before she closed her eyes, looked grim and bleak in the grey sunless morning. She went down to the dining room and poured herself a cup of tea, then sat in the corner and searched the contacts list on her mobile phone for anyone whom she would be comfortable enough to call for support.

From all the names on the list, she found only one that was trustworthy and would possibly help; it was the owner of the loft she rented at the time she had met her husband, he was a pleasant middle-aged gentleman in his mid-fifties that said on different occasions in the past that she should call him if she would ever need help. It's been a very long time since they spoke, thus, he was quite surprised when she called him, but after listening patiently to her story, as she did burst into tears twice, he then invited her to stay at his house as a guest until she could sort herself out. He appeared to be harmless, and she also had the impression that he always fancied her, so she ran up to her room, had a shower, put make-up on, and took two pills with a glass of water, then headed to his house.

9

The house was located in a nice neighbourhood in the northern part of the city. It consisted of detached and semi-detached houses with newish, semi-prestige cars on the driveways, which suggested that they belonged to middle-class, financially comfortable residents. She recalled that he told her that the loft she had lived in was just an investment he had made for retirement; his regular income came from two convenience stores that he owned. The house was dark, she knocked on the door anyway; there was no answer. She tried to peek in through the curtained windows but couldn't see anyone inside. "Why did he invite me if he is not at home?" She wondered, and then she remembered that it was Friday morning. He was probably at work and didn't think that she would get there so fast. "I have nowhere else I can go now, so I might as well stay here and wait." She bought a packet of cigarettes and a bottle of water in the corner shop that she spotted a couple of streets away and then sat in her car to wait for him. By the time he came home, she had smoked half of the pack, and her clothes stank of cigarettes' smell. It was already dark outside and no one was around, so she changed her clothes quickly in the car and sprayed some perfume on her neck, then went and knocked on his door again.
"Hi," She said when the door opened. "Thank you so much for inviting me, I had no one else to turn to."
He smiled at her, "Come in, come in, it's freezing out here! Where are all your belongings?"

"I don't have much, just a few suitcases in the car." She pointed at her car that was parked on the other side of the street.

"Ok, bring the car here; there is space for two on the driveway. I'll help you take your stuff inside; I guess you'll be staying for a while, at least until you'll sort yourself out."

"Thank you so much again. I hope it's not an inconvenience, and I don't want to be a burden. I'll try to find a place and a job as soon as possible."

"Nonsense, you can stay as long as you need, it's a big house, and since my divorce, I've been living here by myself as we didn't have children. So there is plenty of space for you. Now, chop-chop, let's get your stuff inside, we don't want to get sick."

After they got the suitcases inside, he pointed at the second floor and said, "The guest room is on the right side at the end of the hall, there are clean sheets and towels in the cupboard. Make yourself comfortable. I'm going to fix something to eat, I'll call you when it's ready and you can tell me what happened over dinner."

"Ok, thanks again."

"You can stop thanking me." He said with a smile, "You are here now, enjoy your stay." He disappeared into the kitchen.

The guest room was the size of a standard hotel room, decorated in a bit of an old fashion style. There was a woman's touch in the soft colours and design; it looked like he didn't change it since his wife left. It was a much smaller bedroom than what she was used to, but she knew that she must start to get used to a drop in her lifestyle. She sat on the bed thinking about what to tell him; she couldn't tell him that her husband kicked her out because she lied to him, and she definitely did not plan to tell him about the other tablets she was taking. This man was such a nice guy, and she really wanted him to trust her. It is funny how a lie leads to another lie that leads to more lies, until a whole building of lies crops up like a Jenga game, and then crashes down when the blocks/lies are starting to come out.

The dinner was simple but tasty; pasta with Bolognese sauce and garlic bread. They ate in silence and when they finished he poured them another glass of wine and asked gently, "So, what happened?"

"Well, yesterday I found out that my husband has been cheating on me with his secretary since last year. When I confronted him about it, he lashed out and threw me out of the house. He doesn't want to see or hear from me and wants a divorce."

"How can he throw you out of your own house?"

"Before we got married I signed a prenup which stated that in case of divorce I will be entitled only to the property and finance that was in my name, and all this time he put everything in his name. I didn't mind it, because he always gave me enough money to do everything I wanted to do." She started to cry; "Now I have nothing except the car outside."

"What a bastard! I'm so sorry, if I was younger, I would go and knock his lights out. Anyway, you can stay here as long as you need." He poured the rest of the bottle into their glasses then raised his glass for a toast, "May your husband become bankrupt and choked on his own vomit."

She laughed, the first time in days, and raised her glass, "I'll salute to that! I'm really grateful for everything and will look for a job and a flat as soon as I get my head straight."

The following days she made some phone calls and queries about jobs and flats, but, as she didn't have any qualification and very minimal work experience, only from years ago, there were only non-skilled jobs with a minimum salary available for her. The only flats she could afford were dumps in the rough area of the city that were not really suitable for human living. Her host was very caring and affectionate, and he made her feel at home. She found herself more and more fond of him. Eventually, she stopped searching and made herself busy on the house and on him, she wanted to thank him for his generosity, so she cleaned and tidy-up the house and the garden, and made sure that dinner was always ready when he came back from work. The rest of her time she spent watching reality programs on the TV. One night she came to his bed and made love to him. He was not handsome or attractive; a bit overweight and flabby, but she didn't mind, she wanted to make him happy. Due to his age, he didn't have a very high sex drive and mainly wanted companionship, which made it easier for her to overcome the lack of physical appeal. The next evening, at dinner, he proposed to her and got a yes for an answer.

They got married in the registry office with only a couple of witnesses, no wedding party or a big family gathering. Then they went away for a long weekend at the seaside for a honeymoon; it was a nice and relaxed little holiday. He was an old-fashioned bloke and went out of his way to be romantic; walks on the beach and candlelit dinners at expensive restaurants. She liked him, but didn't have a "Woman's" love for him, the antidepressants that she continued to take made her somewhat emotionless and numb, for her, it was as good as it can get, and she felt lucky and thankful.

Not long after they have begun their normal life as a married couple, she started to see changes in his behaviour and attitude towards her, in the beginning, there were only a few minor things and remarks which he showed his dissatisfaction; the living room was not tidy enough, dinner didn't have enough salt, or her top showed more skin than it should. She thought for a while, that it was only a bit of a stress release as the economy at the time was on a slowdown and heading towards a recession, which put some pressure on his business, so she didn't pay too much attention to his moaning and groaning.

After six months of playing the perfect housewife, but with much less money to spend than in her previous marriage, she became bored and felt that she needed some more interaction with other people. One evening after dinner she came up behind him and put her arms around his chest, "Babe, I'm feeling a bit cramped and useless spending all my days in the house, maybe I can come to work and help you in the shops sometimes?"

He glanced at her with a sceptical look for a minute, and then smiled, "Of course you can, there is actually a vacancy for a position behind the till in one of my stores at the moment, you can work there as long as the housework is done and dinner is on the table when I return from work." Then added, "I've asked you before not to call me babe! I'm not a young lad anymore."

She gave him a kiss on his cheek, "thank you, you will not regret it."

That night she went out of her way to please him.

Working in the shop and meeting different people, although they were only customers, were the happy times in that period of her life. She got on well with the staff and as she was the boss's wife, the store manager didn't bother her much. Her husband was also benevolent and kind to her at work and never told her off or embarrassed her in front of the staff or the clients. At home, though, it was another story; the business continued to struggle, and he gradually became more and more abusive and rude towards her, often as soon as he came back from work. Nothing that she did was good enough for him; "There is a crease on my shirt!" Dinner is over-cooked!" "You've put on weight lately! I'm sure you don't want to be a fat bitch!" "The house and garden look like a tip!"

One evening she had to run and lock herself in the bedroom after he threw a full dinner plate at the wall, and shouted, "Can't you make a decent dinner? You bloody useless cow! All I ask is a clean house and an edible dinner when I come home!" After he had calmed down, he knocked on the bedroom door and apologised for his behaviour, excusing it with a bad day at work…then asked her to clean up the mess in the dining room. She opened the door, said that it was fine and gave him a hug, then went to clean the Dining room. "He is working so hard, the shops are not doing so well." She thought and blamed herself as always, "I am a useless cow; he helped me and loved me, and that's how I repay him? Making a rubbish dinner? I need to do better, so at least at home he will be happy." The self-loathing made her blind to how frequent those outbursts occurred and the increase in intensity. She could not see when it started to build up. The writing was on the wall; it was inevitable that the verbal abuse would eventually become physical, then, by the time it did happen, she was emotionally too weak to fight back or to leave.

The growing atmosphere of almost terror at home turned her life into an ominous routine; taking her cocktail of painkillers and antidepressants as soon as she returned from work, then doing the housework, making dinner, getting shouted at or occasionally being slapped, watching his programs on TV, then falling asleep exhausted with him snoring in the background. Once in a few weeks when he had the urge, she was laying on her back staring at the ceiling waiting for him to come, then when he turned to the other side and fell asleep. She would get up and sneak on her tiptoes to the bathroom to wash as she could not stand his smell on her anymore. Every Sunday she had to go with him to church, and sit in the service for an hour trying not to yawn, then provide fake smiles and have boring small talks with the ladies. Then after dinner, he usually went to the pub for a few pints. It would give her a couple of hours alone in the house where she could do whatever she wanted to do, which normally ended with her staring at a stupid talent show on TV. She accepted this life and said to herself that at least she was not alone like her mum. Going to work was her escape; for six hours she could be her vibrant self again, have a laugh with the staff and charm the customers, even if it was pretence as inside she felt empty and hollow, it made her life somewhat more bearable.

Nine years passed by in this forsaken existence, no special occasions except Christmas with his old tedious mother and the odd weekend, once in a blue moon, where he would take her to the seaside; always to the same town and the same B&B. She didn't have friends outside work and she visited her mother very infrequently. Her siblings tried to do an intervention with her once, but she didn't want to listen and waved them off. They could see the blue and black marks on her arms and face that she struggled to hide; they could see how she was gradually fading into the void. The fire that used to burn within her was gone, and she was ashamed of what her life had turned into and felt that she didn't deserve their care, so she pushed them away. One could not really articulate into words the melancholy and despair of sheer loneliness, and she was not far from it when her mum decided that she'd had enough, and threw herself under a train on new year's eve.

After the funeral, her brother and sister sat her down and said to her that as things are, both of them have houses and are financially comfortable, so they decided to give her their mum's house and the small savings that she had left. Nevertheless, there were two conditions; she should leave her husband immediately and move back to the village, and stop "cold turkey" taking the prescription medication.

She tried to retaliate, "Why do you try to control my life? My husband is a good man; he is working very hard, and I'm not an addict, I just take a tablet when I have a headache."

Her sister grabbed her arm and pulled up the sleeve pointing to the clear black finger marks where her husband had held her violently before grabbing her throat and tossing her on the living room floor two days earlier. "Is this what a good man does?" She pulled her to the mirror in the hall and forced her to look at herself. "Look at your neck, is this what a good man does?" "Look at your eyes, your face, your body, look at what the drugs have done to you. This is your wake-up call and last chance to sort your life out sis!"

For a long moment, she looked at the image of the woman that was reflected back from the mirror: the empty lifeless eyes, pale face, and the frail body. She could hardly recognise herself. Then and there, she made up her mind to take their offer and open a new page in her life. She was not going to be a victim anymore.

The next morning, as soon as her husband's car disappeared up the road, she packed her clothes and left a note, "I'm leaving you, please don't come looking for me, if you will, I'll call the police. I don't want anything from you except your signature on the divorce papers that will be sent to you. You are a horrible and violent man! I hope you'll get what you deserve." She left the bed untidy, dirty dishes in the sink, put the note on the dining table, then got into her car and left her second marriage behind.

It was the first time in years she felt hope and confidence that she could make it by herself. There was a lot of work to do physically and emotionally, a lot of healing, twenty-five years of self-torment. She was terrified but adamant to take this opportunity and not fuck it up this time.

Her siblings were already waiting for her at their mother's house and helped her with the suitcases, and then they sat in the living room with the deed for the house. Her brother said, "We are so happy that you decided to take up the offer, you know that we love you and will help you as much as we can, but it's up to you to do the work."

Her sister added, "Before we sign the deed to your name and transfer the money, we need to write a plan for your rehabilitation. All we want is for you to be happy." Her brother nodded his head smiling and pressed her hand with his.

She had the urge to tell them; "Leave me alone, are your lives so perfect? I can sort out my shit by myself and don't need your pity." Nevertheless, she understood what was on the line and decided to be smart this time and keep her mouth shut.

10

"How can I tell him about my wasted life? I don't want to let him down." "Should I use the magic of my charm on him? It's never failed me before." "He is not like other men, and will probably read through me and not fall for these ploys." "Maybe I should just tell him everything? But he will be so disappointed in me and I don't think I'll be able to take it again."

All those questions pestered her since she woke up that morning and while she walked toward his parents' house. As she knocked on the door she made up her mind to just go with the flow and see what happens.

"The door is open!" a voice came from the house followed by a few swear words. She pressed the door handle and walked inside; a smell of fried bacon filled her nostrils, she stood at the entrance to the kitchen and watched him struggling with breakfast; on the stove were two pans with eggs and bacon, and a pot of baked beans, he tried, unsuccessfully, to manage all of it at the same time, but only succeed to burn his fingers and stick the eggs to the pan. Quite a few "Fucks" and "Bloody hells" were thrown in the air during the process which amused her greatly. "Good old clumsy Ziggy." She thought, and then said, "Do you need some help Zigs?"

"Morning!" he waved his hand. "Ouch! For fuck sake! Stupid bloody pan!" he grumbled and sucked his burnt finger. "I'm ok, please sit down, breakfast will be ready shortly."

"Oh, stop being silly and let me help, it's obvious that cooking is not your forte." She took the spatula from his hand, "You can make the coffee and sort out the table, and I'll deal with this before you burn all your fingers and most importantly, my food."

He looked like he was going to oppose her so she slapped his bum and smiled at him, "Chop-chop, stop looking at me and get to work Ziggster, I need my morning coffee."

He finally gave up and put the coffee pod in the machine, "I could never say no to you. Good morning Pippi! I hope you had a nice evening yesterday."

"As nice as it can be to serve food and drinks to horny tight-arse villagers that are constantly checking out my backside but don't leave tips. Anyway let's not start with all the polite small talk, how come you left your family and your job? You were never the type of person who runs away." She put the bacon and eggs on the plates and looked back and shook her head. "Breakfast is ready and the table is not set, mate, you are slacking!"

While they sat and ate he told her the reasons why he left his life. She listened and wanted to say to him, "You are a bloody wanker Z, you have everything and you are throwing it away. Look at my life, I had it, I had the world at my feet, but I blew it, please don't repeat my mistakes." But she was so happy to be near him again and deep inside had the hope that he would save her, so she didn't say much.

When they finished eating, they put the dishes in the dishwasher, took their coffees and sat outside on the bench looking out, enjoying the sunny morning and the silence. "Let's go for a walk to our old spot near the river." He suggested. "You are not in a hurry to go somewhere? Are you?"

"I'm free the whole day, off work today. I would love to go there. I haven't been there for years." It was a little lie,

234

as in the last three years she went there often to sit, relax and contemplate. "Should we take bikes like old times?"

"We just had breakfast and I'm too full to ride now, so walking will be better."

"Ok you lazy sod, on your feet."

They walked for half an hour talking about the old times; exciting episodes and funny memories from school days. When they reached the place where the river curved sharply to the north, they walked carefully on the large dead log that rested across the river like a bridge, and sat down side by side on the middle with their legs hanging, like they used to do thirty years ago.

He took a deep breath and asked, "What happened that week at your father's?"

She looked at him with a serious look and said, "I can tell you, but I'll have to kill you   after." Then a smile appeared on her face and she grabbed his hand pretending to pull him off the log.

"Stop it Pippi! I'm serious, I have the right to know, and it's about time you tell me."

"Well Zigs, what do you think happened?" She provoked him with her old defiant attitude, he could see, though, that down under she was struggling and was debating with herself what to tell him. He had some ideas of what could have happened to her; maybe she was raped, sexually abused, mugged or had been physically assaulted. Nevertheless, he didn't want to say it out loud.

"I don't know, just tell me please."

They sat quietly for a few minutes; he felt that she was torn inside. Suddenly her body loosens down and he knew that she came to a decision. "You probably think and imagine the worst about that week, you are wrong, I didn't get raped or abused or attacked, nothing like that happened."

"So why did you push me away? Why did you change?"

"I was ashamed, that's why. Are you happy now?" Her hands were shaking and she seemed like she was going to burst into tears, but she took a deep breath and pulled herself together. "I'm sorry; I didn't mean to say that." She looked at him and took another breath, "When I went to visit my dad I used to play outside with the kids from the neighbourhood. There was one boy, just a couple of years older than me, which I fell head over heels for. He was handsome, athletic, he was great on the skateboard and much cooler than the village kids here, and he gave me a lot of attention. So I thought he liked me too. To keep it short, two days before I came back home, he convinced me to have sex with him. I was a virgin, only thirteen, but wanted to be loved and to experience stuff; you know me, always jumping head first before checking the water. I was excited to become a "woman" and didn't think much before sleeping with him on a dirty mattress on the floor of his parent's garage. As soon as he finished he got up and left the garage without saying a word and subsequently until I left he totally ignored me. I felt dirty and ashamed; I thought that I had done something wrong, that I wasn't good enough and didn't satisfy him. I was too young for sex and not emotionally ready. My confidence was shattered. He was a wanker who took advantage of me for his own satisfaction but he was only a kid himself, and I wanted it, he didn't force it on me. I was just not ready…"

She paused, she looked so fragile and he wanted to hold her in his arms, but he kept his arms by his side and waited for her to continue.

"The rest of my life since then, until I moved back here three years ago, I tried to redeem myself by gratifying and please the men that surrounded me; boys in school, colleagues, friends, husbands, partners, fuck buddies, my bosses. I mastered the art of being who those men wanted me to be; I was charming, exciting and sexy. The men used it and loved it. Inside, though, I was so insecure, and all those years I put on a mask and dismissed who I really was and what I wanted. My escape was in alcohol in my early twenties, then, for a long time, it was a prescription medication. I got cleaned up and started to mend myself only after my mum passed away after I moved back to the village. So this is it, the story of my life. A huge failure, not what you expected hey?"

He held her hand and squeezed it gently, "I'm so sorry Pip if I only knew…"

She straightened her back, pulled her hand from his hand and looked at him with a defying glare, "I don't want or need anyone's pity, I made my own bed and the bad choices were mine, but I'm ok now. I'm sorry that I'm not who you imagined me to be all those years, just a waiter in a pub that doesn't have much standing for her, and with a poor portfolio of achievements."

"I didn't mean it like that Pips, I meant that if you just told me back then I could have helped."

"You were a thirteen-year-old boy Z, how could you help? My mum should have spotted what was going on with me, but she was too busy with her looks, and her reputation in the village, to notice her own teenage daughter's emotional state. Ignorant cow!

"Maybe there is a reason for all of this that led us here." He smiled. "You are not just a waitress…you know, everybody has issues, but it's all about dealing with them and coming out with the upper hand. It seems to me that you are on the right track. Meeting you again is definitely not a let-down." He said those words, but inside question marks started to pop out.

"Yeah right, please don't patronise me. What issues do you have or had in your life Ziggy? With your amazing parents, perfect little family, success in your job, friends, and money? You achieved what most people want, which issues are you talking about? Also, come out with the upper hand? You are so naïve, mate. I learn to live with my past mistakes and to accept and forgive myself; I'm not trying to win or tame life again, I'm just living side by side with my past and trying not to grab the bull by the horns, they are sharp."

They sat for a long time in uncomfortable silence.

"I'm sorry Ziggy; I didn't mean to be a bitch. I know you just tried to make me feel   better." She kissed him softly on his lips and said to his ear. "You are still lovely Zigman." Then she pushed him until he lost his balance, just before he fell to the water she grabbed his shoulders and saved him, giggling in the process.

"Bloody hell Pip! The water is probably freezing; do you want me to catch pneumonia?"

"Oh, stop being a grouch; we are getting too serious and emotional. We should have some fun today like old times." She got up on her feet and held out her hand toward him, "Come on, let's head back." He grabbed her hand and stood up. They kept holding hands while walking in silence each one in his/her own thoughts.

"I went to visit my mum yesterday after we talked." He broke the silence. "She is not in good condition, it's hard for me to see her like that. By the way, she remembers you and was asking why you are not coming to visit our house anymore? She thinks that we are still thirteen."

"Bless her, I should go to see her, she is such an amazing woman, she was always so good to me." She squeezed his hand to show sympathy.

"I also met Button on the bus on the way back from my mum yesterday, do you remember her?"

"The little pudgy girl who had a crush on you in school? Of course, I remember, what became of her?"

He stopped and started to throw pebbles at the river, making them jump a few times on the water. "Come on Pip, let's see if you can still beat me, but I'm warning you, I had some practice over the years with my son."

"Ok mister, but don't whine if you'll lose." She said while picking up a few pebbles.

"Well," he said, "Apparently Button is not chubby anymore; she is quite an attractive woman, with a successful career, a happy marriage and children. She has done better than both of us."

"Good on her." She said, but he could hear a bit of envy in her voice though.

They hang about on the river bank for a while, competing who can make a pebble jump more times on the water like thirty years hadn't passed since the last time they played there. Eventually, he dropped the stones and raised his hands; "I give up, you're too good."

She patted him on his cheek; "keep practising mate; you might beat me one day. Let's start to head back; it looks like it's going to spit soon"

"Would you like to stay for dinner?" He asked when they got back to the house.

"Sure, I don't have any plans for this evening, do you have anything to drink?"

"I think there are a couple of beers left in the fridge, but we can go to the village and get some wine for dinner."

"Ok, but let's walk fast, I don't want to get soaked."

The closest shop that sold alcohol was the corner shop that he visited two days ago. He wasn't very keen to see that awful bloke again, but they didn't have much choice as the closest shop apart from this one was quite a long walk; on the other side of the village.

When they opened the door it made the noise of bells but the chap didn't even bother to take his eyes off his phone to see who came in. "He is probably looking at porn," Pippi whispered in his ear. "I wouldn't be surprised." He answered quietly. They picked up two bottles of merlot and a few bags of snacks and went to pay. The guy unwillingly scanned the items, still looking at his mobile, then with an annoying expression of inconvenience he looked on the till and then at them. "It's 9.90 please."

"I'll pay for that." he said to Pippi, then took out a tenner and gave to the guy, "keep the change matey."

"You're so kind." The chap answered with sarcasm and looked at Pippi checking her out. "I know you... you used to party hard...I'm going to finish work in half an hour, I can join you two and we can party, you used to love it remember?" he nodded his head with an obnoxious grin on his face, "Yeah man, good times."

A switch turned inside of him, all the anger and frustration burst out and he had done something he had never done before and didn't think he had in him; Mr Hyde suddenly came out of him, he grabbed the guy's shirt, pulled him over the counter and threw him on the shop's floor, then started to kick and punch him. Looking back, he couldn't apprehend where the strength came from; he was never a strong man and always tried to avoid anything related to competition or conflict that involved physical aptitude, but the fury that the lad engendered out of him gave him a boost of power and if Pippi hadn't pulled him away and pushed him out of the shop, he would have probably killed the poor fella.

"What the hell are you doing Ziggy? Are you fucking crazy?" she shouted, "Come on; let's get away from here before he will call the police."

"Hold on for a sec." he opened the shop's door and looked at the battered man that lay on the floor. "You know you deserved it mate, just take it as a lesson in respect to women." He looked around the shop and couldn't see any CCTV cameras that can incriminate him, so he took the carrier bag with the drinks that were luckily still undamaged on the counter and stepped out back to Pippi.

His face was red and he tried to get his breath back while they walked away. "We're lucky that the guy is stupid and didn't install CCTV cameras."

"What was that Ziggs? You totally lost your mind!"

"I don't know, I'm sorry, he was such an arsehole and I couldn't control myself." He said after calming down a bit. "I don't know what came over me; I've never been in a fight or hit anyone before. I've hated this guy since I saw him with you on prom night, and he shouldn't have talked to you like that now. Sorry Pip, we should have just ignored him and walked away."

"Well," she smiled, "thanks for standing up for me." After a few seconds of silence, she added; "It is sexy though, this side of you, Mr bad boy."

When they got to the top of the street they saw a car parking next to his parent's house, it was almost dark outside and they couldn't see the colour of the car.

"I didn't invite anyone, I wonder who it is." He mumbled. Although he knew that it could be only one person.

He increased his strides.

"Slow down man, I'm not going to chase you!" She grabbed his belt from behind.

As soon as they entered the driveway the driver's side door of the car opened and a woman stepped out. She was in her early forties; a brunette with a Bob haircut that never goes out of fashion, an average height, slim built with a flexible and strong body from years of Yoga and Pilates classes. She wore a tracksuit and looked like she got out of the house in a rush. "This is an attractive and well-maintained woman." Pippy couldn't help thinking, "Even with a tracksuit she looks chic."

11

"Shit, it's my wife." he said in a low voice, "Please get in the house, Pip, I'll come in in a minute."

"Hi, I'm…" Pippy started to say to the woman while reaching for a handshake.

"I think I know who you are." The woman cut her off ignoring the hand. "I would like to speak to my husband alone please."

"What are you doing here?" he asked after Pippy entered the house.

"I'm not sure what is going on with you but I want you to come back home." We can talk and sort out the issues."

He looked at her and shook his head, "You should go home V."

"Can we sit and talk first before you throw away twenty years of marriage?"

He took a long breath and pointed to the old garden bench, "Ok, Let's sit over there but not for long, my guest is waiting and I don't want to be rude. I don't think there is much to talk about anymore anyway."

They sat on the bench in silence for a while, then she turned to him and said; "Talk to me babe, what's going on? If it is a mid-life crisis why can't you just buy a Harley or run a marathon? Why do you want to throw away everything we've built together? I know that we like different things and we are very different people, but we are a team and we always worked things out together. We are a family, in good times and in bad times. Please talk to me; you can't just walk away without explanation, your son needs you even if he doesn't show it...and so do I."

She had a tear coming down on her cheek and he had a passing twitch of regret, which he instantly repressed. He hesitated for a couple of seconds, weighing his words. "I'm sorry V but it's going on for too long and I cannot live like that anymore."

"What is going on too long? This is the problem; you don't share! You hold everything in and expect me to read your mind. Well, I have news for you; I'm not telepathic and if anything bothers you or if something I do disturbs you, then you should say it."

She put her hand on his hand and squeezed gently, "Hey, please tell me what's wrong, babe."

"What do you want me to tell you? It's everything; my job bores me to death, my friends become so tedious with the same conversations, same jokes and stories."

"If this is what you feel about your job, change it! You have been working in the same place for the last twenty years; maybe it's time to look for something else? You have enough transferable skills and we are quite comfortable financially, what would you like to do?"

He moved uneasily. "I don't know what I want to do; you are tackling me with awkward questions!"

"Well, whatever you choose, I will support you. And about your friends; if you don't like them and they are so tedious, why do you keep hanging out with them?"

"I don't know, they are inviting me and I feel bad to say no. We have been friends for years and did have great times before...but it's not only this, our son is growing up and doesn't really need me anymore. As a matter of fact; he can't really stand me or my presence, and I don't like what he is becoming. Unfortunately, I don't have much say in his life anymore. Every time I try to say something to him or to put a limitation on him, he runs to you and gets what he wants. He is a selfish spoiled brat that thinks he can do whatever he likes, wouldn't listen, and totally disregards me. We are like two strangers that live under one roof. In the last few years, I've lost him. We used to be very close, do you remember? But...well, life's a bitch"

"He is a teenager, D! A perfectly normal teenager, that's what they are like; they are selfish, they are rebellious, and they are disrespectful in our eyes. We were the same, just with less technology. If the red hair that is waiting for you in the house is who I think she is; according to your stories, she was all of the above and more as a teenager. Maybe you should try to talk to him on his level, about the things that interest him. I'm sure you'll get much more positive responses from him."

"Do you want me to suddenly start to use social media and play video games? Come on, you know me better Vic."

She moved her hand away, then turned and looked into the eyes. "Yes! If you really want to win him back maybe you should show more interest in his life. Also, when you limit him or set a new ground rule, it will be helpful if you inform me about it so I will not overturn it without consulting you. You know, he does love you; he works hard and achieves brilliant grades in school so you'll be proud of him. Try to look over your self-pity and you might see what a lovely boy we raised." You also crumble and give up every time I disagree or have a different opinion than yours; if it's regarding him or about anything else in our life. I know that you don't like confrontations, nevertheless, not every disagreement has to lead to confrontation, and we can talk and get to a mutual ground."

He stood up, walked around a bit pondering what to say, and sat down again.

"You hit the nail on its head now; there is us, you and I; I don't think there are actually us anymore, we live together physically but it seems like we live separate lives. We are doing the regular things to show to ourselves and to the surrounding that we are still a family, but I don't think we loved or even liked each other for years. Tell me the truth; do you enjoy my company? Do you feel any excitement around me or in activities that we are doing together? Even the sex once a week, became a task. Everything that we are doing in our marriage in order to maintain a healthy relationship and to prevent us from sinking into a mind-numbing routine became a task with time, day and length. The marriage became a mind-numbing routine. Even the holidays which we insist on going jointly, and should be fun times away that brings us together come to be the loneliest times in a year for me. I'm sorry it is coming to this, but it's not the life I signed for and I want out."

He could see by her body language that she was getting angry and tense. She opened her mouth to say something nasty, but succeeded to control herself and answered quietly; "Why have you never said this until now? This is the problem; you don't talk or get angry or emotional. You don't say when something bothers you, and you don't fight for things or show disapproval for other things. The most you do is sulk for a bit, on rare occasions, but then you carry on like everything is ok. How do you expect me I know what you feel if you never share?"

"You know me, I don't like arguments."

"Don't you think that we can have disagreements in a conversation without turning it into an argument? Come on! We have lived together for so many years and we have compromised to make it work. I could see in the last few years that you are not happy, but I thought it's a phase that will pass. I did try to talk to you a couple of times but every time I asked you crawled deeper into your shell, so I stopped and let it blow away which apparently didn't."

"You know B; even though you are a miserable twat lately I still love you and don't want you to leave, but you need to grow up and understand that this is life; you chose to have a family for the good and the bad that this life entails. The routine that seemingly burdens you so much is a part of every family's life. A long relationship like ours often tends to go off the boil and become banal if they are not spiced up regularly. Both of us neglected us for a while now, I wasn't sensible to what was going on with you, but also you didn't see me or was interested in my life for a long time. I have issues and problems too; I'm getting older and my body is not what it used to be. You don't make me feel very desirable and attractive. You know, I could choose anybody I wanted back in the days, with a flip of my finger I could have better looking, richer, cooler men than you, but I've chosen to share my life and have a family with you and I have never regretted it and I have never looked for love and affection elsewhere even when you showed no interest in me."

"So why did you choose me then, when you could pick anyone, Vic? Why did you stick with me?"

"You moron, it's because I loved you! Even when you made it impossible for me lately, I waited and hoped that you'll pull yourself together and sort your shit out."

"It's good that we open it all out now, you can come home and we can start to work things out, you don't need to leave, please don't break this family apart."

He was quiet for a few minutes, then got up and said, "I'm sorry but it's too late." He started to walk toward the house, then, before he opened the door he turned; "Go home Victoria." Then he turned back to enter the house.

"Danny," she said calmly. He stopped but didn't look back. "The house door is open to you for the next three days. After that, it will be closed forever."

He nodded his head, entered the house and closed the door behind him.

She stood in the living room and looked at him with tension in her eyes, the carrier bags with the groceries still in her hands. They kept quiet until they heard the car driving away.

"It's over." He said

She put the bags down and hugged him, "I'm sorry it went this way, but, well, it's quite clear that she didn't make you happy."

"Yeah, I guess you're right." He didn't feel relieved or free though, and it made him uneasy.

She pulled away and lifted the carrier bag, "Thank god she is finally gone. I'm starving and need some alcohol in me. I'm going to fix us some dinner, you can be useful and poor me some of this wine meanwhile, you heartbreaker you. We are going to have the night you dreamed about since school." Then she turned away to the kitchen and started to prepare the dinner.

He poured two glasses of wine, handed one to her, and then sat down on his father's old reclining armchair in the living room. The old smell of sweat, cigarettes and Old spice aftershave throw him years back to a memory of his dad sitting there after work, sipping from a bottle of cold beer and watching his favourite detective series on the telly, the white foam of the beer used to hang from his thick moustache after every sip. He missed his dad; although he was a strict and demanding dad, he was also happy to teach and guide with patience and love. Whenever he or his brother struggled with something; if it was homework or inflating the tire of a bike, his dad would leave whatever he was doing, no matter how important it was, and help them until they knew what they were doing. He was a funny and loving man, and loved people; his biggest joy was to host BBQ evenings in the summer to family and friends when the weather permitted. He used to entertain the guests with songs and funny stories while flipping burgers and sausages. When he spotted a guest with an empty bottle or glass he used to leave the BBQ and actually run to replace it with a full bottle or fill the glass. Everybody in the village loved and respected his dad. On many occasions in the past, he wished he could be more like him; a person that everything was clear to him, his place in the world, his expectations... life was simple, the joys were the little things that life offered. The heavy self-doubts and frustrations did not have a place in his dad's being. The old armchair had the essence of the old man, almost as if he was still alive.

The sudden flirtatious behaviour of Pippi somehow confused him. Even though he remembered her mood swings from back in the adolescent years, he was not used to this flip between the vulnerable wounded women who fight to recover that he saw just a few hours earlier to the suggestive evocative men-eater that she has transformed too. He was attracted and put off at the same time. It seemed as old Pippi emerges as a defence mechanism when the real Pippi feels vulnerable or threatened. The sudden appearance of his wife clearly struck a chord and the alluring siren came out.

He looked at her wiggling her bum and humming to the music that came from the radio in the kitchen. Then he took a large sip from his glass and got up, he approached her and turned her gently toward him then kissed her lips softly.

"What are you doing Ziggs?"

He pulled back and she looked at him with a strange expression.

"Oh, sorry...I thought you wanted this." He mumbled and felt the blood rushing to his face.

"It's ok, relax, I liked it." She started to laugh. "You're such a blusher, it's like nothing has changed since our first kiss. Do you remember? On the bench outside, you were so clumsy."

"Well, I'm sure there is some improvement." He said and kissed her again.

"There is definitely some improvement." She looked a bit flushed. "Now piss-off and go to do the table, dinner is ready."

The dinner she made was splendid; a tender sirloin steak that they bought from the butcher after the thrilling visit to the corner shop, with roasted new potatoes in mint seasoning and parsnip and green beans on the side. During dinner, they devoured two bottles of wine while having a light conversation about anything but the elephant in the room. All this time she didn't take her eyes off him and made him feel that everything he said mattered and was important, she laughed when he was telling jokes and wowed when he told her about things he had done. Her body language was inviting and alluring; she touched his hand or patted his shoulder at the right times. He could still see glimpses of sadness in her eyes every now and then, but he was almost bewitched by the attention and the fondness that she showed him, and by the sexual aura that surrounded her.

After they finished the second bottle they cleared the table, both were a bit tipsy, he opened the last bottle and put on the old turntable record player one of his mum's records; a female sixties folk singer, which was her favourite. Then they slouched on the settee, looking at each other and drinking the wine.

"Why are you sitting so far, Ziggy? Come a bit closer." He moved a bit closer to her until their shoulders touched each other.

She turned to face him and caressed his hair softly. "You know, it is the first time in years that I feel comfortable around a man. How did I push you away all those years

249

ago? I'm sorry I was such a bitch, I was fucked up…but now we are here, we can make up for those years." Then her hands travelled down his shirt and started to undress him.

He wanted to stop her, tell her that they only met again yesterday and they should slow down. But he couldn't; the environment together with the wine made him too aroused and excited to stop. Above all, it was the unfulfilled yearning that was finally becoming true. So he allowed her to convince him that it all meant to be and let himself be carried away.

12

The night was not magical as he had imagined it would be. When they made love something was missing; the ecstatic feeling of unification of two bodies and souls did not happen, at least for him. He felt that she was trying too much instead of going with the flow and let the stream take them away. She was almost adamant to give him the best pleasure he ever had and to show him her skills in bed. It wasn't a disaster, though, and was one of the nicest nights he had in years. Nonetheless, it left him a bit disappointed.

After she turned over and fell asleep he laid on his back with his eyes open, not able to sleep. He was confused and overwhelmed, not sure how he was feeling. The sudden appearance of his wife and their conversation took him off balance and messed up all that he felt about his family and life, it made him question his actions and behaviour.
Making love to Pippy felt more like a one night stand than coming back home. She was exciting, unpredictable and fun, but under all of this she was sad and damaged; life and the choices she had made took their toll on her and left battle scars that couldn't be erased or totally heal. However, after they came to a climax he didn't feel the urge to cuddle with her or spoon together. The feeling of running away together, supporting each other, and rebuilding together their broken life wasn't there anymore. Less than a day ago he had a hope that she can give him back some of the joy and spontaneity and he can help her

gain back her self confidence and trust in men. But the previous day made him realise that he was dwelling on the past; Pippy was a dream, a fantasy. The woman that was sleeping next to him wasn't that twelve years old girl anymore. Her worst fear was to become like her mum and it consumed her and drove most of her choices as an adult. Nevertheless, after the rebellions, the escapes, the places she has seen and the people she has met, at 42 years old, she turned to be like her mum; an uneducated lonely village girl with low self-esteem that lives to satisfy others. Only, Pippy had no children or friends who cared for her.

He looked at her and thought, "Is it love what I feel for her or just compassion? Maybe it's a wistful love and yearning for the girl I knew thirty years ago…I don't really know the beaten-up woman that is laying here. Those last couple of days were just a fool's wish that was based on silly nostalgia. It was stupid and immature of me to think that people don't change and we can go back to be like those two kids sitting on the garden bench kissing for the first time."

He realised that although a life with her can be compelling and intoxicating, he would be a caretaker and will have to endure mood swings and deal with an addiction. The evening and night showed him that even after three years of self-therapy, she still believes that fast thrills and charm is all she needs to catch and hold onto a man. Maybe that is all she knows. He suddenly understood that he doesn't need the excitement of living on the edge, he never really needed it. After hearing his wife, who put a mirror in front of him which gave him some perspective and made him understand that the culpability of many of the faults he sees in his life is on him. Joy and spontaneity can be present in his family life but he must nourish them.

"All I need is to bloody grow up, grow some balls, and deal with issues like an adult instead of hiding or running away like a twat."

Maybe she is right and he shouldn't throw away twenty years of marriage and try to work out the differences between them? Maybe he should try to connect more with his son and show more interest in his life. They are financially comfortable enough for him to look for a different career; he is young enough to start again.

How can I do it to Pippy again? She got hurt so many times and just found her feet again. Though he didn't actually promise her anything, last night was initiated by her; he wanted to give them more time to get to know each other but she has tempted him when she was aware that he can't resist her.

"It was a stupid mistake! I should go back home and ask Vic to forgive me." He thought. "But how can I do it without hurting Pippy? I can't fuck up my life, though, and give up my family for a woman I hardly know after only one night together. She is an adult and has to understand, I'm sure she will bounce back. She will probably see it as a one-nighter also and will continue with her life."

The rest of the night he was tossing and turning; the thoughts about what he should say to his wife when she'll open the door and how to say it, and the fear of Pippi's reaction when he will tell her his decision, kept the sleep away. Eventually, he gave up trying to sleep; he got up and made himself a cup of tea, then went outside and sat on the bench to watch the sunrise and wait until Pippy wakes up. It was quite nippy outside, so he put on his dad's heavy old house robe and warmed his hand with the teacup by holding it with both while drinking slowly. The sky was scattered with light airy clouds, which were not typical of the season and created glorious orange-pink dawn.

While sitting and watching the incredible light show in the sky that gradually revealed the world out of the darkness, he knew that everything will be fine, everything will land in its place and there is nothing to worry about.

When Pippy got up she found him in the kitchen making scrambled eggs and sausages.

"Good morning Pip, breakfast will be ready soon, do you want coffee or tea?"

She hugged him from behind and kissed his cheek. "Good morning lover boy, I had a lovely time last night."

He turned and smiled at her. "Me too, now, go and brush your teeth and wash up before food will get cold."

Her hand moved toward his groin and she whispered with a sexy voice in his ear, "Should we have a rerun before breakfast?"

He moved her hand gently and pointed to the bathroom. "Don't be silly, breakfast is the most important meal of the day, we need the energy. Come on, chop-chop, it's almost done."

She smacked his bum and walked toward the bathroom. "Alright, alright, don't get your knickers in a twist, I'll be right back. But you better have the energy for some action after breakfast, old man". She closed the bathroom door behind her and shouted, "By the way, coffee please!"

After 15 minutes she came out smelling lovely after a shower, she took her plate, a fork, and the coffee cup from the table and sat on the wide window sill of the large window that faced the garden.

"It's a beautiful morning, isn't it Zigs?" She ate some egg from her plate. "Amm, that's nice. I thought you can't cook."

"Don't you want to sit on the table Pip?"

"I'm quite comfortable here, thanks." She took a sip of coffee. "I love this house."

The rest of the breakfast they ate in silence, each one in their own thoughts. When they finished eating he took the plates and put them in the sink.

"Another coffee?" He asked after he finished washing the dishes.

"Yeah, don't mind if I do."

"Alright, but let's drink it outside and get some fresh air."

After ten minutes he came out with two mugs of coffee and sat on the bench next to her.

"Pippy, I need to tell you something."

She looked at him and started laughing. "Sorry, but you look so serious and confused." Then she gave him a kiss on his cheek and held his hand. "Ok, ok, carry on, I'm listening."

He pushed her gently away from him until they looked at each other then took a big breath. "I had a great time last night, you know that, right? Probably the best I had in years. But, after thinking about it the whole night, as I couldn't sleep, I decided to go back home to my wife and son." He paused and looked at her reaction, then continued. "I don't want that you'll feel that I have messed you about and used you; I'm not this kind of guy. But I'm sure you can agree that even with all our past from 30 years ago, we actually know each other for only two days. I realised that to throw away 25 years of marriage, a family, friends, and everything I have worked for and built all my life, just because I'm facing some difficulties and frustrations, will be irresponsible, weak, and immature. It's not how my parents brought me up. You are wonderful, but we hardly know each other. To leave everything I have behind and run away with someone you barely know sounds nice and romantic for a book or a film, not for real-life though. I think I need to fight more for what I want and need within the life I have built and I need to start to look more at other's needs also, instead of only my own. I'm so sorry if I misled you Pip."

She looked at him, nothing moved on her face except the colour that ran out of it. It was like a white death mask framed by ginger hair. After a few seconds of looking at him without any expression, she suddenly burst out into loud laughter. When she calmed down she reached with her hand and caressed his cheek.

"Oh Ziggy, you are so sweet and naive; we had a nice day and lovely night, we closed the circle. I gave you what you have longed for since school and I also had a lot of fun. I can't believe that you really think that I want to run away with you and have a "happy ever after". You were never my type anyway, and I'm good and happy by myself at the moment. Last night was for old times' sake, I've never wanted to be more than a mate with you. Anyway, Ziggs," She got up and gave him a quick hug. "I do need to go now; I still have a few chores to do today. I hope everything will work out fine for you with your wife. Come and say hello next time you'll come down."

As she turned away decisively with body language that tried to project pride and started to walk away, he saw the gutted look in her eyes; the same despaired sad look she had on prom night when she saw him looking at her with the two lads.

He sat there gobsmacked, unsure how to take her behaviour. She disappeared around the street corner and he knew that he would never see her again. He got up and walked into the house, closed the curtains and covered the furniture with sheets, and then he took out the rubbish bag, locked the door and started to walk to the village. Before exiting the garden, he stopped and looked for a few seconds at the house. "This is the last time I'll ever be in this house, I'm not going to come back to the village again, I have nothing left for me here." He thought, and then headed to the bus stop.

13

He woke up and looked at the clock with urgency; the clock showed 9am. "Bugger! Shit! I'm late for work! He mumbled and jumped off the bed, put on the trousers and slipped into the shirt without bather to open the buttons. Then he ran to the bathroom to brush his teeth. When he got out of the bathroom sorting out his tie his wife was in the bedroom tidying the bed up.

She looked at him baffled. "Where are you going dressed like that D? It's Saturday!"

He stopped and looked confused for a moment, "Oh fuck, I was sure it's a working day."

"Oh babe, it's so typical for you. Come on, take those clothes off and I'll fix you some breakfast. You're so funny! You even forgot that you are working from home now. By the way, there is a package for you on the kitchen table; it came with the post this morning. Did you buy something online?"

"Not that I recall. I'll be down in a jiff babe."

After she left the room he sat on the bed smiling to himself, thinking what a plonker he is. He took off the clothes and put on jogging bottoms and a T-shirt and his house robe on top.

Things changed in the last 8 weeks since he came back; he left his job and decided to start writing a book. At the same time, he started to work part-time for a charity organisation that raises funds for Dementia and Alzheimer's research. His relationship with his wife was improving; they spent more time talking and discussing issues that in the past they held in, they often debated and disagreed, but they were more open to compromises than previously. He tried to communicate with his son more and get involved in his life; it wasn't easy and the progress was slow, but there was progress. They even went once for a football game together and spent a couple of evenings playing video games together and actually enjoyed each other's company.

Life looked promising and it seemed that with a bit of work everything will fall into its place sooner or later.

He went down to the kitchen, hugged his wife from the back, gave her a wet kiss on her lips and opened her robe admiring what was revealed.

"Hey! Down boy! We are not alone; wait until he goes out with his mates, babe." She slapped his hand and closed her robe to cover her body, then handed a plate with an omelette, bacon and baked beans.

"Sit down and eat your breakfast young man, I need to run to the market fast, to get a few ingredients for dinner. The pup has a sleepover at his mate's tonight and we'll have the house to ourselves. I'm planning to cook a special pre-Christmas meal for you with a special dessert. See you later! Love you!" She gave him a peck on his cheek and headed to the door. "Oh, I left your parcel on the table."

He kept staring at the door for a while thinking about the day he returned; how terrified he was and worried about her reaction; is she going to take him back or shut the door in his face? He sat in the train station most of the day. In the early evening, after he had a whole speech in his head where he apologized and begged her to take him back; he finally found the courage to face her and headed home. When he eventually arrived at the house, his stomach was in a twist and he could barely breathe. He knocked on the door and she opened the door and looked at him from top to bottom without expression on her face. When he opened his mouth to talk she moved to the side and signalled him to come in.

"Are you hungry? There is some leftover from dinner if you want."

The first few days were awkward; she was quite cold and distant and he was walking on eggshells. Slowly in time, they started to talk and be more comfortable around each other. Nevertheless, she didn't allow him to apologize, every time he tried she changed the subject, eventually, she said, "I love you and we can have a fresh start, I can also forget what happened, but I will not give you the satisfaction of apology and forgiveness. You shouldn't forget and will need to live with it.

After he finished his breakfast he took the parcel that was a large envelope, wondering what is it and who is it from as he couldn't recall ordering or buying anything online. It was addressed to his parent's house in the village but diverted and been sent to his house as per the request he put in the village post office. The sender's name was Lauren Cunningham. He didn't recognize the name and became quite curious, so he tore off the envelope and checked the content. Inside he found a small note and the village's weekly newspaper dated from 2 weeks ago. The note was short and basic;

"Hi Danny, I'm not sure if you've been informed...open page 4 of the newspaper.
I'm really sorry.
Lauren (Button)"

He opened on page 4 of the newspaper, on the bottom he saw a short article with an old photo of Pippi that looked as it was taken on a holiday 15 year earlier; she was smiling and looked happy.
He started to read;

"On Monday 29th November Pippa Mclean was found dead in her house in 12 Orchid Lane. The police have been called to the house after her manager reported that she didn't attend work for a week and didn't answer his calls. The neighbours also reported a bad smell coming from her house. The large number of painkillers and antidepressants found in the house and Miss Mclean's history suggested that she had taken her own life.

Mclean grew up in the village and was the daughter of Diane Mclean who also had a similar tragedy and took her own life 3 years ago. Miss Mclean did not have her own family and lived by herself; she left behind a brother and sister. Her siblings decided not to have an autopsy and to cremate her body in a small ceremony for family only."

He put the paper on the table and shook his head.
"Oh, Pippi! What have you done?"

Yaron Broon was born and raised in Israel, in a Kibbutz. After a national service in the paratroops in the IDF, he decided to become a professional dancer. He danced in a number of companies and projects in Israel and Europe. For extra income at that period, he also worked as a busker and nude model. After his career as a dancer ended, he worked for two years as a tour guide on camels excursions in the heart of the desert in the south of Israel. He then relocated and settled down to start a new life in England.

By the age of 50, divorced plus one, he decided to fulfil a lifelong ambition to write and publish his first book.

Printed in Great Britain
by Amazon

12773204R00149